STOLEN

Jennifer Mackenzie Dunbar

This book is a work of fiction. References to real people, events, establishments, organisations, letters or locales are intended only to provide a sense of authenticityand are used fictitiously. All other characters, and all incidents and dialogue, are drawn from the writer's imagination and are not to be construed as real.

STOLEN. Copyright © 2025 by Jennifer Mackenzie Dunbar. All rights reserved. Printed in Australia. No part of this book may be used or reproduced in any manner whatsoever without written permission except in the case of brief quotations embodied in critical articles and reviews. The unlicensed use of this work for training generative AI is not permitted.

FIRST EDITION

ISBNs:
978-0-6485043-2-0 (print)
978-0-6485043-3-7 (eBook)

Cover design by Kim Lock.

Dedicated to my Nanna, who said her skin was
dark because she was part Spanish.

Dedicated to all the other children who were taken
because their skin was not dark enough.

WARNING: The language in this novel reflects that used at the historical time in which it is set. In particular the word 'native' was commonly used to describe the Aboriginal people who owned and inhabited the land that became known as South Australia.

Stolen has been read by a cultural sensitivity consultant, Courtney Hunter-Hebberman, and deemed not offensive.

Such is the degraded state of the native Australian,
and such the difficulties of taming, educating, and
Christianising these bond slaves of Satan.
Signed Augustus Adelaide

Port Arthur, South Australia
Once they got hold of our old ancestors, they brought them back
here. They put them up in the prison here. Removed the rock.
Stuck the gun through and started shooting them. And that's
how they dealt with the 'Aboriginal problem' in those days.

Storyteller: Quentin Agius
Aboriginal Cultural Tours
South Australia
2022

CHAPTER 1

Echunga Creek 1841

The snake slid over my outstretched arm, his spiky tongue testing the air, yellow eyes staring. A king. Silent. Calm. I turned to granite, still and strong. He slithered away, leaving no trace.

There, in my favourite hiding place between the tents and the creek, amongst the spiky long grass, I could be anything I wanted to be.

In the distance, men, hopeful of flecks of gold, cursed as their pans drained to nothing but worthless rubble. A hot wind carried the dull toll of the school bell, and the freshly filled creek warbled like a happy magpie in the rain.

The creek, our only source of water, was watched and revered like a newborn. Our most precious belonging, Ma once said. Then she'd sung her Rose of Tralee song, soft and teary.

I'd taken my time over my porridge that morning and played with the twins, hoping Ma would let me wag school. But she said if I stayed home, I'd have to help with the chores, washing the grit from Da's digging clothes and collecting the kindling. So I'd set out with Joseph instead, letting him get ahead before I veered off towards the creek and slid, like the snake, into the long grass.

Joseph liked school. 'It's the only way we'll make a go of it in the colony,' he said. But the teacher, Mr Humphage, had smelly breath and the other girls laughed at the holes in my knickers when I hung upside down from my favourite hook-shaped branch. I much preferred being at the creek. It smelt good and didn't tease me. It laughed when I did and cried too when I was sad. The creek knew all my secret thoughts.

A strand of grass tickled my nose as I watched the clumpy clouds come together. I gave each clump a family name from our Meetings: Hogan, Hastings, Mayfield. Laffer, our name, I saved for the last cloud to join up. It had six bumps, one for each of us: Ma, Da, Joseph, Polly, Thomas, and one for me—Annese. Slowly the cloud families joined up, making a thick, strong, and quiet grey cover, just like we did on First Days, when the Society of Friends gathered, heads bowed. Safe together in God's company. We were mostly silent at the Meetings, which suited me because words, even simple words, got muddled when I tried to use them. That's why I'm mostly silent.

When the quiet time is up at the Meetings, the families say their goodbyes and move apart, walking to their separate homes, like the clouds letting in the sun. The Hastings, all ten of them, go to their small stone cottage. Friend Hogan goes to his public house on his own, and the Mayfields to their new grand house on the hill. We Laffers return to our tent near the creek.

I rolled onto my belly, my cheek in the dirt. A bee hovered, his low, threatening buzz so loud I imagined him flying into my ear, filling my head with honey. So I made myself into a strip of bark, pinky-brown, soft and thin. He darted away joining his family at the yellow-orange dandelion patch.

Staying still and quiet is the one thing I'm good at, like a tawny frogmouth pretending to be a branch or a butterfly on a petal.

Joseph told me the other children think I'm strange; quiet and starey like a snake.

'They think you're stupid too, cos you don't talk or play games.'

But I didn't understand their games, so I kept to myself. Anyway, being quiet had a good side. At night, in our tent, I'd close my eyes, let my breath go in and out, and listen. That's how I would find out the stories Ma and Da and Macca tried to keep from us children.

The bee safely gone, I rolled onto my side, propping myself up on my elbow. Three magpies called out, loud then soft, alone then together, as if discussing something serious. The clouds had almost disappeared, leaving just the open sky, like one big blanket stretching over everything. Ma said the sky in South Australia was too big and too blue. But it's never just blue. I can see purple and yellow, and grey too. And how could it be *too* big? It had to cover all the animals and the rocks and the trees and all the people. And the natives.

I liked how it just went up and up into Forever.

'It goes on until it gets to heaven,' Joseph said.

I was turning my head, looking from one side of the sky to the other, stretching my eyes wide then making them squinty, trying to find God or Jesus or the Ghost. That's when I saw her: her arms and legs curled along the twisted branch of a tree, her skin as brown as Friend Hastings' bay horse. She stared back, her eyes showing the white bits. Watching me. Waiting. I made my eyes squinty again and she turned into a possum. She didn't look away even when the voices came from down near the creek, loud then soft again. A bigger girl's laugh, a young man's rumble. Instead, she smiled, her teeth like the white keys of Mayfield's piano.

The voices got louder, merrier. Moving onto my hands and knees, my eyes just above the grass, I could see that the male voice was Macca's and the laughing one a young native woman. Her breasts were uncovered and she had a flappy cloth covering her down below parts. She flicked water at him and chortled like the magpies as he pulled a basket from the creek, catching an eel as it tried to jump out. He passed it to her but she waved her hand, her words clattering river pebbles. Macca nodded and put it into his bag. She turned towards the possum-girl.

'Kiani,' she called.

The younger girl slid down from the tree, a heron now, her legs like spindles weaving through the grass, across the rocks to the creek bed. Her chest was flat like mine and she had no hair down below.

Macca lowered his head and walked away a little, like he did with Friend Hastings' skittish horse. The girl, Kiani, slid behind the young woman and peeped out at him as he raised his hand in farewell.

'*Nunka.*'

'*Nunka,*' the sister replied and then said more rattling-pebble words to the girl as they walked up the creek in the direction of the native camp.

I dropped back onto my belly as small as a mouse. Macca whistled as he passed me, so close I could hear his breath going in.

He was three steps away before I rolled over just enough to peek at his back.

'You better be getting on home too, Annese Laffer,' he said, walking on without turning. 'Your Ma'll be after giving you a skelping when she finds out you havna' been at your lessons.'

I sat up, dusting off my pinafore and, pulling grass seeds from my hair, I ran to catch up with him, slipping my hand into his.

'Aye,' he continued, 'and she'll no' be pleased wi' me being down here either.'

I'd heard enough at nights to know that Macca was out of favour with most of the Friends for being too familiar with the natives. Ma said no good could come of it. Da said there was no harm if it was only with the men.

'We'll tell her you've been helping me with the fishing. Just you and me.'

'Fishing,' I repeated, taking his hand. 'Just you and me.'

He laughed from deep inside his chest and tweaked my nose.

'You might not speak much, but you're a clever one for sure, Annese. A tad sly too, if I'm not mistaken. And that's not a bad thing in my book. Don't let them Quakers tell you otherwise.'

I didn't know what book he meant, but I was pretty sure it wasn't the Bible because he didn't read that. As we walked, I thought about the possum-girl. Blending. Belonging. As if everything around her was part of her, and she of it. I thought too of the other woman's laugh, free and joyful. I hadn't heard laughter like that for a long time.

Macca's words 'just you and me' lit a glow within me, making me feel special, not strange, as if together we knew things others didn't. Important things.

The crack of a gun split the air. Macca flinched, his grip tightening on my hand. Three kangaroos bounded towards us before veering off, leaping the creek and disappearing into the bush. We both turned, searching the path along the creek for the native people. But they were gone.

CHAPTER 2

The adults used different voices at night when they thought I was asleep. I didn't always understand all their words, but I could tell from the sound of their voices if they were sad or happy, angry or sorry. That night, the night after I first saw Kiani, their talk was about Friend Hastings.

'His kindness will be his undoing,' Da said in his sad and sorry voice.

I didn't know a person could come undone but I closed my eyes and imagined Friend Hastings being pulled apart, like an old woolly jumper, disappearing row by row, and rolled into a ball ready to be made into someone else.

'His brother, Stephen, is the better worker, and *cannier*,' Ma said. I didn't know what 'cannier' meant either, but she said it as if it was a good thing. 'His stories certainly grow bigger in the retelling,' she added, laughing as she spoke.

'There's no harm in him,' Da said.

'I'm no' so sure,' Macca said. 'Be careful around him, Joshua.'

Macca was the only person, other than Ma, who called Da 'Joshua'. The other adults called him Friend Laffer. I wondered if Da had to be careful in case Friend Stephen's stories got so big, they'd knock him over.

'He's no' the honest man his brother is.' Macca's voice was somewhere between happy and sad.

Even though Macca wasn't in our family and didn't go to the Meetings, Da spoke to him like kin. Ma said he was mature beyond

6

his sixteen years because his family had been torn apart by the greedy landlords back in Scotland.

I figured the landlords must have been very strong, and mean, to tear a family apart. I knew Scotland was a country far away next to England where we'd come from, and near Ireland too, where Ma grew up and her daddy still lived.

***

I played with Kiani often after that first day, always at the place where the creek got wide. I usually went with Macca on Saturday afternoons when Ma told me to get out from under her feet, or when the school was shut down because Mr Humphage had a cold. But sometimes I skipped school and went on my own. I never told Ma but she soon cottoned on and took Macca to task.

'Nothing good can come of it. They're heathens. Who knows what their superstitious ways will bring on us?' She crossed herself then and said her Blessed Mary prayer.

Macca laughed. 'And what would that be you're doing right there, Kitty Laffer?' He mimicked her actions. 'Who's being superstitious now?'

I'd noticed that he could laugh at Ma and get away with it. She'd just pretend to slap him and call him a *fallen protesting*—or something like that.

'You can do as you like Macca, but don't involve Annese.'

'You're the boss, Kitty, but I think they're good for her. They understand her quietness, which is more than I can say for most around here. She's learning to understand their ways too. How are we ever going to share this land together if we don't try to understand them?'

Ma looked at me with her worried face. She'd encouraged me to be friends with the Hastings girls. They'd been kind at first, but when I didn't understand what they were giggling about, they'd wander off, leaving me to climb trees on my own.

'G'wan then,' Ma said, looking at me. 'But remember, you're only to play with this Kiani you talk about when Macca is nearby.'

That was how Kiani became my first friend. We climbed trees and splashed about in the waterhole. She showed me how to pick the reeds and chew them for her sister Ngama's weaving. I taught her to skip rope. We swapped words too. She was much better at remembering my words than I was hers. She called me *yirki*, which Macca said was a small animal that lived underground.

'Because you are good at hiding,' he teased.

We taught each other our words for the trees. I had only a few— she-oak, eucalyptus, and wattle—but Kiani had many more, as if each tree had a meaning of its own.

Kurra, kungngurri, mangalya.

We even taught each other the names in our families. I tried to say *Ngama*, although Kiani laughed and shook her head. But she quickly got hold of how to say 'Kitty' and said it over and over again.

'Kitty,' she'd said smiling and patting her chest. 'Kitty.'

***

I was heading to the creek without Macca one morning when Joseph caught up with me.

'I know where you're going.'

I shrugged and kept walking.

'Ma said we're not to play with the natives on our own. We'll be in trouble if she finds out.'

'Go away then.' I didn't want him to come. I didn't want to share Kiani. But he came anyway.

We pushed through the wattles and, for the first time, I was glad Kiani and Ngama weren't there. I was beginning to climb a tree when Joseph pointed upstream.

'Let's go and spy on them - the natives.'

I'd never been to where Kiani lived, although I'd seen it from a distance and knew Macca went there sometimes. Da called it their camp, although it was better than any camp I'd seen. They had real homes, made of logs and bark. Even I knew camps were made of tents and things that could be moved.

Joseph grabbed my foot before I got to the second branch. 'If you don't come, I'll tell Ma that you sometimes skip school to come here alone.'

I kicked his hand away but didn't climb any further.

'Come on, Annese, it'll be fun to spy on them. They're on Friend Hastings' land so it's not as if we're trespassing.'

The thought of spying on Kiani made me squirmy inside, the way I felt when I lied to Ma about eating the butter straight from the paddle. But Joseph was already picking his way through the reed beds. I ran after him.

'How can they be on Friend Hastings' land if they were already living here when we came?'

'He paid for it. He gave money to the South Australia Company before he came here from Chichester. Some of that money paid our way out here so Da could do the work on their farm. Ma said her and Da were told it was empty here in South Australia. No towns. No houses. No farms. Nothing.'

'Well then, they was lied to. The natives were here. In their houses. They still are here.'

Joseph shrugged. 'All I know is that all the land hereabouts belongs to the Hastings now. Da says it's only through their good nature, being Quakers and all, that they let the natives stay. He says the natives will probably just up and move one day.'

We found a spot behind a fallen tree trunk where we could see the camp without being in the open. But one of the native men, about Macca's age, stood up and shouted out in their language, pointing in our direction. I felt Joseph stiffen beside me, getting ready to run. But I could see Ngama, so I climbed on top of the log and waved.

Joseph pulled at my skirt, a terrified look on his face. I laughed at him, bathing in his reluctant admiration as he too stood.

An old woman, sitting on the ground with six other women, spoke to the young man without looking our way. Her voice rose and fell like a magpie talking, waiting in between warbles as if giving him time to think before she added the next instruction. I expected him to argue back like Joseph did to Ma of late. But he didn't. An old man, sitting by the fire, shouted out and threw his head back as if summoning the boy to join him. He turned to take one more look at us and obeyed the old man's instruction.

Ngama and the women laughed then, sharing a joke. I wondered if it was about us or the boy. I'd seen Ma and Mrs Hastings do the same thing, after they'd disciplined one of us children, as if their harsh words were only for show, to hide their amusement in our antics.

The women were bare from the waist up. Some had breasts that hung like the sacks Da carried the cheese in; those on the younger ones were smaller, tighter. Like melons. Ngama and two of the other women were weaving grass into baskets; the rest stripped reeds and put them in a pile. Around them, a dozen or so naked children tumbled and played chasey.

The sun was overhead now, burning my face and hands. Below my layers of clothes, I could feel the sweat running down my legs and under my arms. While we watched, a cool breeze sprang up. I imagined how it would feel on my body if I too was naked. I longed to undress and let the air caress my skin, gentle and caring.

Ngama turned and called *yirki*, Kiani's my name.

'*Nunka.*' I waved again and she raised her hand too. Joseph stared at me, his admiration spreading to a grin. It was the same look I'd seen when I'd recited a whole section of the Bible without looking.

The old man called out to Ngama and she turned back to her work.

Joseph pulled at my dress. 'Come on, Annese. We're too late for school. Let's go for a swim.'

***

That night I couldn't stop thinking about Kiani's little town.

'Ma, how much did Friend Hastings pay the natives for the land?'

She laughed and shook her head. 'You sure can find words when you want to.'

'Joseph said their campground and the creek belong to Friend Hastings now?'

She frowned before answering. 'Seems they do. He was told it was as good as empty here. That nobody was farming the land. That's what we were all told too. That's why we came, to have land of our own.'

'They lied.'

'Lie is a big word Annese. Maybe they made a mistake.' She put down the pot she'd been scrubbing, sighing as she shook her head. 'And it's too late now. There's no going back, Annese. We'll all just have to learn to live together, alongside each other.'

I liked that idea because that would mean I could keep playing with Kiani. 'So we will share, like you tell me to do with Joseph and the twins?'

A worried look crossed her face. 'Don't you be asking these questions outside of here. You understand?' She hesitated before going on. 'They'll be Christianised soon enough. We'll teach them how to sow crops and fence in stock and make proper use of the land, and soon they'll be able to buy some for themselves.'

I wanted to ask what Kiani's family would need to do to be Christianised. And how long it would take for them to buy their land back. But I knew from the look on Ma's face that it was time to stop my questions.

***

Two days after Joseph and I spied on the natives' camp, Friend Stephen Hastings came visiting after supper. As usual, Macca had eaten with us and was about to go back to his tent when Friend Stephen arrived. The twins, Polly and Thomas, were already asleep in their cot, and Joseph and I were supposed to be at our bible reading inside the tent. But we snuffed the candle out and stayed quiet so Ma didn't notice us listening.

Friend Stephen was younger than his brother Friend Ernest. He wasn't married. Maybe that was why he looked so different. Stephen was sharp, Ernest was saggy.

I liked Friend Ernest better. At the Meetings, he'd wink at me and once he gave me a boiled sweet. Friend Stephen laughed a lot, but his eyes didn't squint up like his brother's, and the sound came from his throat, not his belly. He kept looking at everyone when he laughed too—to see if they were sharing his joke, I guess.

Ma welcomed Stephen with a glass of rum. Quakers mostly didn't drink, but Ma said the Catholic in her couldn't deny a visitor a dram. She had one too and, when Macca held out his tin mug, she gave him a large dash. Only Da went without.

They were sitting outside around the fireplace and Friend Stephen was relaying the news from Adelaide Town. He did his half-laugh as he made fun of all those who'd been in trouble with the law. Ma giggled at his stories and asked him about who'd arrived on the latest boat, what marriages were being planned, and if any babies had been born.

After his second rum, Friend Stephen's face grew stormy and his voice changed from soft to hard, from sand to gravel.

'There was trouble up there last week. Hordes of natives came from both south and east, hundreds of them, camped in one big group, up near the German village at Klemzig. Two nights and two days they sang, if you can call what they do singing. They did their dancing too, stamping and clapping those sticks together, beating on drums made of rolled-up possum fur. *Corroboree*, they call it. Satanic rituals, if you ask me.'

I crept outside and curled up in the annexe. I wanted to hear more about the dancing and singing. Kiani's family had a *corroboree* once and we watched all day as other people came along the Onkaparinga River to join them. I'd fallen asleep listening to the hypnotic sounds.

I saw Macca straighten up. He'd not said anything since Friend Stephen had arrived, but now he was alert.

'When they finished their dancing,' Friend Stephen continued, 'they sent five men up to talk to Cawthorne. Each was painted all over with ochre and carried a spear. One of them said something in his broken English and then yabbered on in their mumbo jumbo, shouting and carrying on. Then he threw a huge stone—a crystal covered with fat, someone said. He threw it right at Cawthorne's feet.'

He was speaking loudly now, as if he was angry. 'They're not to be trusted when they're in a mob like that. Savages, through and through.'

Macca put down his rum.

'So did you hear what he said to Cawthorne?' Macca's voice was like a challenge.

Friend Stephen's face went stern for just a second before his sideways grin returned.

'Not this again, Macleod. How could I tell what they said? They don't speak God's language.' He turned to Da with his hands outstretched as if asking him to be on his side, against Macca.

'Is that what you call it, God's language?' Macca's voice was raised now. 'Christianise. Civilise. Protect. They're the words we hide behind to justify the destruction we're doing.'

Friend Stephen flicked his hands as if dismissing him.

'I was there too. You're only telling half the story, Hastings,' Macca said. 'I wonder why that is?' I could hear Macca trying to keep his mad inside.

Seeing me hiding, Ma stood. 'Get to bed, Annese.' She turned to Macca and Friend Stephen and added, 'And you two can lower your voices.'

'What did thou hear, Macca?' Da asked in his gentle way, as I crept as slowly as I could back into the tent, not wanting to miss a word. 'What did they say?'

Ma remained standing, her hands on her hips, her back to me. I went back into the annexe and crouched down so I couldn't be seen but could still hear.

Macca's voice went soft again. 'Their leader was a man I've seen around often enough in Adelaide Town. They call him King Rodney. He spoke in English as good as some white folk I know. He said "You have taken away our Country. Killed the emus, the kangaroo and the possums".'

I heard Friend Stephen scoff. 'You're a fool, Macleod.'

I expected Macca's voice to go angry again and I peeked around the canvas. But he kept talking, quiet and serious, looking only at Da.

'He said, "The emus, the kangaroos, and the possums all go when white man sit down here." I swear Joshua, he said it as clear as that. And there is not one of us who can deny that what he says is true.'

Friend Stephen laughed hard and loud. 'And what if they have? We've brought our own food.'

'You may laugh, Hastings,' Macca shouted, 'but you and your brother and all the landholders here have never known what it is to have your land taken from you. I've seen the destruction it brings firsthand.'

His voice cracked then and I stood to see his face. He wasn't crying, but it was clear he wanted to. Joseph came up behind me and I grabbed his hand. I'd never seen Macca this sad.

'My family was driven from their land by men just like you. And now you, no, we, are doing exactly the same to these people.'

Da raised his hand trying to get Macca to sit again. 'I don't know the answer, Macca. We have to trust God to guide us. I'm afraid that it's the way it's always been: the strong conquer the weak. Here in the colony, you have the chance to be on the side of the winners, Macca.'

Macca shook his head and was about to sit but Friend Stephen was not to be silenced.

'Angry young men like you need to be very careful, Macleod. It's one thing getting your pleasure from a native, but don't believe for one minute that you know them. You'll end up with a spear in your side if you're not careful.'

Macca lunged at him then, but Ma was quick to get between them. 'Enough! Take your argument away from our home.'

'Kitty's right,' Da said laying a hand on Stephen's shoulder while Ma edged Macca backwards. 'If there's one thing we should all agree on, it's that no good can come of fighting. We must pray for guidance about how we can lead our native brothers into God's flock.'

Friend Stephen sat back down. Macca put on his hat and began heading towards his tent before turning. I'd never before seen tears on a man's face.

'Maybe they're already part of God's flock, Joshua. Maybe they know Him better than any of us.'

CHAPTER 3

I woke the next morning to find one of Macca's strange stone dolls beneath my pillow. He'd shown it to me once before, along with another one almost the same.

'My mother gave one to me and one to my brother the day we left the old country,' he had said. 'She said they were for our safe keeping. But my brother died at sea, his body thrown into the deep.' He had given one to me to look at, turning the other over and over. 'It's the only possession of his that I kept.'

Wiping the sleep from my eyes, I took the doll to Ma. 'I have to find Macca and give it back. It's from his Ma, for his safekeeping.'

'He's gone, Annese. Macca had to leave.' Her voice cracked and she turned away, wiping her eyes on her apron. 'He brought the doll early this morning and said to tell you it's for your safekeeping now.'

'When's he coming back? You have to find him, Ma, and tell him to come back,' I said, angry she'd just let him go. I needed to ask if he meant that the doll would keep me safe or was I to keep it safe for him? I needed to take his hand and go to the creek. I needed to hear his laugh and see his eyes dancing when he smiled.

'I can't do that, Annese,' Ma said. 'He's not family. He's his own man. Most likely he'll never come back. That's the way it is in the colonies, Annese. People come, and people go.'

My body flooded with sadness and anger. I ran and ran until it felt as if my heart would burst. I ran into the bush until the pain turned from a knife's edge into a heavy rock holding me down. I screamed at the sky and threw rocks at the creek.

It was Da who found me there. He sat beside me, silent like in the Meetings, waiting until I was moved to talk.

'But Macca is family, Da.'

'I think thou art right, Annese. Family comes in many shapes.'

'Did he go because of what Friend Stephen said about getting his pleasure and getting a spear in his side?'

Even though I wasn't sure what 'his pleasure' meant, I knew he didn't mean just going fishing at the creek.

'Much was said last night that should not have been said. There is no need for thou to be concerned, Annese.' After a pause, he said, 'Have I ever told thou when we first met Macca?'

He'd told me a dozen times but I shook my head and snuggled against him.

'Macca jumped ship in Adelaide. It was the first English-speaking port they'd visited since his brother had died. I found him hiding in the bush up behind Holdfast Bay. He was all broken up about his brother. Your Ma and I took him under our wings.'

Under our wings. He always said that. I knew they didn't really have wings but I wondered if, just for Macca, they'd changed into pelicans and stood on each side of him, their feathered arms stretched over and around him. I wiped my eyes and sniffed.

'Did you and Ma put him back together?'

'I guess we did, with the blessing of the Lord,' Da said. 'We used our love, our kind words, and strong hands and he slowly got whole again.'

That night I pulled the doll from under my pillow and made a promise to the baby Jesus that I would always use kind words and use my hands to do a good deed every day if he would bring Macca back. Not the broken, angry Macca, but the strong and smiling one. The Macca I loved.

I prayed too that Kiani's family still had their emus and kangaroos and possums.

***

Ma let me skip school the day Macca left. She sent me to collect nettles for the soup but I snuck down to the creek, in case God had already brought Macca back. But he wasn't there. Ngami's fishing traps were gone too.

I listened for the usual sounds coming from Kiani's camp, straining to hear voices singing or calling out. I listened as hard as I could for stones struck against each other, children squealing. But there was just the screeching of a dozen black cockatoos. They turned and swooped above me then surged as one towards the camp and back again. Over and over they went, crying out, until I felt a sadness grow inside me again, like a sponge filling with muddy water.

The next time they headed upstream, I followed, using the track Kiani's people had worn beside the creek, stopping at the fallen tree. An eerie silence greeted me. The cockatoos settled, decorating a tree-like black flags, watching over me.

Kiani's town was empty.

How could so many people just disappear? Did they have to go to find their animals scared off by the white men like Macca said the man told Mr Cawthorne? If they were still close by, maybe Ngama and Kiani would come back to the fishing hole.

My sadness filled me—and my anger too. Kiani was my only friend after Macca. It wasn't fair. I missed her already.

I crept forward, scanning as I went in case one of her people appeared and surprised me. The stones covering the fire pit were still warm. The earth around it was smoothed, brushed free of footprints. Their tools and baskets were gone too. Just their houses, the *wurlies*, stood strong and firm.

I snuck into one and lay down. I could smell Kiani in the earthen floor and see Ngama's face in the firmness of the branches that wound together to keep out the rain and the dust and the wind. Some branches were as round as Joseph's legs; others, skinny and wispy, filled in the gaps so I could hardly see the sky. The smell of eucalypt stroked me and my sadness got smaller. I closed my eyes and listened as the low hum of the *wurlie* sang to me. I felt my body lift from the ground, as a cushion of happiness enveloped me.

I heard Kiani's gentle voice: *Tidda*—Sister. We will survive.

***

Voices outside the wurlie snapped me back into my body. I peeked through a gap. The cockatoos fled from their tree, snatching branches as they did and throwing them at the intruders.

Da and Friend Stephen. Relief that it was not Kiani's family, who might be angry I was in their house, quickly turned to fear at being caught.

'They've maybe gone further up the creek,' Da said.

'Suppose young Macleod went with them,' Friend Stephen said, laughing his mean laugh. 'He's got a yen for lubra, they say.'

'Mind thy words.' Da's raised voice told me he was properly angry. 'He said he was going to the whaling at Encounter Bay. Said he missed being near the sea. Thou have no need to add to his woes by blackening his name.'

'Settle yourself, Friend Laffer. I meant no harm. But I'd stay well clear of the lad if I were you. He's not one of us. Presbyterian, he says, but I'm not sure he believes in God at all. How else would he justify his attachment to the savages?'

'It's not ours to judge another man's faith, Stephen. God has made of one blood all the nations of men.'

'Well, I'm glad they're gone and him too. It gives me full access to the creek. I'll be able to expand the dairy. Then there'll be plenty of work for both you and that boy of yours. I could put you into the dairyman's cottage.'

'I appreciate the offer to myself, but Joseph's still young. I want him to keep on with his schooling.'

'And you? Will you stay at the panning now that Macleod has gone?'

Their voices faded as they disappeared into the bush, pushing branches aside, taking the shortest route. I waited until I could no longer hear them before emerging from the *wurlie*. Looking around one last time, I went back along the creek to the fishing hole, dragging a stick as I went. How far was Encounter Bay, and what did 'the whaling' mean? Was it a type of crying?

By the time I got home, Friend Stephen had gone and Da was telling Ma about his offer.

'I'm going to accept. It'll pay more than the field work I do for him now. I'd hoped to make a little from the panning, but what I get is barely worth the trouble. And anyway, it won't be the same without Macca by my side.' His voice was heavy but determined. I sat beside him and took his hand. He was right. Without Macca, nothing was the same.

That night, a wind came up like never before. It felt as if it would blow us away altogether. The tent canvas flapped, frightening the twins who thought it was a ghost trying to get in. I clutched Macca's doll to keep it safe and fell asleep remembering the strength and gentle quietness of Kiani's *wurlie*.

***

The following week, we moved further up the creek to the place they called Echunga Springs. Ma said it would be much easier for everyone and Da said Friend Stephen was as good a boss as any.

We had a proper house now, near the dairy. It was made of slabs of wood nailed together, with mud to fill in the cracks. We didn't have a shingle roof—ours was covered only with cow hides but mostly it kept the rain out. The floor was just dirt when we first moved in, but Da and Joseph brought rocks from along the creek and dug them into the ground to make it as flat as they could. It was my job to sweep it every night, and once a week Ma and I would get on our hands and knees to get the dirt out of the grooves. We'd sing her songs as we went. My favourite was *The Rose of Tralee*. Even though it was a sad song, it made me happy to sing with her.

I shared a bed with Polly and Thomas, and Joseph slept on mats on the floor. Polly had the cupboard end of our bed so she wouldn't fall out. On the second night there, I scratched the mud between the skinny branches at my end so I could see the stars and the moon. I looked for the diamond they called the Southern Cross. Macca had once told me he'd sleep under the stars every night if he could.

It was a crescent moon and I wondered if Macca was looking at it wherever he was. He'd once told me that it was the same moon all over the world. It had been a crescent shape that night too.

'My mother will be looking at it when she goes to bed tonight.' His face had gone all soft and his lips went like jelly. 'There's no going back.' Even though he was sad not to see his mum again, I was glad he wasn't going back.

Then, as if he wanted to be happier, he ruffled my hair and made his happy smile.

'Do you know that the natives see more stars than us? They use them to tell them when to look for certain food and even work out who they can marry, based on how the stars look in different parts of the land.'

He'd often play his harmonica on those nights and I'd lean against him and feel the vibrations in his chest as the air went in and out.

Polly mumbled in her sleep and I felt that sad longing for him well up within me. A tawny hooted and its mate answered. Even the birds had the one they loved close by.

***

I stopped skipping school now that Kiani had left, and soon I could read well enough, although when I had to read out loud to the class it came out in a whisper and some of the children would laugh at me. My favourite lesson was composition. I liked making up stories, pretending to be someone else. But my writing was still very messy, on account of using my right hand. I could write neat enough with my left hand but the letters sloped the wrong way. Mr Humphage said being left-handed was a sign of the devil and he tied it to the chair if I tried to use it.

He didn't like my stories either. I wrote about talking animals and fairies living in the trees. One day the subject was 'Friends', so I wrote about Kiani and how she could change into a possum and then a heron. Mr Humphage said I was to stop writing nonsense and keep to the subjects he gave us. I knew better than to tell him it was the truth.

The classroom was crowded, with thirty of us all crammed into one room. Da said it was because more and more families were taking up the chance to get out of Adelaide, where the water supply was putrid.

Today, Mr Humphage had told us younger children to practise our loops and hooks, but a hot wind was blowing dust in and my writing just got messier the more I tried. My left hand kept wanting to take over so I sat on it so it didn't get tied down again. I could hear Mr Humphage's droning voice on the other side of the room. He was talking about Kiani's people.

'The Australian Aboriginal is an example of a primitive race. They are not civilised. They don't farm the land to produce excess. They make no attempt to extract a fraction of profit. They merely subsist.'

I'd heard of *exist*, but what was *subsist*? I could tell *merely subsisting* was not a good thing in Mr Humphage's opinion. When he said it, his voice went snarly like it did when someone broke wind.

'It is regrettable, but soon the natives will all be gone.' Now his voice went round and strong—as if he'd won an argument. 'Races which are of a low mentality and are weak in constitution rapidly die out when their Country comes to be occupied by a race that is more vigorous and robust.'

My stomach clenched. Did he mean that one day Kiani's people would all die? And if he did, why did he look so pleased? Da always said pride was a sin, but Mr Humphage looked very proud, his chest thrust forward and his head wobbling like a rooster.

'You only have to look at nature to see how it selects the strong. It lets the weak ones perish.' It was the same as Da had said to Macca, although he had said it sad.

My thoughts floated out of the classroom to the stringybark trees and the birds, and then down to the creek. Did he mean looking to *this* nature? I tried to imagine Mr Humphage climbing trees to get to the honey like Ngama did, or squatting by the creek to pull in the fish traps. Surely, if nature had to select, it would select Kiani and her people?

'You are born in an exciting time, children,' Mr Humphage went on. 'We will follow the work of Mr Darwin. He is providing many answers to the question of why the natives of this and other countries are disappearing. If it weren't for the goodness of we colonial Christians, their children would starve.'

He wrote *goodness of Christians* on the board and he went on to talk about more boring things. A kookaburra landed in the tree just outside the classroom. It looked at him and laughed. I wanted to laugh at him too, because his waistcoat didn't meet anymore except for the top button. One day it would pop clean off.

Kiani and Ngama hadn't ever looked hungry. Although their legs were skinny, they were strong. Ngama's breasts were firm and round; her teeth big and white. Kiani could run like the wind. None of Kiani's family were as rotund as Mr Humphage, but I didn't believe her people would starve, not if they were allowed to live near the creek.

I remembered Ngama's fish basket and the small squirming fish— *galaxias* Macca called them—their eyes bright and their tiny scales shiny. She'd put the smallest ones back in the creek and only part-fill her woven basket. One day we'd made a campfire nearby and roasted them over the coals. Ngama and Kiani ate theirs whole but, seeing me squirm at the idea, Macca pulled the head off mine and scooped out the inside. It was the tastiest thing I'd ever eaten. One day they caught a *rakali*. It looked like a rat and they took that back to their camp too.

Kiani had shown me how to find and pick bush cherries. At first, Ma refused to use them but Macca made her taste one and we had them often after that. It had been the same with the yam daisy that grew like tiny potatoes. They'd become a regular on our table, at least when Macca was living nearby; he knew the best places to find them.

'Annese Laffer, what are you doing?'

I flinched, surprised to find myself in the classroom.

'Loops and hooks,' I stuttered. The children laughed and Joseph gave me one of his angry squints.

'Well, get on with it then.'

***

Most days the girls played close to the school building, while the boys kicked a ball around in the paddock next door. That's where they were when a big fight broke out between Michael Hastings and Fred Sanders. I'd thought them to be best of friends, but Fred said that Michael's father, Friend Ernest, owed lots of people money. Then Michael accused Fred of being unchristian and greedy. Soon they were rolling around in the dust, throwing punches. We all stood around watching until Mr Humphage pulled them apart. That night Da and Ma spoke in lowered voices.

'A bailiff arrived in the wee hours of the morning to take over Friend Ernest's farm. They turned him out, Elizabeth too, and all the children. Just like that. Their cottage belongs to Friend Hogan now.'

'That rogue Hogan should be ashamed,' Ma said. I'd noticed of late she'd stopped using the title 'Friend' unless she was in their company. Da teased her and said she was going back to her papist ways.

'Hogan's not one to show mercy when it comes to a debt. Do you think he'll take the dairy off the Hastings too?' Ma asked. 'What would we do then?'

'Well, I suppose I'll have to work for Friend Hogan. Thou mustn't fret, Kitty. We've made it this far—we'll just keep going. Perhaps…' Da hadn't finished before Ma flew into a temper.

'What? Just keep going? Do you think it's that simple? Have you not heard that there are more and more people arriving in the colony every day, all looking for work? There's plenty of folk already in the destitute home. Some have even had to put their children in there or have them boarded out with wealthier families.'

'Thou have no need to fear, Kitty. Mayfield's farm is going from strength to strength. I've heard they are taking on more domestics.'

'Is that what you'd have me do? Be a servant again? Did I come all this way to be what I could have been back home?'

Da sighed and rubbed his head. 'It's not what I want either, Kitty. But maybe just for a while, if it comes to it.'

Ma slapped her hands on her knees, the way she did when she was saying yes but meaning no. 'Well that's it settled then. I'll do Mrs Mayfield's dirty laundry and Annese will have to leave off school and look after the twins when I'm not here. That's what we've come to!'

'We'll find a way, Kitty. I want both Annese and Joseph to stay in school as long as they can. Joseph is doing well and Annese is learning too. She has a good mind, no matter what others think.'

They fell into the silence then. But not like the silence at the Meetings. An angry silence, where words filled the air without coming out of their mouths.

CHAPTER 4

Mrs Mayfield let Ma take the twins with her to the laundry, but soon they got bored being inside all the time when Ma was cleaning and began running off into the bush when she wasn't watching. One of the other workers said she should try tying them to the big gum tree in the middle of the yard, but when she did, she'd come home crying, saying she couldn't bear to see them held back like dogs.

That evening Ma and Da were quiet as we ate our dinner. When Joseph and I got up to clear the plates, they told us to sit back down.

'Times are hard, as I am sure you have heard,' Ma said. 'We have decided that you will take it in turns to go to school, so that one of you can stay at home with the twins while we work. It'll only be until we sort something else out.'

But they didn't sort anything out, and soon Joseph had to leave school to work in the dairy with Da. I only went to school once a week when I wasn't needed to look after Polly and Thomas.

'Don't let me hear you've been anywhere near the creek,' Ma would say as she left each morning. 'Those two will be in there and drowned as soon as you turn your back.'

But even with all three of them working, we were still often short of money for food. Mr Hogan wouldn't always pay Da and Joseph properly. He said it was because of something called the depression. Often, he'd let them take milk, butter, and cheese instead of money, and it was lucky he did, for it was all we'd have for days on end.

Every so often, Ma got work for me at the Mayfields' too, so we took the twins and tied them to a tree while we were both too busy to watch them. It was on one of those days that Mrs Mayfield took Ma aside, leaving me to load the sheets on my own. I had to stand on a stool next to a window to paddle them into the water from the boiler after throwing in the Reckitt's blue bag.

'I hate seeing them tied up as much as you,' I heard Mrs Mayfield say.

'What else can I do? We need for Annese to work to…'

'I know times are tough for you.' Mrs Mayfield was holding Ma's hands now. 'I know you're doing your best but it can't go on. The twins are pale and tired.'

'That's just how they are,' Ma said, but her shoulders were droopy. She and Da had said the same thing the day before. 'If you could give us more hours…'

I put the paddle down and peered out. Ma was wiping her eyes with her apron.

'I wish I could, but we're struggling too. Mr Mayfield says that the whole colony is in debt and that I need to think about letting most of our help go.'

They worked in silence for a time until all the sheets were hung.

'I've heard that some people are having their children boarded out for a time,' Mrs Mayfield said. 'They could go to a good Christian home.'

Ma drew herself up straight as she saw me watching. Her jaw set and a frown I knew well to avoid formed on her brow. 'I'll not have anyone else raise my children. I'd sooner starve myself.'

She grabbed the basket, tossed it into the laundry, and headed to where the twins were tied.

'And what good would that do?' Mrs Mayfield implored. 'Think about it, Kitty. It'd only be until things change for you. I'm sure you'd be able to visit them.'

'Thanks for your advice, Mrs Mayfield,' Ma called over her shoulder. 'Annese and I will just finish this load. It'll be just me here in the morning.'

***

Joseph and I didn't go with our parents the day Polly and Thomas went away; we said our goodbyes at the door. Ma told Joseph and me to hold our feelings till they were well away, so as not to upset them. They were happily playing with the dolls I'd made each of them from some scraps and two pegs I'd found on the ground at the Mayfield's; too little to know what was happening.

Da said the twins would only be gone for a month. I didn't know what a month felt like and hoped it was something to do with how long it took for a moth to grow and break out of its wee bed and spread its wings. When I asked Joseph, he said it was the time it took for the moon to grow from nothing to the big white ball then back small again.

'That can't be right,' I said, stamping my foot. 'You're lying, Joseph Laffer. Ma and Da would not let Polly and Thomas out of their sight for that long.'

I decided to ask Margaret Mayfield. She was eighteen, so I figured she knew more than Joseph. She was writing in her notebook when I approached her. I'd practised and practised the words I would use to ask her, but still, when I got alongside her, they got stuck and I just stared. I'd always been a little afraid of her because of the nasty words I'd heard her use on a few occasions. Ma said she needed to take charge of her tongue or she'd always be on a shelf, but I couldn't imagine her fitting on a shelf.

'What is it, Annese?' she said, covering the page she was writing on with her arm.

I eventually got enough words out to ask my question. 'How long will the twins be gone for?'

She shrugged as if I'd asked about the weather or the time of day.

'A month?' I asked. This time my voice was strong so she couldn't ignore me.

'Oh, they'll be gone much longer than that,' she said, her chin raised and smiling as if she knew a secret. 'Some children stay at the asylum for good if they don't get boarded out. The girls get trained as domestics and the boys as farm workers. Father says it's what the colony needs.'

The asylum? For good? I knew that meant forever. I looked at her, hoping I was wrong, but Margaret just gave me an unfriendly smile. A rage filled me. I tried to kick her but she was much taller than me and grabbed me by my hair.

'And you'd better watch that temper of yours, Annese Laffer, or you'll be taken too.'

***

A dark spirit took over my parents after the twins left. They looked mostly the same, but there was nothing shining out from them anymore. I'd heard about how the fairies in Ireland, the *good people* Ma called them, took good babies and replaced them with naughty ones. But this was the first time I'd realised adults could be swapped too. I was sure that the *good people* had come and swapped our happy, whole parents for these sad broken ones.

Ma still woke me every morning, cooked my porridge, and said her prayers with me. But this swapped person didn't have Ma's cornflower blue eyes that danced even when she was cross. This woman's eyes were dull grey and didn't change, no matter what the time of day. The lines at the ends of her eyes didn't crinkle up when she smiled either, and she had saggy skin, like a rotten apple. Her mouth was always turned down now and she didn't sing her Irish songs anymore.

The Da person was thinner, as if a worm had gone in and hollowed him out. His voice too, when he spoke, for he rarely did now, was no longer a contented warbling magpie but a faded and lost cry, like the end of a crow's call. Others noticed that they'd changed too. At the Meetings, the Friends greeted them as usual but with a wet sadness in their voices.

I began telling funny stories to make the Ma-lady laugh. Her mouth would smile and she'd pat me on the head, but her eyes got even sadder. I offered the Da-man my supper because I could see he was hungering for something.

'No, Annese, it's yours,' he said. 'Eat it and be thankful. The good Lord knows I couldn't bear to lose another child.'

'We haven't lost them. We know where they are,' I shouted. 'You've just got to get right again so we can go and get them back.'

It was the first time I'd ever been truly angry at him and I expected him to wallop me. But he pulled me to him and squeezed me so tight, I thought I would break. His body shuddered and I thought maybe he had hiccups until he let me go and I saw the tears. The emptiness inside me turned into a balloon so big I couldn't swallow.

Joseph tugged at me. 'Come on Annese, leave him be. Let's go to the creek.'

At the creek, we threw stones in silence until I could bear it no longer.

'It's my fault they were taken, isn't it? Mrs Mayfield told Ma I wasn't capable of looking after them.'

He shook his head. 'It's not because of just one thing. It's Da's work drying up and Ma having to work too. It's happening all over the colony.'

His words soothed me because I didn't want it to be my fault. We continued to throw stones. The plopping noise as they fell into the water went into me, rubbing away some of the hurt.

'What's happened to our parents, the real ones? Where have they gone?'

'I don't know,' he said. 'Why do you expect me to know everything? I don't know anything. I don't know anything anymore.'

I reached out to touch his hand but he brushed me aside and turned into an angry kookaburra killing a snake. His eyes were fierce now, as he smashed and smashed. His pain drove a spear deep into me. I tried to touch him again but he pushed me so hard I fell over, hitting my head. Everything went black for a moment and, when I could see again, Joseph had gone.

That was the first time I wove myself a cloak of eagle feathers. Opening my arms wide, I took three steps and soared away leaving the pain behind.

CHAPTER 5

Now that the twins weren't with us, I helped Ma in the Mayfield's laundry most days. I didn't get paid, but when I helped, Ma could do extra loads and Mrs Mayfield would give her more money—money that would bring the twins back.

I'd just finished hanging out a basket of towels, propping the line with the forked stick, when I saw Margaret sitting on a bench under a tree. She had an ink pot and a pen and was frantically writing in her notebook. Catching me watching, she slammed it shut.

'Don't be so nosey, Annese Laffer. Have you never seen anyone writing before?'

She watched me from under her scowl as I sidled closer. I could tell my curiosity pleased her. She had something I wanted. She kept it firmly shut.

But I wasn't interested in her words. It was the notebook I was drawn to. I'd never seen anything so beautiful: its cover of red leather, the edges of the pages marbled like grapeseed oil on water. I longed to hold it, the cover resting on one hand as I stroked each page.

As I edged closer, she opened it, quickly flicking over the pages she'd written on, and, watching me, she slowly turned the clean pages. Endless sheets of creamy paper. I yearned to fill it with my own creations—not words like Margaret, but shapes, big and small, hard and soft, some shadowy some firm. I wanted to make lines, some curved and some straight. I yearned to draw the twists of the trees and the sharp edges of the reeds; to create something that would not be wiped away.

I stepped forward. Margaret waited until I was alongside her before she slammed it shut again.

'If you must know,' she said, contemptuous and proud, 'I'm writing a letter, an important letter, back to the old country. Mother says that I must keep a copy of all my letters for our records. One day they will tell the history of our colony.'

For our records… the history of our colony. I gasped. I'd heard Da talk about the history of the old country, of Kings and Queens and Quakers long dead. Of Captain Cook and Matthew Flinders who'd discovered Australia for the Crown. But I didn't know a girl like Margaret might write about such things.

Margaret basked in my admiration. 'If you must know,' she said again, looking at me with pride, 'I write my letters out here in this notebook first, then I write them out again on single pieces of quality paper Father gets from Mr Thomas's stationery store. I don't suppose your family writes letters, Annese.'

I could have told her Da wrote once a month to his brother in Chichester, although he didn't write on such glorious paper as in her notebook. His paper was worn from use as a wrapping and he wrote on both sides, filling every space. He wrote to his brother about our family and of the Meetings, subjects I am sure Margaret would deem unimportant.

I felt my anger rise and imagined throwing the ink over her, spoiling the neat pinafore that Ma had laundered and ironed for her. I wanted to scratch her with her pen, grab the notebook, and run.

Maybe guessing my thoughts, she stood hurriedly and went inside, the notebook held tightly against her bosom.

***

When the notebook turned up in the wash basket a few days later, I knew it was by mistake. I knew she would not have left it there so carelessly. I knew I should have given it straight back to her.

But I could still feel the sting of her rudeness, the offence of her disdain.

I tucked it beneath my pinafore.

Telling Ma I didn't feel well, I went home ahead of her. Joseph and Da were still at the dairy. I had the hut to myself. Taking the notebook out, I thrilled at the weight of it, as if it contained something magical. Its pages smelt like the shavings at the wood mill and the hard cover, as red as a parrot's breast, was bumpy yet silky to touch. Some pages had been carefully cut out so only one of the pages had Margaret's words on it. Her writing was tiny and squashy and the ink had smudged, probably from the steam in the laundry. I tried to read it but could only make out a couple of words. Anyway, it was not her words I coveted.

I ripped the used page out, folded it, and put it alongside Macca's doll in the old spice tin under my bed. Taking in my left hand the fat pencil Da used to record the rainfall, I began making my own marks on the first page of this glorious notebook. I drew shapes of all sorts and wispy swirls. I made circles large and small and thick bold dashes, sudden curious dots, strong and certain squares, disappearing spirals, sad teardrops, sparkling stars.

I'd never felt anything like this before—the exhilaration of the movement, the joy of making a lasting creation.

Hearing Ma coming across the garden, I shoved the notebook under my mattress and grabbed the broom.

***

Knowing my hiding place for the notebook would soon be discovered, I found a better one in a tree down by the creek. It had been burnt out long ago, leaving a hollow big enough for me to sit in cross-legged. Using a smooth stone as a table, I drew on one page and then another, my left hand released and carefree, my eyes rejoicing in my creations. I drew my pain, I drew my joy, my love, my fury. I drew all the things within me I had no words for.

***

Nothing was said about the notebook at the next big laundry day or the next. Weeks passed and still no one asked about it. I came to believe that maybe it had not been a mistake. Maybe Margaret had thrown it aside.

It was about three weeks later, however, when Ma and I arrived one day to the sound of Margaret's bossy voice coming through the bush. At first, I feared I'd been found out. But instead, as we drew nearer, my heart leapt with joy to see a native girl standing with Margaret. She wore civilised clothes, although she kept pulling at the lacing as if trying to free herself.

"Kiani!' I called out, breaking into a run before Ma could grab my arm. But I soon saw my mistake. This girl was taller and older than Kiani. Her head was not dropped as Kiani's surely would have been if Margaret had been admonishing her.

'You must understand, Tottie,' Margaret said, her voice raised, her words fake-kind. 'You are not to come into the parlour, nor are you to follow us around. My beloved brother-in-law, Mr Peters, has, from the goodness of his heart, asked that we take you in to teach you to be useful, to instruct how you're to behave in civilised company. It is a wonderful opportunity for you. But that does not mean you can mix with us as an equal.'

I expected to see the girl grimace or even curtsy, but she turned her back on Margaret, walked to where the she-oak trees formed a shelter, and sat, glaring at Margaret, her pinafore hooked between her legs. She began chanting then, a low rhythmical sound. Hypnotic. I imagined she was calling up some form of magic against Margaret.

I smothered a laugh, wishing I was brave enough to glare and sing spells against her.

I fully expected Margaret to begin shouting, as I'd seen her do often enough at an impertinent servant. Instead, she threw her hands in the air and returned to the house.

The girl's chanting dropped to a low humming. Ma pulled at me. 'Stop staring Annese. We have work to do.'

I collected a large basket of sheets from the laundry and set about hanging them. Perhaps seeing me struggling with an extra heavy sheet, Tottie ambled across the yard, taking one end from me. I couldn't take my eyes off her. She was taller than any girl I'd ever met. Her skin shone like a newly groomed horse; her black eyes made all the more striking by the whiteness around them. Her teeth were wide and strong, her lips generous. Her wide nose flared as she drew breath and her broad brow allowed for no nonsense. She smiled at me, pulled a comic face, and laughed at my stare.

'Do you know how I can get to *kurra murka*?' she asked. I gasped. She spoke perfect English with a lilt the same as Ma's.

I shook my head. Her smile disappeared; her scowl deepened.

'I… I don't know what a *kurra murka* is.'

Her laugh came out gritty. 'It's the place where my family live.'

A place. My mind raced back to a day in the classroom when we looked at something called an atlas.

'I can ask my brother to look in the book at school.'

Tottie's face softened again, but she still had her stubborn look as we hauled the sheet onto the line and put on pegs. Taking another from the basket, she passed me one end. Her quietness gave me the confidence to keep talking.

'Were you born at *kurra murka*?'

'No. My true Country is *tommeginne* Country. My mother's Country.'

We pegged that sheet and I picked up a pillowcase. 'Your father from tomme…' I attempted, remembering my stumbling attempts with Kiani to pronounce her words.

'No. He's from Ireland. A convict.'

A convict, from Ireland, Ma's home country. How could a native in South Australia have a convict father from Ireland? The shock of it made me drop the pillowcase and I cursed out loud.

Tottie laughed at my cursing and picked up the soiled pillowcase, putting it aside. 'He stole a horse and they sent him to Van Diemen's Land.'

Her story sounded like a fairytale. A faraway place with a strange sounding name, convicts, stolen horses, and Ireland. I found my words coming easily now, as if a cocoon of safety had been woven around us.

'Is it far away—your *kurra murka*?'

'Not too far, I think. It's that way.' She pointed in the direction the sun set. 'West. The land of *narungga* people. Here *peramangk*,' she said spreading her arms.

'Why did you leave your parents?'

She fell silent then and we'd pegged two more sheets before she answered.

'I was taken. Two fishermen came inland from Oyster Bay. They took me and my brother from our parents. They said an escaped convict had no right to be having half-native children.'

Her voice trailed off and she turned from me and began her chant again. I lifted another sheet from the basket. Her chanting stopped and she passed me the pegs.

'Thanks, Tottie.'

She reeled around and glared. 'Not Tottie. I am Tottengarr.'

'Tottengarr.' The name, proud and strong, rolled from me. I nodded. It suited her much better than Tottie.

'Your name?' Her voice, soft now, reminded me of Kiani.

'Annese. Annese Laffer.'

We worked in silence until the basket was empty.

'Those men kept me on Kangaroo Island until they had no more need of me. Then they put me on a boat. They kept my brother with them. Mr Peters found me at the beach he called Rapid Bay.

'On your own!'

Her jaw tightened. 'Yes, on my own. They left me there; on Country I knew nothing about.'

'What is this?'

We both jumped; we'd not heard Margaret approaching. 'Answer me. What is the meaning of this?' She pointed to the dirty pillowcase.

I began to explain 'I, I...'

Tottengarr stepped between us. 'I dropped it, miss. Sorry, miss.'

Apologetic words, but her face stayed firm. My hands trembled, fearing Margaret's reaction. If she got any crosser, I would own up. But Tottengarr's stance seemed to transfix her.

'Very well. Go and make yourself useful in the kitchen, Tottie. Annese, you can scrub the pillowcase your lubra friend dropped.' *Lubra* came out like a sneer. I knew it just meant native woman, but Margaret's was the same sneer I'd heard when Friend Stephen said it.

Walking back to the house behind Margaret, Tottengarr began mimicking her bossy walk, her bottom swinging from side to side. Tears ran down my face as I pushed my laughter down. For the second time that day, I wished I was as brave as Tottengarr.

***

That night I heard Ma telling Da about Tottengarr.

'Her father is an ex-convict from County Cork. He was on Flinders Island working as a sealer. That's where he took up with one of the native women.'

'So how is this Tottengarr here all on her own?

'Apparently, he took her mother to live on Kangaroo Island and then onto the mainland near Oyster Bay. That's where she was taken from them.'

Da shook his head. 'And then they just left her at Rapid Bay, thou says? Imagine doing that to a child. Poor wee thing.'

Ma laughed. 'She's hardly wee. Some say she is kin to Tarenorerer, the woman they called the Amazon. I'd believe it too, the way she stands up to Margaret Mayfield.'

'Still, why would they take her away from her mother and father?' Da said. 'It's not right, Kitty.'

'What's right doesn't come into it, Joshua. Wasn't right when they as good as took our children from us either. But they still did it.'

'That was different, Kitty. We agreed. We …'

Their voices blurred to a murmur. That night I dreamt of being lost and alone on a beach. In the distance, I could see Polly, Thomas, Macca, Kiani, and Tottengarr, but they all ignored me. I had let them all down.

***

Tottengarr was nowhere to be seen when I next went to the Mayfields'. One of the kitchen girls told me Margaret had arranged for her to be sent up to Adelaide to the new training school.

'It's for the native children, so they can learn enough reading and numbers to get work and be useful citizens. But rumour has it, Tottie ran away the very first night she was there. They think she might have stowed away on a boat going west.'

'Annese Laffer, you're not here to gossip.' Margaret stood, hands on hips, at the door. I grabbed the mop and went back to join Ma in the laundry. Mrs Mayfield was there.

'Have you been able to get to see your twins yet, Kitty? Are they being treated well?'

'Oh, the twins are doing fine,' replied Ma, her voice snappy as if she was trying to sound happy.

'I'm glad to hear it. You did the right thing.'

'Oh yes. The right thing,' Ma repeated, hauling the sheets into the boiler. 'They're as happy as children could possibly be at their boarding-out home.' She pushed the words out, cold and hard now, like there was something she was not telling.

Joseph walked with me to school the next day. He got to go once a week, like me, now Ma had regular work. I told him what Ma had said.

'They're as happy as any children could possibly be. They'll be home soon.' I made the last bit up but I was sure it was right.

I thought he'd be pleased, but he stormed ahead. I ran to catch up and grabbed his arm. 'What's wrong with you? Aren't you happy that they'll be with us again soon?'

He reeled around. 'Are you so stupid to believe that? Have you not noticed that Ma eats less every mealtime so we can eat proper? How can they come back if there's not enough food for them?'

'I can feed them with some of my food. I'll play with them and teach them to talk.'

'Da told Friend Stephen that unless we can give them a room of their own and feed them three times a day, the Governor will not return them. Da has asked Friend Stephen to help get them back because he doesn't know what else to do.'

'But they can't keep them. They're ours, not the Govenor's.'

He took my hand and squeezed it as we walked on. 'Not everything makes sense Annese. The sooner you learn that, the better.'

We arrived at school in plenty of time but my mind was too full of hurt and confusion to concentrate. Who was lying—Ma or Joseph? Ma's pushed-out voice when she said *as happy as any children could possibly be* to Mrs Mayfield still echoed in my head. My legs began twitching and my head shaking as I tried to get rid of the hard thoughts. I didn't even realise I was kicking the chair in front of me when Mr Humphage came beside me, cane in hand.

'Stop that, Annese Laffer, or I'll stop it for you.'

Everything around me turned red. I leapt up and tipped the desk over, sending my slate and chalk flying. Running out of the room, I caught sight of Joseph staring at me, aghast.

'You're a liar, Joseph Laffer,' I screamed.

I ran and I screamed until my insides burned dry. I ran and I screamed until my head emptied. I ran and I screamed until I became an eagle and soared away.

***

The kookaburras were announcing the end of the day away when Da found me at the creek. He sat beside me and together we skipped stones across the water.

'We all miss them, Annese, but right now we don't have enough to give them.'

'So you'll bring them home soon?'

Da sighed. It took him a long time to answer. 'The authorities want us to have a two-bedroom cottage and be bringing in enough to have milk and bread for them every day. Now that Ma has regular work at the Mayfields', and with thou helping out too, it will happen in the blink of an eye, thou'll see.'

I blinked my eyes ten times, although I figured it was just one of those expressions Joseph had told me about.

'We won't leave them at the boarding-out place a day longer than we have to. Just until we get on our feet.'

I said the words to make sure I had it right. 'But how will we know when we are on our feet?'

Da tousled my hair. 'Enough questions, Annese. Come on, let's get thee home. Thou are to go to work with Ma for the rest of the week, until Mr Humphage calms down. Thou sure surprised him. Thou are quiet, so he thought thou didn't have a temper. I told him us quiet ones are the worst. When we're riled, there's no stopping us.'

I snuggled into him, glad to be like him.

That night I prayed that we would get a bigger cottage and have a big party when the twins came home. I didn't pray for Macca, or Kiani or Tottengarr, because there wasn't enough room inside me for them that night.

CHAPTER 6

Da had never missed his fat pencil. I'd sharpened it as best I could with a blade I found at the dairy. But it was soon too small to hold, so I resorted to using charcoal. I'd get it on my face sometimes and Ma would ask what I'd been up to. I'd tell her I'd been cleaning a pot or tidying the fireplace. I figured they weren't lies, just saving my face.

When I finished with the notebook for the day, I'd wrap it round with sheets of soft bark and put it at the back of the hollowed tree behind the stone.

I must have been humming the day Joseph caught me. I'd just finished hiding the notebook when he appeared from behind a tree.

'So this is where you disappear to.'

If I'd acted normal, as if it were just any old hiding place, I might have fooled him. But the suddenness of his appearance caught me by surprise and I used the words I'd heard the boys at school say.

'Bugger off, Joseph.'

I expected him to scold me for bad language. Even that would have been better than what happened. He laughed and tweaked my nose.

'What are you hiding?'

I tried to grab him as he ran past me towards the hollowed tree.

'I wasn't hiding anything. I was drawing,' I said as he re-appeared with the notebook, flicking through the pages.

'Where did you get this?'

'Margaret Mayfield gave it to me.' I tried to grab it from him but he held it high above his head.

'*Gave* it to you or you stole it?'

'She…doesn't want it anymore. She threw it away.'

Joseph ran his hands over the glossy cover. 'I doubt that. Let's see what Ma has to say.'

'No. Please, Joseph, it's mine. Margaret probably has plenty more just like it.' But my pleas only fuelled his sense of triumph.

'You're in big trouble now, Annese.'

Ma was peeling potatoes in the yard. She wiped her hands and took the notebook from Joseph, looking carefully at every page filled with my designs.

'Did you do these?'

There was no point denying it. I nodded.

'I didn't know you could do this. Your drawings are beautiful.'

My heart swelled. I'd never been good at anything much before. But my delight was short-lived.

'But you'll have to take it back and apologise. It's the right thing to do. I'm sure Margaret will forgive you if you say sorry.'

I noticed a crease form above her eyebrows and her mouth turned down. Her words fell from her, as if even she wasn't sure she believed them.

'It's the right thing to do,' she said quietly as if trying to convince herself.

The next day wasn't a laundry day but we went anyway, right up to the Mayfields' front door. Florrie, the house maid, told us to wait and went to find Margaret. She was already cross when she arrived, as if we'd interrupted something important. Seeing the notebook she snatched it from Ma, flipping through it several times, her face turning the colour of a parrot's breast.

Ma pulled me closer. 'Annese found it and thought you'd thrown it away. She should have asked. Say sorry, Annese.'

'Sorry, Margaret,' I muttered. 'It was in the sheets on a big wash day. I thought you didn't want it anymore.'

I heard Ma sigh and felt her stand a little taller. She'd made me practise my sorry words over and over on the way there. But Margaret grabbed me by the arm and waved the notebook at me.

'And where's my letter? There was a letter in it. What have you done with it?'

Ma stiffened and I knew if I hung my head, she would know the truth. So I looked straight at her, avoiding Margaret's rage. I made my eyes wide.

'Nothing, Ma.' The word came out quivering and I shook my head. I had to make Ma believe me.

'Nothing. What do you mean nothing?' Margaret screeched, scaring a willy wagtail. He hopped a little further away but kept watch over us. I looked at his curious eyes and wondered if he knew the truth.

Ma prodded me. 'Was there a letter, Annese?'

'Nothing else in it.' My voice was still wobbly but I managed all the words in order.

Margaret's eyes narrowed. 'Where's my letter?' she yelled. 'It was private and personal. What have you done with it?' She turned on Ma now and threw the notebook at her feet. 'Tell her to answer me, Mrs Laffer.'

I looked to Ma to save me, but, instead of love, I saw fear in her eyes. My voice came out sharp as an axe now.

'No letter. Only blank pages.' I made my eyes squinty too.

Margaret stepped forward and pushed me to the ground. 'You're a liar. A liar and a thief. People think that you're simple, but I know you're as sly as a fox.' Her words hit me in the chest like the legs of a fighting kangaroo.

'And you, Mrs Laffer, should know better than to let her get away with it.'

Ma's hands trembled. 'I swear, Miss Margaret, I only saw the notebook yesterday and there was no letter in it. Just Annese's scribblings.' Her voice was pleading now. 'Annese may be a little off with the fairies at times, but she is not a liar. If she says there was no letter, there was no letter.'

Margaret began to walk back into the house before reeling around, a new look on her face, like the big rocks beside the creek. My stomach churned.

'You're liars. Irish liars. Father always said that no good would come from Friend Laffer marrying a Catholic. Go, both of you—and don't come back.'

That night Ma and Da went out under the stars to talk. I could not hear all the words but I did hear Ma crying. At times they were loud and then they went quiet. I heard my name a few times but mostly they talked about Polly and Thomas. I heard them say the name Mrs Scholz several times.

'Just because she has money doesn't mean she'll look after them,' Ma said.

'Eliza Hastings knows her. She says she is kind and gentle. She's well educated too; a patron of the arts, she said.'

'You say she has no children of her own?'

Da nodded. 'She will take them on, but only if we agree to not try to take them back. We can see them but she says she couldn't manage the grief of giving them back to us. She already thinks of them as her own.'

'Her grief! What about ours? No. There must be another way. We must get Friend Stephen and Friend Ernest to help us.'

***

By the time I woke the next morning, everyone was already going about their chores. Ma was in the garden; Da and Joseph building a wood pile with the mallee stumps from the trees they'd recently cut down. With them all out of the hut, I put my plan into action.

I took the tin from under my mattress. A soothing waft of cinnamon and star anise—the spice I was named after—greeted me. Taking

Margaret's letter from underneath Macca's doll, I tucked it into my underwear and went to the stove. But the day was hot and no fire had been lit. I was about to tear it up and put it in the pig scraps when Ma came up behind me and grabbed it out of my hands. I needed to pee but I squirmed from one foot to the other watching her face, waiting to be scolded.

But instead, she shook her head as she read. 'Poor Tottie. Accused of stealing. That explains why they sent her away. And Macca… no wonder he left in a hurry.'

She passed it back to me. 'Light a fire, Annese. No good can come of returning it. If Margaret ever learns that you kept this, it'd be the end of us. You've already brought so much trouble to this family; we don't need any more. Burn it.'

I took it from her, still squirming to hold in my pee.

'Oh for goodness' sake, go to the lavvy first.'

As I rushed past her towards the toilet, she thrust the letter down my pinafore. 'Make sure you burn it when you finish out there.' And then as an afterthought, she added, 'Don't mention it to anyone—not even your father or Joseph. Best keep it our secret.'

I took it out while sitting on the lavvy, wondering what was so important that the burning of it needed to be a secret. I scanned it to see if I could find Macca's name in among the writing. I looked for a capital M and soon found *Malcolm Macleod,* which I remembered was his real name. Why was Margaret writing about Macca? Did she know where he was? Did it say anything about why he'd left? But I couldn't make out any more of the words.

I looked for a T for Tottie too, but couldn't find one. Why did Ma say 'poor Tottie?'

Joseph had lit the fire and was unloading more wood when I got back. I went to my bed and took out Macca's doll, pretending to play with it.

'You're too old for dolls,' he said. 'Come and help me with this wood.'

I kissed the doll and, glancing behind me, took the letter from my pinafore, putting it in the tin with the doll on top. It seemed to smile at me as if it too was saying *our secret*.

***

Ma never asked me if I burned the letter. I should have felt ashamed for deceiving her but somehow, it just made me feel clever. And powerful.

CHAPTER 7

Not long after I hid the letter, Macca came for a visit. He was truly a man now, with a full beard and browned skin. His eyes still glinted when he smiled, although he was mostly sad and quiet. He reached into his pocket and gave Ma a wad of money.

'For all the times you fed me when I had nothing, Kitty. Take it.'

Ma tried to push it back but he wouldn't have it. 'Buy this one some ribbons for that mop of hair.'

He went to ruffle my hair like he used to but stopped. He looked at me differently now, as if he wanted to tease me. He was different too. Sad. I asked him to go to the creek with me but he shook his head and grew even more morose.

'Too many memories at that place,' he said. It wasn't until around the fire that night that I understood what he meant.

'Is it Stephen Hastings thou worked for at Encounter Bay?' Da asked him.

'Right enough. I left here for Encounter Bay looking for work. But even there, Hastings had his say in who gained employment and who didn't.'

'So where did thou go after that?' Da asked as we all took our tin-cup of tea and settled around Macca.

'A place called Port Fairy, following the whaling work.'

'I'm told it's a dangerous business.'

Macca nodded. 'Probably as frightening as it gets. The boat we go out in is only as long as your hut. Six of us row to where the beasts are offshore. There's also a steerer harpoonist on board. Once we are within striking distance, the work really starts. The harpoonist stands and thrusts the weapon. If he jags a whale, we are pulled miles offshore before it slows enough for us to drag it to shore.'

'You could die out there,' Ma gasped, her hand to her cheek. 'Why do you do such work, Macca?'

Macca took his time to answer. 'Maybe that's it, Kitty. The chance that it will all be over.' He said it with such seriousness that not even Da had his usual wise response.

'There are things you should know, Joshua. Before I left for Port Fairy, I came across the tribe who had once lived on this land hereabouts. They told me that they moved to near Encounter Bay after Stephen Hastings threatened to poison the water hole here.'

Da held up his hand. 'Enough, Macca. Not in front of these two.' He nodded towards me and Joseph. 'Friend Stephen has his faults but I'm sure he'd never do such a thing. Thou has no proof.'

The memory of Stephen Hastings's words when I hid in Kiani's people's house came back to me. *Well, I'm glad they're gone and him too. It gives me full access to the creek.*

'No proof other than the words of the people he threatened,' Macca said. 'Are their words not proof?' The bitterness in his voice was cutting, but Da did not respond in kind.

'We will agree to disagree on the subject of Friend Hastings. He is my employer and I find him to be an honest man.'

Macca shrugged. 'Many of them are still living near Encounter Bay. I came back that way only yesterday.'

Still near here! My heart leapt. 'Kiani?' My voice was thin with both hope and fear.

Macca turned to me and nodded. 'Kiani, yes, but…'

'Ngama?' All eyes were on me now.

A cloud covered Macca's face. 'No. Ngama was taken by the sealers soon after her family moved to Encounter Bay. They'd come across from Kangaroo Island and took five of the young women—to help them find food and water, they said. Ngama has not been seen since. Her family holds no hope for her survival. They believe the island is where the spirits of their dead people go.'

My mind whirled. I could not accept what he was saying. Ngama taken and likely dead? She was young, her body and spirit full of life.

I looked up, expecting to see my sadness reflected in the faces of my family but it was only Macca's eyes that met mine.

'I miss her too, Annese. Every day. But Kiani is alive.' His voice took on that forced happiness adults use for children.

My feelings soared between sadness for Ngama and joy that Kiani was still nearby and with her family. I jumped up and ran. I needed to be on my own. I wanted to go to the creek, but the night was moonless and, as Macca had said, there were too many memories there.

It was Macca who came after me. We had no words, so we sat in silence and watched as a shooting star fell from heaven. I prayed it was Ngama coming back from the island of the spirits.

***

Soon after Macca's visit, Da got word from Friend Stephen about the twins. He called us all together as soon as he arrived home.

'He even met with the Governor. With only me and Joseph working now, they will not let them return. He says there is no more he can do. They want them to stay with Mrs Scholz. Polly and Thomas have been with her for two months now and the Governor's report says they are happy and have plenty to eat. We can visit as often as we like and when they are sixteen, they can make up their own minds.'

Ma's face hardened. 'So, what did you tell him, Joshua Laffer?' She made no attempt at hiding her anger.

Da looked at her and shook his head before turning to us.

'Thy mother says it must be me who tells thee. I said we will do what we must for the twins' welfare. If that means them going to another home until they are sixteen, with a person who can provide them with good food in their bellies and a solid roof over their heads, then so be it. We must reconcile ourselves, Kitty. We need to relinquish them into Mrs Scholz's care.'

'So that's it then, children. We are relinquishing them.' She pushed past Da and went to the wood pile. Her angry chopping lasted until dark, when she went straight to their bed. Da slept under the stars that night.

I waited for two days before I asked Ma what relinquishing meant. 'Is it like connecting up again, like re-linking the gate chain?' I crossed my fingers hoping it was, because that would mean the twins would be coming home soon. In the past, when I'd asked her when they'd be home, she'd answer 'as soon as we can' or, if she was cross with me for being away with the fairies, she'd say 'when you learn to do as you're told instead of watching the clouds all day.'

'No, Annese. It means giving them up. Letting them go. It means Polly and Thomas will live with Mrs Scholz until they're grown and can fend for themselves.' Her eyes filled with tears and her voice wobbled.

I stared at her, angry and confused. 'But you said they'd be home soon if I did as I was told and didn't watch the clouds. And I haven't, hardly at all.' It was true. Why, just the day before, I'd ignored them, even when they were gathering in the sky like dragons.

'I'm sorry, Annese, but the fact of the matter is, we can't provide for them now that I have no work.'

'Thanks to you, Annese.' Joseph had come up behind me. His words slapped my face. He was right. It was all my fault. If I hadn't taken the notebook, Ma would still be in work. If I hadn't lied about the letter, the twins would be coming home.

My head swirled as the prospect of a future without Polly and Thomas pulled me under. I couldn't breathe.

'Are you all right, Annese? Annese!'
Ma caught me as I fell.

***

My school days came to an end on my eleventh birthday and I began working alongside Ma when she eventually found work at the Hogan Arms. She served beer and rum to the regular coachmen and passing travellers, while I mostly cleaned rooms and helped in the kitchen.

Working at the Hogan Arms didn't bring back the old Ma, but she was better than when the twins first left. I could tell that she enjoyed the banter of the customers. And, at night, she'd report back the news brought from Adelaide Town. She said it reminded her of the public houses she'd gone to as a child with her father.

'There's much talk about the construction of a proper road to connect the Town to the port. It'll open up all that unused land along the way. There's new farming areas opening up too. A Mr Weaver and a Mr Hart have bought land on Yorke Peninsula. They hope to find copper there.'

On another occasion, she said all the talk was about the New Queen's Theatre. 'They're putting on a new drama, *The Warlock of the Glen*. The last act has a white person singing with a face painted black. Can you imagine that?'

At first, I'd join her in the bar whenever I could, to hear the news firsthand. I loved watching the different ways the men spoke and interacted. I'd mimic them as I watched them, re-enacting their boisterous antics. After a while though, Ma said I needed to stick to my chores.

'The men find your ways unnerving.'

'My ways?'

'You don't answer their questions and you copy them behind their backs. They think you're mocking them.'

From then on, I found myself doing only those chores that didn't require me to talk to anyone. Happy with that arrangement, I would answer the whistler birds as they called from high in the trees. *Eechung. Eechung.* On rainy days, I'd pretend I was underwater and push through the damp air, a fish swimming upstream.

One day, I overheard Mr Hogan asking Ma about me. They were sitting under a tree near the room I was cleaning. Hearing my name, I curled up below the window and listened.

'Is she simple, Kitty? Some say she's a dullard.'

I didn't know what a dullard was, but I was pleased to hear Ma's response.

'No. In fact, she's as sharp as a tack. She understands everything you say, but her words don't come out quickly enough most times. You would have seen her practising; talking to herself. Sometimes she'll answer a question you asked her minutes later. Most people don't have the patience to wait. Even I get frustrated. Joshua is much better with her than I am.'

'So she can talk?'

'Oh yes, although she'll try to get away with just saying one or two words if she can. I sometimes wonder if we've let her get lazy that way. Not pushing her to say whole sentences.'

'Do you think she'll ever make it on her own? You know, get married and run a house?'

'Aye, if she finds the right man who can tolerate her oddness, she'll make a good wife. She's handy at making things, putting things together. She has a notebook full of drawings, shapes, and patterns mostly. They're quite something.'

They finished their tea and went back to the bar, but their words kept going around in my head. I'd never imagined that my ways would stop me getting married. Margaret Mayfield was the only older girl I knew who hadn't married. They called her a spinster. I didn't want to be like her.

I knew people found my quietness strange. They seemed to mind that I spent so much time on my own in the bush. It was true I could spend hours at a time up a tree or lying on the ground watching the clouds chase each other across the sky. Sometimes I'd make a tunnel with my hand, listening to the sounds coming up from below; the earth talking to me. One day I was following a mouse in the grass, pretending I was a cat, readying to pounce, when Joseph grabbed me by the arm and hauled me to my feet.

'You're too old to be doing those things,' he said. 'It's not ladylike.'

'Why do I have to be like a lady? You get to climb trees still. Why can't I?'

'Others talk about you. They say you're loony.'

I knew without asking who he was referring to. 'Margaret Mayfield, you mean. Why do you care what she says?'

'Not just her. Everybody.'

'Not everybody. Not Ma. Not Da. Not Macca. Not Friend Ernest Hastings or Mrs Stephen. Not Mr Sanders. Not…'

I could have gone on because I knew well enough those that thought me strange and those that didn't.

'Stop, Annese. You know what I mean. Some say you should be taken before you become a danger.'

His words landed on me like a pail of cold water.

'Taken where?'

'I don't know where, Annese, but it's what they say. Can't you at least try to act properly?' He'd said it with a cracked voice, sad not angry, and walked away, hitting out with the stick he was carrying.

Taken? Like Polly and Thomas? I tried to shrug off his words but they grew inside me. So I stopped climbing trees or looking at the clouds when others could see me. I began using my words as best I could too, mimicking others to try to fit in. Laughing when they laughed, even if I didn't understand the joke. It was exhausting, and some days I had to spend the whole day in bed and just sink into myself, like a sunflower waiting to be watered.

***

I took to asking Da and Ma to tell me stories about the twins. It was the only way I knew to make my memory of them stay in my head. Sometimes it made them sad, but they said it didn't matter. They said it was the right thing to do, to keep thinking and talking about them. My favourite was Ma's story about when she found out it was twins she was carrying.

'At first, I was worried—I didn't know how to manage two babies at a time. But as my belly grew, I was happy they were in there together. Do you remember how they always had to hold hands to go to sleep?'

I did remember that and much, much more.

'I'm sorry for stealing the notebook, Ma. I'm sorry I made them get taken.' I was about to tell her that I had disobeyed her and kept the letter but she pulled me to her, burying me in her bosom.

'It wasn't your fault, Annese. There's plenty of others I could blame, but you won't hear their names from my lips. Anyway,' she said setting me back on the stool and drying her eyes, 'we'll be seeing them soon enough. I won't go another Christmas without seeing their shiny faces. And this time, you and Joseph must come too.'

A trip to Adelaide Town both excited and terrified me. I'd only been there twice, once to see a dentist and the other when I'd broken my arm falling from a tree. I knew it took the best part of a day to get there—more in bad weather—and that the trip was uncomfortable. But the thought of seeing Polly and Thomas far outweighed my fears.

Friend Stephen offered to take us, along with a load of wool bales. Da left for Adelaide after tea. 'There's not room for us all on the dray. It's a full moon. I'll walk and get to the Mount Barker turnoff tonight. If you leave early tomorrow morning, you'll probably catch up with me somewhere near Crafers.'

Friend Stephen drove the two horses and Ma sat up front with him, while Joseph and I sat amongst the bales. It was bumpier at the back but, on top of one bale with another on each side, I had a cosy ride. Surrounded by the smell of sheep and lanolin from the wool, I drifted off, waking occasionally to swat away a fly. By the time we saw Da, Joseph had had enough of the jarring of the dray. Da climbed aboard and Ma came to the back with me, while Joseph ran alongside. The descent down from Crafers had Ma and me clinging to each other, Ma saying her prayers to Mary out loud. She wasn't supposed to; the Friends didn't believe in Mary the way Ma did.

Once we were on flat ground with a proper cleared road again, I climbed on top of the bales to get a better view. I couldn't believe the number of houses I saw before me. Many were grand like the Mayfield's, others little huts like ours. The nearer we got to the river, the closer together all the buildings came. Horses and sulkies went in all directions. Shops selling all manner of things—hats, drapery, shoes, saddles, piping, and brooms—lined the dusty streets. The people were muddled together too. Some women wore large things under their skirts to make their bottoms bigger and some men wore fancy hats. I tried to imagine them walking around at Echunga like that, but I couldn't. I think even Margaret Mayfield would have found them comical.

Dozens of children ran unsupervised in the streets, in and out between carts and drays. But they were outnumbered by dogs of all breeds in all conditions. I caught a glimpse of some natives sitting in groups, just like they had at their camp on the creek, but these all wore proper clothes. It should have made them look more civilised, I suppose, but to me, they just looked silly.

Mr Hastings dropped us at a small park near the German Hospital. The twins were already there with Mrs Scholz. I knew immediately it was them, even though they had changed so much. Not babies anymore, both tall and plumpish. I ran ahead, my arms outstretched to hug them, one in each arm as I'd always done. Polly ran to me, but Thomas held back and turned to Mrs Scholz, his manner formal and angry.

'Mutter, wer ist das?'

'Sie ist deine Schwester, Thomas. '

'Nein, Polly ist meine Schwester.'

His words came out hard and flat and took the wind from me. Even though I knew not a word of German, I understood.

He did not want me as his sister. Me, who had washed his mucky bottom and fed mashed oats into his gaping mouth. Me, who had coached him to take his first steps and rocked him to sleep when his tiny baby teeth inflamed his gums. Now he looked at me as if I was a stranger—no, worse—an enemy.

I stood back, unable to meet his accusatory stare, certain that he somehow knew it was my fault they'd been taken.

We all sat on rugs and, at Mrs Scholz's prompting, Thomas offered Ma a piece of cake.

'Try some, Mrs Laffer,' he said. I gasped. Mrs Laffer? He called Ma 'Mrs Laffer'. A look of confusion crossed her face, but she covered it quickly and took a slice.

'It's a traditional German cake, made from potatoes.' Mrs Scholz's words were strange, thick, and pushy, but she had the bluest eyes I'd ever seen. They smiled as she talked.

When Thomas came to me, he put the plate down before me and turned away. His rudeness met its mark.

Da asked Mrs Scholz about her farm in the Barossa and Ma talked to Polly about her school. Joseph and Thomas were having an awkward conversation about cricket. How could they all act as if this was a normal family get-together? My head spun and I felt as if I would gag on the stodgy cake.

'Annese, Polly is talking to you.' I heard Joseph's voice through the fog. He prodded me and I realised Polly was beside me with two dolls. I'd never held a real doll. I'd seen Margaret Mayfield's china one, which she kept in a glass cabinet, but I didn't know what I was supposed to do with the one Polly was now passing to me. I took it from her as gently as I could.

It was made of cotton and had a face stitched on, the lips like a little red bow. I ran my hand over its hair, so soft I wondered if it was real.

Its dress, a simple straight down tunic, was decorated with pink and blue flowers, with long bloomers poking out beneath it. Its feet were like two prongs, with tiny bits of leather sewn on as shoes. The arms were pointed too, with no fingers.

Polly held the other doll up for me to see. Made of wood, its hair was painted on, glossy black, and parted in the middle. Its clothes were much more elaborate than the one I held: the shiny blue skirt matched the colour of Mrs Scholz's and was trimmed with lace. Above it was a silky white top with the tiniest stitching I'd ever seen. A crocheted lace shawl, draped around the shoulders, was fixed with a threepenny coin of all things. It had proper feet with black shoes painted on. But what fascinated me the most were the long fingers, etched into the wood. I longed to touch them but dared not.

'I brought them both from my home country,' Mrs Scholz said. 'They're Polly's now.'

'Do you want to play schools with me, Annese?' Polly asked. 'My doll can be the teacher and yours the student.'

I looked to Ma for guidance; I'd never played with real dolls before. Her face went sad before she nodded. 'Polly will show you what to do, Annese. Just have fun.'

We sat on the lawn and Polly used a funny bossy voice as if it came from her teacher doll and I answered her questions in my whispered voice. I knew this was the wrong way around, with me being the older sister by more than three years. But Polly was so happy and confident no one seemed to notice.

The afternoon came to an end too soon. I realised as we said goodbye that a part of me had been hoping Ma and Da would change their minds and that we would take the twins with us. Instead, what I heard was them telling Mrs Scholz that they were grateful for her kindness.

'We could never have given them what you have provided. We are forever in your debt.' *In her debt*. But it was us who had given her something. We had given her part of our family.

'They have brought me great joy that, at one time, I thought I would never know,' Mrs Scholz said. 'It is not your fault that circumstances conspired against you.'

Her voice was soft and kind. *Circumstances. Conspired.* I felt as if an axe had hit me as we walked away, our lives wrenched apart once again.

Da placed a consoling arm around Ma's shoulders and we headed to our accommodation at the City Bridge Hotel. I could see Ma was weeping and I fell behind, trying to avoid the misery that engulfed us all. A gust of hot wind from the north swirled dust around me and I prayed that it would carry me away. Away from the hurt I'd caused everyone. But it left me alone as I placed one foot in front of the other.

My hell was to be here on earth.

Through the heat of my shame, I heard a familiar voice calling my name.

'Annese. *yirki.*'

I looked ahead to my family but they were engrossed in their own thoughts.

'Annese. Sister.'

A young native, with a child on her lap, waved to me. She was with the group I'd seen earlier, sitting under a tree. It was not until she smiled and called something in her own language that I recognised Kiani. She had the body of a woman but her face was still that of the girl from the creek.

Despite my despair, I felt a surge of joy. Checking that Ma and Da were not looking, I stopped and waved back. A settler family walked between us and I saw the mother pull her children to her as they neared Kiani and her group. One of the older native women called something out and the group laughed, reminding me of Ngama's laugh. I looked for her, then I remembered Macca's story. Ngama had been taken.

Kiani called again, the children around her giggling just as she and I had once done splashing in the creek. I remembered how we'd both screamed with delight when a frog had jumped towards us from under a rock we'd turned over.

She beckoned me. 'Kiani. Tidda.'

I felt the heaviness of the day lift and called back, about to walk to her when Da gently took my arm. I tried to wave again but he tightened his hold and guided me away.

'That time has finished, Annese,' he said, his voice like cotton wool. 'It's best thou leave the natives to themselves.'

CHAPTER 8

The number of people in Echunga grew fourfold on market days. Ma had left early to prepare for extra customers and I was walking to work on my own, when Jonathon Hastings caught up with me. He was a friend of Joseph's and, of all the Hastings boys, the best looking.

'Off to work, Annese?' he asked.

Annoyed at his attention, I nodded and walked faster, hoping he'd understand I didn't want his company.

He seemed not to notice and kept walking beside me. 'I'm soon to start work too at the wheelwright's. My brother has been given work at the nursery—he has green thumbs, they say.'

I'd never looked at his brother's thumbs, but I'm sure I would have noticed if they were green.

'Green?' The word escaped me before I could hold my curiosity back.

'Just a saying. It means he can make things grow better than most.'

We'd almost reached the Hogan Arms when four men, farmers by the look of them, jostled past us and pushed me against Jonathon. I could smell the drink already on their breath. Jonathon caught me by the elbow and set me straight, as embarrassed as I was by the contact. He stepped away from me but not before his gaze dropped briefly to my chest. I was still tiny compared with other girls but I'd noticed boys paying more attention to me lately.

My bleeding had started two months before and it seemed that now, even more was expected of me. After the last Meeting, Margaret's little sister, Nancy, said if I took more care with my hair I'd be quite pretty. I wasn't sure that I wanted to be *quite pretty* if it meant brushing my hair all the time. Ma and I had only one brush between us and I often forgot to use it; then Ma had to pull at my tangles till my eyes watered.

The Mayfield girls went to Adelaide Town once a year to have their hair done at Mr Schumann's. They told me that there was a separate treatment room for ladies. They would spend a whole day there being shampooed and pampered and come home looking like the girls in a magazine a woman had once left at the Inn.

'Is thou going to my cousin's wedding?' Jonathon asked.

I shrugged. Jonathon was the only person my age who still said 'thou' instead of 'you'. The other boys teased him, but I rather liked it.

We had been invited to the wedding—all the Friends had—but Ma told them we were unable to attend. It wasn't because we had another engagement but because we had no fancy clothes other than our First Day clothes.

'I'll not provide Margaret Mayfield with the satisfaction of seeing us so poorly equipped,' she'd said as she tore up the invitation.

When I didn't answer Jonathon for this second time, he turned away towards the wheelwright's. 'I'd be pleased to see thou there.'

Only Macca had ever told me he was pleased to see me before. I knew half the girls my age would have welcomed Jonathon's interest, but it just made me feel awkward.

Readying myself to clean the rooms, I found myself wondering if Macca liked girls with fancy hair styles and fashionable clothes. I doubted it, but still, I snuck a look at my image as I passed the mirror in the bathroom and imagined what I would look like if I ever went to the Mayfields' fancy hair salon.

'Annese, stop your dilly-dallying. You're going to have to help me in the bar today.'

Ma was standing, hands on hips, a frantic look on her face. 'They're coming in droves. Leave the rooms until after lunch.'

The bar was dimly lit, but I could see that the men who had jostled us were now lined up along the bar, halfway through a beer.

'Reckon that James Brown will get away with it, the killings at Avenue Range?' one asked another.

'Reckon so. The only witnesses have scarpered. He expected his overseer, Eastwood, to speak for him but he's disappeared too, along with all the blacks.'

I filled their glasses as requested and counted the coins. 'I'm not a lover of the natives, but it don't seem right that he'll walk just like that. Nine of them, there was, killed: one an old blind man, the rest women and children. One an infant, they say. All partially burnt then buried on top of each other.'

My stomach lurched at the thought of charred bodies. I stood open-mouthed, waiting to find out more.

'In retaliation for a few stolen sheep. Brown denies it was him but even the magistrate said that there was little question of the extent of the butchery or who the butcher was. But without any evidence…'

Nine of them. I knew they were talking about Kiani's people but was it her family? Where was Avenue Range? Was she one of those bodies? Even if I could have found the words to ask, I doubted these men would know which family it was. Was it stories like this that had brought sadness to Macca?

'Annese!' Ma had returned from clearing a table. Her angry voice cut through my stupor. She snatched the coins from me and threw them in the till. 'Go clear the other tables and then help in the kitchen. And you lot just remember who is around before you start with your stories.'

***

It was almost a year before I saw Kiani and her family again. They'd arrived quietly overnight, about fifty of them. We could hear them from our hut and, as soon as Ma left for work, I went to watch them at their old camp site. All day they chanted as the men painted themselves with ochre, the women daubing themselves with what looked like a mixture of charcoal and fat. I kept my distance as they gathered around something that I soon realised was a body, wrapped in branches and leaves. Some of the men lifted it between them, their chanting rising and falling.

It was then that I finally saw Kiani. She didn't look at me even when I stepped out from my hiding place. They circled many times over an area beside the creek before they lowered the body into a hole in the ground. There was no crying, just the hypnotic drone of voices coming together from a sadness deep inside.

They disappeared as quickly and as quietly as they'd arrived, and I thought it would be the last time I'd see Kiani. Our worlds had drifted so far apart.

***

Da took work at the new quarry and, with us all in work—Joseph at the dairy and Ma and me at the Hogan Arms—we were able to make the hut more comfortable.

Joseph made bricks from mud to put along the west and south sides and I helped him put up new corrugated iron to fully enclose the lean-to. Da redid the thatch on the roof.

Every six months or so, Ma and Da visited the twins. They came home with stories of how well they were both coping with all the changes.

'They are so grown up for their age. Polly takes control of our visits like a hostess and Thomas is so polite. It must be the German way, I suppose,' Da said.

'And the way of those with money,' Ma said, her resentment obvious to all.

'Now, Kitty. We agreed. She's a good Christian woman and is bringing them up to become successful young people in a modern world. There's even talk she may take them to Europe for a time. Imagine that.'

Ma and Da always asked if Joseph and I wanted to go with them, but Joseph hated going to Adelaide and would say he needed to stay at home to feed the chickens and milk the cow. I'd ask to stay home too, to cook for him I said, but we all knew it was an excuse. The truth was, I was afraid Thomas's contempt for me would by now have spread to Polly, and I couldn't bear to be rejected by her too. I'd convinced myself they'd been told about the stolen notebook and letter, and that they knew my actions had led to Ma's dismissal and their removal.

Margaret's letter was still in the tin. I hadn't dared look at it again, telling myself no good could come of it. Her notebook I'd filled long ago, but I kept that too. Ma once offered to buy me another one but I said no; I felt guilty about her hard-earned money going on such a luxury.

Not long after we got the new roof, word began to be passed around that things were getting worse in the colony. Farming was not proving as productive as once expected. Crops had failed due to drought and the government had overspent and were now calling in debts. Hundreds of men were leaving the colony for the goldfields in the east, and travellers who'd once used the Hogan Arms as a stop-off point, now had to save their coins and camped at the creek.

Mr Hogan called Ma aside as we were about to leave one day. 'The banks are foreclosing on those who have over-speculated. With so many men already away at the goldfields, the hotel is losing money. I have to cut down on staff. I'm afraid I can't keep both you and Annese on.'

'But our family relies on us both having an income. Joseph and Joshua barely make a living between them. And what about our cottage? We've just made it comfortable.' I heard the distress in her voice.

'I'm sorry, Mrs Laffer. At the end of the day, I'm a businessman and must ensure I am staying afloat myself. Would Mr Laffer and Joseph consider going to the goldfields? I've heard there's plenty of men making their fortune there.'

'And plenty more who've lost everything, leaving their wives and children to fend for themselves,' Ma said, her voice angry now, like a screeching black cockatoo.

'If there is anything I can do…' Mr Hogan continued.

She put her hands on her hips and pointed her chin upwards, a sign all our family knew meant to keep our thoughts to ourselves.

'We've no need of your charity. We'll make our own way as we've always done.'

I'd listened often enough to her views on how the rich get richer at the expense of the poor. Up until recently, she'd been of the opinion that Mr Hogan was different from most rich men but, just two nights earlier, Joseph brought home a story of how Friend Hogan had evicted a recently widowed woman and her seven children.

'After years of keeping up with her rent, she'd defaulted. But only twice. He swooped in, they say, and the woman and her children are now living in the destitute asylum in Adelaide.'

Her eviction disturbed us all. We all talked long into the night. Joseph had been itching to leave for the goldfields for months but would not do so without Da.

'It's our only hope,' he said. 'I'll go on my own Da, if you won't go.' I could tell from his face that it was not what he wanted. By the time we went to bed, it had been agreed.

'We'll leave next week for Bendigo,' Da said to Ma. 'Thou and Annese should go to Adelaide Town, Kitty. With so many men gone, there's work there for those who are prepared to do it.'

Ma shook her head, not to say no but from despair. 'You know I hate the place,' she said. 'It's dusty for nine months of the year and muddy the rest. And I'm not so sure about there being work now that the South Australia Company has seen fit to bring over even more girls from Ireland. They've taken up most of the domestic jobs, and those who don't find legal employment resort to street work. Is that the life you want for your daughter?'

'Kitty, that's enough,' Da scolded, glancing at me.

'Well, it's true. Many of them were supposed to go on to Melbourne but they get off the boats in Adelaide, with no way to support themselves other than revert to what women have had to revert to since time began. There's even a quadrangle sectioned off near the destitute asylum for them; the Female Immigration Depot, they call it. I don't want Annese being influenced by the likes of them.'

Da nodded as he always does when he can't think of a solution to a problem. 'I've heard those stories too, Kitty. It's a far cry from what we all hoped for when we came here.'

The very next First Day, Da and Joseph packed the tent and a bag each and left to make the journey on foot to Bendigo.

'We will be less hindered in that way so it should only take us six weeks, providing we come across no trouble. Those travelling on horse are doing it in four, though some of their time is spent finding a suitable track.'

'Don't forget to write us once you're there. Address it to the Hogan Arms, for we'll not know where we'll be. It will get forwarded from there.'

CHAPTER 9

Friend Hogan allowed Ma and me to stay on at the cottage for another month before we too had to leave. He helped Ma find a position with a Mrs Bartholomew, the wife of a wealthy pastoralist who'd taken out a special survey of land near a town called Clare. Mrs Bartholomew stayed mostly in Adelaide Town though, awaiting the building of their homestead. Ma's job came with a room at the back of their house on East Terrace and Mrs Bartholomew agreed to me staying with Ma until I found work.

'Remember, it is only until I need the other bed,' she said to Ma but looking sternly at me.

Ma took the bottom bunk and unpacked her small case. I lingered until she went outside then, after placing the very few clothes I owned in a pile at the end of my bed, I put the tin containing Macca's doll and Margaret's letter under her bunk, pushing it against the wall where I hoped she would not find it.

With businesses all over Adelaide closing down, their proprietors leaving for the goldfields, work was hard to come by. I noticed too that I seemed to annoy people in Adelaide. Most folk in Echunga, who'd known me since I was a child, had become used to my silent ways. Of late, they'd taken it for granted that I would speak only when necessary and then only in as few words as needed. It was only Margaret who either laughed at me or got cross when I didn't promptly answer her demanding questions. The people of Adelaide were not at all patient with me and twice I'd been shuffled out of a shop when I couldn't make my words come out.

Ma's patience with me wore thin at times too. 'Annese, I know you can talk well enough. You have to make more of an attempt. Folk think you're rude. I've even been asked if you're deaf. You'll never find work if you don't make an effort.'

'But I only like talking to you, Da and Joseph.' And Macca, I said to myself, even though it had been over a year since I'd seen him.

'That's fine and dandy, but it annoys people and any likely employer will think you'll not be able to follow directions.'

It seemed she was right, for none of my attempts to find work had been successful. A week after we arrived, I was about to set out again, practising my words as I left, when Ma rushed home. It was not yet noon so I feared something was amiss.

'Hurry, Annese, come and see. Mr Tolmer and the gold escort have arrived.'

Everyone had been talking about the newly formed escort, created to bring gold found by our men back to Adelaide.

We reached the Toll House in time to see the cavalcade rounding the corner. It seemed that everyone in Adelaide Town was there to greet them, all waving flags made from any old rag they could find. The troopers at the front and rear of the vehicle carrying the gold had their carbines on their shoulders, lances at the ready although there seemed to be no threat, just jubilation. From a distance, they gave the impression of a well-groomed troop, but this was quickly dispelled as they got closer, their dusty clothes and faces so bronzed they resembled the very rascals they were sent to resist. But even their dishevelment could not dampen the resolute and triumphant look on their faces. They knew the important duty they'd performed, bringing back the riches of the goldfield to our colony rather than into Melbourne, where its worth to South Australia might be lost forever.

By the time they made it to the Assay Office, a small brass band had been cobbled together and they were heralded in as the heroes they were.

'This'll show those eastern states that we are not just pious do-gooders,' I heard one man say. 'Soon, our buildings will be as grand as those in Melbourne.'

Ma's enthusiasm stopped short of us joining the partying that ensued. She went back to work, sending me to our room. 'Best stay inside today, Annese. Those men may be heroes but they've been on the road for weeks. There'll only be two things on their minds.'

Alone in our room, I was practising my talking out loud as I would in a conversation when I heard a gentle knock at the door. Remembering Ma's instruction and not knowing anybody who would come calling, I did not answer.

The knock grew louder. 'I know you're in there, Annese, I can hear you talking. I just saw Jonathon Hastings and he told me where I would find you.'

The man's voice had a familiar lilt, similar to Macca's but rougher. 'Open up. It's me, Annese. It's Macca.'

I gingerly opened the door, half expecting to be confronted with a drunken stranger. Relief flooded through me when I recognised his conspiratorial smile, the smile that led me to trust him all those years ago. I threw myself into his arms and our laughter filled the air but he gently pushed me away.

'I think you're a bit too old for that now. But aye, it's good to see you, lassie.'

Questions tumbled from me. 'Where have you been? Why didn't you write? Are you on your own?'

He laughed again and I felt the blush rising on my face. I'd often imagined meeting him again but had long ago convinced myself that my feelings for him were just a childish crush. But now, with him standing before me, a surge of love flooded through me, warming in ways I was too embarrassed to think about.

'So many questions,' Macca said. 'Come on. Grab your bonnet. I'm taking you to the tea rooms.'

The eatery was at the other end of the town and I revelled in the curious eyes upon us as we walked. We certainly made an odd couple. Him so tall, scruffy, and striking; me short, tidy, and plain. Him very loud, me so very quiet.

He opened the door for me to enter and, for the first time, I truly felt like an adult in his presence. I'd never been inside the tea rooms. They were what Ma called a genteel establishment. The smell of cinnamon buns and coffee mixed with the various perfumes of the customers, mostly ladies with fancy hair styles who I'd seen along the streets of Adelaide, but never met.

One of the walls was covered with decorative mirrors. Catching sight of my reflection, I at first thought it was Ma who gazed back at me—the younger, playful Ma. But there was Macca's image behind me. I pushed a stray hair back into my bonnet and smiled at the image, happier than I'd been for a very long time.

We found a quiet table in the far corner and Macca ordered tea with scones, jam, and cream. A shyness descended on me then; not my usual quietness, but a hesitancy, as if everything I said now really mattered. I needed to show him I was not the child he once teased. I needed him to see me as someone who he could truly love.

Macca didn't seem to notice my apprehension. 'So, which of your questions should I answer first?'

Words stuck in my mouth now and I cursed my affliction. I wanted to impress him but all I was doing was showing him that I really was a dullard.

'Where have you been?' I whispered.

He gave me a curious look then, as if trying to understand the change in my mood. He deliberated too, but rather than demand I speak up or simply ignore me like most others did, he proceeded to tell me about his adventures in the intervening years.

'After I left you last time at Echunga, I went with a whaling boat to Thistle Island near Port Lincoln. It was all but deserted. Just a white man living off the land with his Aboriginal wife and two children, a boy and a girl. Their water had all but run out so we offered to bring them back to Adelaide but he asked to go to Oyster Bay. I reckon he may have been hiding from the law, an escaped convict maybe.'

'Was the girl called Tottengarr?' My words came out fast and loud.

He sat back in his chair. 'Yes, I do believe she was called that. A very tall girl, as I recall. Why, do you know her?'

My words flowed now. 'She worked for a time at the Mayfields'. She spoke English as well as you and me.'

'Yes, I'm sure that was her then. How on earth…?'

'She was found by Mr Peters, abandoned, at Cape Jervis, poor girl. But she got no sympathy from Margaret Mayfield. She had her sent her to Adelaide, to go to the native school, but Tottengarr ran away.'

Macca was nodding excitedly now. 'Fancy you remembering all that, Annese.'

I could see he regretted his words as soon as they were out of his mouth.

'I don't mean …'

'I'm not a dullard, Macca.'

He grabbed my hand. 'I'm sorry, Annese. I know better than anyone how bright you are. I just meant that I'm surprised you took such notice. And heartened that you're happy to talk about what is happening to the Aboriginal people. Most folk don't. They pretend they don't see or don't care. Only some of us are concerned about how they're being treated.'

I blushed at the attention then, and once again caught Macca looking at me with those different eyes.

'For the past three months, I've been part of John McLaren's team while he surveyed the best route through to the goldfields at Mount Alexander from South Australia. With the help of the local Aboriginal people, we were able to sink wells every ten miles so that Commissioner

Tolmer and his men had water for the entire journey. The Aboriginal people get no pay for their work, just meagre rations.'

He looked up holding my gaze as if deciding what to say next. 'I've seen some terrible things, Annese. Things I can't talk to anyone about.'

I heard the sadness in his words. A loneliness too. 'Are you still… alone?'

He came back from his bleak mood. 'Are you asking me if I'm married, Miss Annese?' he teased.

I felt a fierce blush burning up my neck and into my face. Was I? I remembered Friend Stephen's words—*a yen for lubra*.

'Are you?'

He dropped his head a little and rubbed his beard. 'No. Not married, Annese.'

I was about to change the subject when he looked up, the sadness clear again now. 'I was in love once but it could never have gone forward. And anyway, she is gone now.'

He stared at me then as if willing me to understand him.

'Ngama?'

He nodded.

I took his hand. 'It's alright. Just between us,' I said, repeating the words he had said to me all those years ago.

He laughed. Not quite his merry laugh but one of admiration. 'You always did know more than everyone thought. Oh Annese,' he said, squeezing my hand, 'I'm so happy to see you again.'

A silence fell between us until the waitress came to clear our cups. He let go of my hand then.

'Let's go down by the river,' he suggested. 'Away from prying eyes.'

We walked to the place where the river bends and slows down. Taking a flask from his pocket, he took two long swigs.

'So why are you back in Adelaide?' I asked.

'I'm with the gold escort. I joined in Bendigo. He was recruiting men who knew how to handle themselves and had experience riding across long distances.'

'Bendigo! Did you see Da and Joseph?'

'No. Are they there now? I didn't know to look for them. The miners' camps go for miles, Annese. It's like a city of its own.'

'Is it true Tolmer's escort is going to change the fortunes of the colony?'

'It may well do. His armed escort certainly allayed the fears of many a miner.'

'Is it true that now the money for any gold found will go to the miners' families and be spent here?' I couldn't keep the hope from my voice, as I imagined how Ma and my life would change if I could get work and we could find a wee cottage together.

'Yes, that was Mr Tinline's idea, to store the gold as ingots at an Assay Office in Adelaide to boost the economy here, not just Melbourne.'

'So you will be off again soon?' I tried to keep the sadness from my voice.

'I'm afraid so, Miss Laffer.' He tweaked my nose as he used to do but then ran a finger down my cheek before pulling away, shaking his head as if dispelling a thought.

I longed to take his hand to my lips but he'd straightened up and was no longer meeting my gaze.

'I'll seek out your father and Joseph next time and bring their findings back safely for your Ma.'

'Would you? Ma said…'

I stopped. Her words were hard for me to repeat. 'Ma said if Da doesn't find gold and I don't get work soon, I could find myself at the mercy of the state. Maybe even in the asylum.'

As if by providence, the bell from the destitute asylum tolled at that very moment. I shivered, trying not to think about what my life would be: separated from my family, locked in every night, unable to see the stars or the sunset. With no trees to breathe their kind words to me, no warm grass to stroke my skin.

'I'll not let that happen.'

His words were certain but I knew he said them more from a place of hope.

We watched as a steady stream of women and men, all dressed in grey, both young and old, walked from various establishments and returned to their pitiable accommodation. Two of them were native girls with lighter skin, half-castes as they were called. They held hands like children and leaned into each other as if they were one, protecting each other from the strange cruel world around them.

'When was it you last saw Kiani?' Macca asked, his voice quiet.

'I saw her at Echunga. She was with her family for a burial ceremony. I didn't talk to her. She was different somehow. Like she was taken up with the ceremony. Anyway, Da says those days have gone, when we can get along together.'

'Does he now? Well, in a way, I agree. He's right, but not for the right reasons.'

'They say they're destined to die out. Is that what you think too?'

As painful as it was to be talking about Kiani and her people like this, I was relieved to finally have someone I trusted to ask these questions.

'Destined to be driven to their extermination more like.' There was pure bitterness in Macca's voice now.

I remembered the conversation I'd overheard at the Hogan Arms and the image of burnt bodies flashed before me. 'I heard tell of a killing at Avenue Range. Who is allowing all this to happen?

A stiffness entered Macca now and his hands formed fists. It was some time before he spoke again and, when he did, a deep melancholy rippled through him.

'We are all doing it, Annese. Not one of us is innocent. We all know what's happening and we do nothing.'

His voice broke to a sob. He pulled the flask from his pocket and drank deeply. 'I've seen men, good Christian men,' he continued, 'do things that no god would ever forgive. Never let anyone tell you that it is we white people who are civilised and the Aboriginal people the primitives. In my experience, it's the opposite.'

The sun sank behind a cloud and I felt his sadness enter me. I leant into him and he pulled me to him; an embrace of friends joined in pain.

We stayed until the moon rose and night fell. 'I must be getting home, Macca. Will you still be in the town tomorrow?'

'Aye, I've one day here before I head off again.'

'Let's meet here at five tomorrow,' I said. 'I'll bring your doll.' He looked confused. 'The one your mother gave you.'

A slow smile spread across his face. 'It's actually a chess piece. You have it still?'

'Of course. You said to keep it.'

'Well, bring it along,' he said finishing off the flask. 'It'll be good to see it again, but it's yours to keep, Annese. I gave the other one, my brother's, to Kiani. I wonder if she still has hers.'

I longed for him to kiss me as we parted but he just made a small play-ful bow, as if I was just any young girl. But his smile told me otherwise.

***

Ma was pacing the room when I arrived home. 'Where have you been? I've been worried sick. You know that Tolmer and his men are in town. There's money being spent on drink like there's no tomorrow.'

I told her about meeting up with Macca. But not about his sadness. Or his drinking.

'You need to be careful around him, too. Did he have anyone with him? A woman?'

She spoke the words with a curl in her voice and I knew exactly what she meant.

'A native woman, you mean?'

Hearing the vexation in my voice she pulled herself up. 'Well—did he? It's what folk say about him.'

'He was alone,' I snapped. 'And what if he did? Is that so wrong?'

'Some say a white man who's lain with a native woman will never enter the kingdom of God.'

'And what do you say, Ma? What does the Bible say? Or your Mother Mary?'

She sank onto the bed beside me. 'I once loved Macca like family. When he just up and left, I missed him terribly. But he came back changed, Annese. And you saw how upset he was about that native woman, the sister of that girl you played with. They say he's a drinker now too.'

I could have told her how he'd smelled of rum and drank from a flask, but that would've felt like a betrayal. I could have told her that he'd seen a lot of bad things that would change anybody and that he had once loved someone, Ngama, but she was gone.

I could have told her that I loved him. But I wanted to savour that feeling as my own.

'And as for friendships with the natives,' Ma went on, 'it can only bring trouble. We're too different. They are not like us, Annese. There's those who have tried to bring them to our ways but they always fail. Look at the young girl the Mayfields took in, Tottie. They gave her a job but she wouldn't work and maybe even stole from them. Then they sent her to get the training she'd need, but she ran away.'

'I'm glad she did. I hope she found her way back to her family. She deserved to do that, surely?'

Ma sighed and nodded. 'I suppose you are right, Annese. Let's hope she is with them still.'

That night I couldn't sleep. Ma's reaction to me seeing Macca had been so different from what I'd expected. She'd always been so protective of him and even argued his case when others had made jokes about him. When had she changed her mind?

But it was not so much these confusing thoughts that kept me awake. It was the haunting, wordless sadness I'd shared with Macca.

Nothing that Ma could say would shift that. Macca's truth had become my truth. I remembered one of my Bible readings and yes, the scales had lifted from my eyes.

I made a vow that night to find Kiani and… and what? What would I do? What could I do?

The next day, I went to the river as arranged, the chess piece in my pocket, but Macca wasn't there. I stayed until the asylum bell tolled and knew he would not be coming. By the time I rose the following morning, I could tell from the quietness in the streets that Tolmer and his men had already left, heading back to the goldfields for another load of bullion; the bullion that everyone hoped would save our colony from ruin. Deep inside me, a voice whispered.

No wealth will bring back the ruined life of Kiani's people.

***

My vow to find Kiani was easy to make, but harder to do. For a while I looked at every dark face I came across, hoping to see her. I even approached one native woman who I heard speaking some broken English and said 'Kiani,' trying to get the sound to resemble Kiani's own way of saying it. The woman shook her head and called over her shoulder to her friends. They shrugged their shoulders and yelled something back, laughing at a joke. I could not help my anger rising at them, for I knew they were laughing at me and my futile attempts to connect with them.

'My friend,' I said a little louder, making awkward hand gestures hoping to make my point.

The woman grabbed my hand and held hers out. 'Sugar?'

Startled, I pulled my hand from hers and was about to walk away when a policeman came to my side. 'Anything wrong, Miss? She giving you trouble?'

'No, I was just…' I knew I could not say I was looking for a friend. He would neither sympathise nor help.

'You lot move on,' he yelled to the group, making them shift from where they sat in the shade to a place upriver where the trees had been cleared and the sun scorched the ground. I knew I should defend them, point out that he'd jumped to a wrong conclusion.

But I remained silent. I did nothing.

I told Ma about the police's actions but not that I'd been searching for Kiani. 'He made them move out into the heat. And she wasn't even harassing me, just asking for something to eat.'

Ma was usually on the side of the downtrodden, so I thought she would at least see the injustice. But she just repeated her warning.

'Leave them be, Annese. It's too hard. It's sad but it's the natural way of things. The strong are meant to outlive the weak.'

I stopped looking for Kiani after that. I tried to tell myself that Macca was wrong to be so sad and Ma was probably right; it was probably the natural way. But still, my heart ached to know Kiani was all right; that she was one of the ones who could keep going.

And then, one day, she arrived at our door.

CHAPTER 10

Although it was a First Day, Ma had gone to work. Mrs Bartholomew had guests arriving and she needed Ma to make up their rooms. I was about to leave for the Meeting when I heard a knock at our door. Hoping it was Macca, I rushed to open it.

'Nunka, Annese.' Kiani's wide white smile tossed aside my disappointment and filled me with joy. She touched my hair and said something in her language—not to me, but as if telling herself a story. I stood back to allow her into our tiny room but she would not enter.

'Bad spirits. Needs smoking.' I'd heard from one of Mrs Bartholomew's maids that the last occupant had been very ill. I wondered now if she'd actually died in there. I'd never felt any unease, but clearly, Kiani did.

She took my hand. '*Yirki.*' It had been her pet name for me all those years ago. 'Hiding no good. River.'

As we walked, she kept turning to me and laughing.

'It is so good to see you, Kiani,' I said, trying to keep up with her long strides.

'Kitty.'

'Ma is working,' I answered, surprised she remembered Ma's name after all these years. 'Ngama?'

A cloud covered her face. She did not answer. A heaviness enveloped her and I knew the answer. Ngama was gone.

'Macca. You see him.'

It didn't sound like a question. Did she know I'd met up with him?

'Yes, I saw him. But he's gone again. Back to the goldfields.' I pointed east and was about to explain to her about the gold escort.

'With Tolmer?' I nodded, surprised at how much she knew of my world and ashamed of how little I knew of hers. She reached into the woven bag she wore around her waist and drew out her carved chess piece, the twin to mine.

'I have this for him. Yours? You still have?'

'Yes. I wanted to give it back to him but he said for me to keep it. He said you were to keep yours too. He wants us to have them, he said.'

'You tell Margaret Mayfield I not steal it.'

'Margaret? What has she to do with anything?'

'You tell her Macca give one to me and one to you.'

'Alright, but I don't think she will listen to me. She…'

She interrupted me. 'Macca needs them back, Annese. To keep him safe.'

'Why?' The urgency in her voice frightened me. 'What has happened?'

She stood and walked away.

'Where will you be?' I called but she kept walking.

She was almost out of sight before I saw Mrs Bartholomew observing me from further up the bank. She was with two other well-dressed women but her eyes did not leave me. I waved, hoping to reassure her, but she looked away.

Kiani's strange demand to tell Margaret that Macca had given us the dolls intrigued me. But I was at a loss about what I could do. I rarely saw Margaret. Ma and I mostly went to the Catholic service at St Thomas's now, although I sometimes went to the Meetings in Adelaide. The Mayfields occasionally came to those, but they more often went to the ones held at their home, Fairfield, near Mount Barker.

When I did see Margaret, I was reluctant to talk to her on any topic, let alone about a false accusation against a native girl. As for Macca *needing* the chess pieces to keep him safe, I was quite sure if he was in trouble, two stone dolls would do little to save him.

Kiani's requests were soon cast to the back of my mind when, about a week after her visit, Ma came home very distressed.

'You'd better sit down, Annese.'

I sat on her bunk and she beside me.

'Mrs Bartholomew came to see me today. She saw you with a native girl. She said she could not risk having any of them associating with her servants.'

My first inclination was to lie but I knew that would have been useless. 'It was just Kiani, Ma. My friend from Echunga.'

'She was here?' The alarm in Ma's voice told me all I needed to know about getting any support from her. I simply nodded.

'She is not your friend, Annese, and never can be. Anyway, it isn't only that. Mrs Bartholemew has taken on three of the Irish girls recently arrived. She says I must share with one of them now.'

I searched her face for reassurance that I would be able to stay too, maybe share her bed. But all I saw was guilt and fear.

'I spoke to Father Ryan for help. He says maybe it's best if you go to...'

'Where?' I demanded. 'Where can I go?"

Ma drew a deep breath. 'The asylum.'

'No.' I grasped her hands my eyes imploring her. 'I can sleep here on the floor. I'll do whatever she says. Any work at all. Please Ma.'

But Ma shook her head. 'Her mind is made up, Annese. It's just for now, until you get work. As soon as you can pay your way or your father sends money back from the goldfields, we'll find our own digs.'

I clung to her and her tears soaked my hair. 'Mother Mary bless my child and keep her from harm,' she prayed.

***

Ma came with me to meet up with Father Murphy at the gate leading into the asylum. My eyes were red with having cried all night. Ma's face was empty again, just as she'd been when the twins were taken. She barely said hello to Father Murphy before giving me one last hug. 'I'm so sorry, Annese. I wish it were me rather than you.' She turned away then and did not look back.

'I've told them of your circumstances, Annese,' Father Murphy was saying. 'You're to be interviewed by Matron before they take you in.'

It had not occurred to me that even the asylum would not automatically give me a home. A shiver of fear ran through me. Where would I sleep? How would I eat?

'I've told them of your condition and it may be enough to persuade them that you are vulnerable and have no one to support you.'

'Condition?'

'It means the way you are.' He spoke slowly and loudly. 'That you can barely speak.'

I realised in that moment that Father Murphy, like many others, thought me a dullard. We'd only met at the door of St Thomas's after Mass and it was Ma who spoke to him on those occasions.

I opened my mouth to persuade him otherwise, to show I could talk as well as the next person if I tried, but quickly closed it again, unsure now if I wasn't better off being thought a dullard if it at least gave me a place to sleep.

'They're already over capacity—that means full, Annese—and mostly only taking abandoned women or those who are with child.'

The matron's office was the first after entering behind the wall. Father Murphy knocked.

'Come.'

She was a tiny woman with an accent similar to Macca's. I'd seen her before at mass although she now wore a uniform with a large belt at her waist. Her grey hair was pulled tightly from her face, giving her a look that matched her steely grey eyes.

'So, Miss Laffer, Father Murphy has told me of your circumstances— your condition.' She looked at her notes. 'Your father and older brother, once gainfully employed, have left you and your mother to try their luck at the goldfields. You've been deserted by them.'

Deserted! I sat forward in my chair trying to summon the courage to protest. Da and Joseph had not deserted us. They would send money when they could. But before I could Matron continued.

'Two of your siblings have already been boarded out.'

She turned to Father Murphy. 'As you know, Father, we are very overcrowded. Another boatload of girls from Ireland arrived just last week. They are in the Immigration area but, as yet, few of them have found employment. Has everything been done to find someone to support this one? Can she not find work?'

'I know well your restrictions, Matron. But as I said, Annese is afflicted in such a way as she will not find work easily.'

'An imbecile then?'

The word landed before me and it took all my energy to stop shouting my protests. The matron was staring at me now.

'Will she be any trouble? Does she become violent?'

'No, no, no. Nothing like that. Just will not speak. I believe she mostly understands what is being said, and will follow the rules of the asylum. She is good with her hands so you could put her to work sewing the hessian bags for the farmers.'

She took my hands in hers and turned them over. 'Well, I can see that she has been used to hard work. Miss Laffer, we will place you in the east wing and provide you with three meals a day. You will be allowed outside the walls for four hours a week. In that time, I would advise that you seek employment. Any dalliances with men will result in your immediate expulsion. Am I clear?'

I nodded, although every fibre of my body told me to turn and run as far and as fast as I could. But to where?

'Here is your uniform. You are to wear it at all times. If you find employment, you can wear whatever is required of you while you are there, but you are to wear this to go to and from your work. That way we can identify you easily.'

'A percentage of your earnings will be taken to cover the costs of your accommodation here. Before then, you are dependent on the mercy of the Church and the good people of the colony.'

I wondered how, even if I was lucky enough to find work, I would ever save enough to pay for my own lodgings.

'Do you understand?' She articulated the question as if I truly was an imbecile.

I nodded. Better to be thought of as an imbecile than be left to sleep on the streets.

'Good. Now wait outside my door. One of the inmates will come and show you to your dormitory. You've missed lunch. Dinner will be at six. Tea and bread. Father Murphy, can you stay? I have the matter of the woman you brought in last week to discuss.'

I stood to leave, expecting him to at least stand to say goodbye, but he avoided looking at me.

'Ma?' I said, tears welling in my eyes.

'Yes, I will tell your mother. Now run along.'

***

The dormitory was lined on both sides by bunk beds, twenty in all. A stale, musty smell prevailed, although I could see that some of the women had attempted to camouflage it by putting bunches of rosemary or lavender, many long past their usefulness, onto the bars of their beds.

I was taken to the bunk furthest from the door. Furthest too, I soon realised, from fresh air.

'That's yours.' The woman who'd escorted me was about Ma's age. She pointed to the top bunk. 'You're lucky, you don't have to share it right now. It's all yours. Luxury.'

I looked to see if she was smiling at her joke but she was not. It was not a joke.

'Get changed. Keep your clothes safe. If you've anything worth taking, it'll likely disappear. I keep my clothes bundled and use them as a pillow. It'll be the only one you have.'

As I watched her leave, a shaft of sunlight came through a high window, falling at my feet. I closed my eyes and felt its warmth. Looking up along it, I felt my body dissolve into tiny dust particles, invisible without the sun. A floating nothingness. There but not there.

Then, just as quickly as it had appeared, the light disappeared and the loathing within consumed me. If only I'd never stolen that notebook. If only I could talk like everyone else. If only I was smart enough to get a job.

Outside, the bell tolled. How long had I been standing there? Pulling off my tunic, I was pulling on an oversized uniform when the blanket on the bunk below mine moved. I jumped backwards, fearing a rat.

Two eyes appeared and a girl rolled from under the covers. At first, I thought she was a very young child but as she emerged, I could see that she was only slightly younger than me. Her cheeks were sunken and her arms, as she pulled her uniform on, were thinner than any I'd ever seen, the bones pushing against her skin. But her belly was bulging, as if, I thought then, full of food.

'Dinner,' she said as she walked, ghost-like, towards the door.

The dining area was filled with a series of long tables and benches. We were given a tin mug of what they called tea as we came in the door. The older woman who'd shown me to the dormitory stood beside baskets of bread chunks, monitoring that we took only one each. As one of the last to arrive, there were few to pick from and each looked as dry as the others. Bread and tea in hand, I made my way to the table and sat at the last available spot on the very end of a bench. I glanced around avoiding eye contact for fear of being expected to make conversation. I was surprised at the number of both very old and very young women. I realised that, from the other side of the wall, I'd only seen the women who worked. The fitter women. I shuddered to think how long some of them had been here and swore that I would not become one of them.

I was surprised that there were no children. I learned later that the women with children were housed elsewhere. While some inmates seemed confident and spoke with strong voices, most hung their heads, shoulders slumped over their meagre meal.

The moment I sat down, the Matron appeared at the door. A silence fell over the already hushed room.

'Bless us, O Lord, these Thy gifts, which we are about to receive from Thy bounty, through Christ our Lord. Amen.'

'Amen.'

A low level of chatter resumed. I could feel those sitting near me eyeing me with curiosity. I heard one of them whisper to another. 'Doesn't talk. An imbecile.'

I raised my head to protest but lowered it again and dunked my bread into the tea. Closing my eyes, I put the still-hard morsel into my mouth and imagined again that I was dust, floating in the air, only visible when the sun shone through me. I convinced myself that I could become unseeable. I could be nothing.

The noise levels grew as the women finished their meal and began filtering outside into the quadrangle. I followed and the rat-girl fell in beside me and, to my surprise, took my hand.

'Leave her alone, Maisie,' one of the older girls called out. 'No one wants your mange.' It was only then that I noticed the scabs around her mouth. My first impulse was to drop her hand, but memories of Ma and Da talking of how poorly Polly and Thomas had been before they'd gone to Mrs Scholz crowded in on me. I clasped her hand tighter.

'Imbecile.' The woman and her friends laughed, leaving us alone.

'Back to your bed, Maisie,' the matron said from behind us. Maisie obeyed and walked away, without so much as a look in my direction. Matron too kept walking and I was alone. Going into the centre of the quadrangle, I looked up into the darkening night sky. A crescent moon had risen and the evening star beside it. I longed to lie on my back to watch as the heavens filled, but I knew it would attract attention. My neck began to ache as my stomach rumbled, the rock-hard bread and tea barely enough to dent my hunger. I joined in the aimless walking around the quadrangle. Alone and invisible.

When the bell rang again, I was thankful to be one of the first to be guided towards the ablutions block where a row of seven stinking toilets were divided from each other by filthy curtains, but open at the front. Finishing, I looked for a bowl to wash my hands but saw instead that we were to wash at a standpipe. Queuing, I saw that some women had a cake of soap in their pockets; others, like me washed with only a splash of water, enough to fill our cupped hands. I wondered what would happen when I had my bleeding, but quickly pushed the thought aside, determined now to find my way out before the next full moon.

I slept through the wake-up bell but when the breakfast bell tolled, Maisie shook me by the shoulder and together we scurried across the yard. We sat together. Perhaps noticing my disappointment to find that breakfast was a repetition of the evening meal, Maisie spoke to me again.

'Soup and mutton for lunch, miss.'

Despite her reassuring words, I noticed she was barely able to eat her bread before she grew weak and made her way back to the dormitory. I was ushered to the workroom and instructed on how to sew hessian bags. They were the same as those we used to fill with barley at harvest time.

'They're for Messers Dunstan, Mayfield, and Hogan,' the work supervisor told me. 'They're all on the Board and give the Governor money for your labour. It's what pays for your upkeep.'

Dunstan. Mayfield. Hogan. All names I knew well from the Meetings. At first, I felt comforted by the notion that people I knew, people with wealth and influence, were in charge. But as my fingers began to bleed, the hessian tearing at my skin, I wondered why they'd not been willing to pay me for this work while I was on the outside of these walls. Even

Da and Joseph might have made good with the income and not left us. Did these men rely on this cheap labour?

At the risk of dispelling the notion that I was an imbecile and threatening the roof over my head, I asked my question.

'How much do they give?'

Unperturbed by my curiosity, perhaps unaware of the label placed on me, the supervisor answered with a laugh.

'Much less than they'd pay their employees, you can be sure of that, miss.'

I couldn't work out if he approved or disapproved of the arrangement, and was wise enough not to ask.

Even though the work was rough on my hands, I came to enjoy its mindless repetitiveness. Several times the supervisor commended me on the fact that my stitches stayed in place, unlike those of others.

'I'll recommend you to Mr Ennis. He may find work for you on the other side of the wall.'

***

On the following Monday, the bell sounded at 11 am, signalling the period when we could leave the asylum, wearing our grey uniform to ensure we could be easily identified. We were to use the time to look for work and return by 4 pm.

The first week I went straight to Mrs Bartholomew's and found Ma in the laundry. I'd planned to tell her about my life behind the wall but when it came to it, I couldn't find the words. Nothing I could say would save her from the guilt and despair she already felt. So instead, I exaggerated the camaraderie between the women and lied to her about our accommodation. I was relieved when, after just ten minutes, one of the other workers came to find Ma.

'You'd best come, Kitty. Mrs B has been asking for you and she's got the hump.'

Ma jumped to her feet and ushered me out the door. 'It's the uniform, love,' she said. 'Mrs Bartholomew isn't keen on you being here. She says it gives the wrong impression.'

The second week, I spent walking along the street in the square mile of Adelaide Town, looking for 'Worker Wanted' signs. But all I saw was the growing number of businesses with boarded-up windows. I noticed a few of the girls from the asylum disappear into the taverns, while others met up with family.

The third Monday, Ma arranged to get an hour off and we walked along the river to where the reed beds grew. Ducks and swans abounded and when a family of new ducklings made their way past us to the water, we hugged each other with delight.

'I've missed you Ma. I'm not sure how long I can …' Again I stopped myself from expressing the horrors of my life. It would be too much for her to bear. 'Have you heard from Da?'

'Not this last month. He's sure to be striking it lucky soon and will send money,' she said. 'Then we'll find a place together with a bed each and running water.'

'And a small cooker of our own.'

Neither of us believed our lies but they were all we had.

The day after the visit with Ma, I noticed Maisie had not risen for breakfast. I shook her shoulder and she flopped onto her back. Her face was a waxy grey. I put my hand to her cheek. She was icy cold.

Two women came to my side when I cried out.

'Get Matron,' one of them instructed the other. As they carried her tiny body away, I realised I didn't even know her last name.

I arrived late at the sewing workshop that day, but rather than being cross, the supervisor was more than usually pleased to see me.

'Mr Ennis is looking for you, Annese. He may have work for you on the outside. Hurry to the office before he finds someone else.'

CHAPTER 11

Mr Ennis looked me up and down. 'There's not much of you but you look healthy enough.'

I shoved my hands into my pockets and stood as tall as I could.

'The shoemaker on Leigh Street, a Mr Isaac Petersen, needs someone to fetch and carry from the tannery and do odd jobs around the workshop. His boy, a nephew I believe, has gone to the goldfields. He said he'd consider giving it to a girl if that was his only choice. And you come recommended.'

He stared at me, waiting for me to respond.

'Well, what have you to say?'

My words, so clear in my head, came out in a jumble. 'Fetch and carry. Odd jobs,' I repeated. 'Good worker. Start tomorrow.'

He harrumphed and shrugged his shoulder. 'Report to Mr Petersen after breakfast tomorrow at 11 Leigh Street.'

I didn't wait for breakfast the next morning and arrived at Mrs Bartholomew's laundry before sunrise. Ma was alone in the laundry and, on hearing my news, filled a tub with warm soapy water.

'You'd better hurry,' she said, 'before the others arrive.'

I stripped and climbed naked into the water. As Ma washed me for the first time that I could remember, I couldn't recall ever feeling so clean and sweet smelling. I wanted to never leave this place of comfort.

But Ma soon had me by the elbow and passed me a towel, before helping me to pull my uniform back over my head.

'Here's the key to my room. Fiona will still be there but tell her who you are and she'll be no bother. Your church pinafore is under the bed.'

'But I'm supposed to wear my uniform.'

'Says who?' Ma said. 'There's them that make the rules and them that sometimes need to break them. This is one of those times, Annese.' Her Irish brogue took over as her chin set in the same defiance I'd seen when she'd stood up for me to Margaret Mayfield.

Rubbing my damp hair one last time, she pushed me out the door. 'And for goodness' sake, when you meet Mr Petersen, make yourself heard.'

***

I entered through the shopfront, where a large clanging bell on the door announced my arrival.

'Out here.' The voice came from an open lean-to, adjoining the shop. The smell of recently tanned leather almost overwhelmed me as I picked my way past rows of boots and shoes. A large bench, with several metal foot-shaped moulds at one end, took up most of the space. Opposite were shelves with rows of tins of various sizes. A man, who I rightly assumed was Mr Petersen, sat at the far end stitching a boot.

'Miss Laffer?' he said, barely looking up.

'Yes. Annese.'

'Laffer,' he said again, waving his hand to indicate a large bucket on the bench. 'Sort into sizes. Put them into the tins.' He indicated the tins on the shelves.

His manner, although gruff, held no malice; he amused rather than scared me. Perhaps I'd found someone who used as few words as me.

The bucket had about two hundred used tacks of all sizes. Picking it up, I looked at him for confirmation but got none. Upending it, I began sorting into size order as requested, keeping aside the ones that

92

were too bent to reuse. The work was repetitive and easy and, best of all, required no talking. To the sound of Mr Petersen tapping, I relaxed into the task and soon finished the sorting.

Taking the other tins from the shelf, three at a time, I was pleased to find them already arranged in strict order according to the length of the tacks they contained. I soon found a home for my assortment. Replacing the tins, I took a handful of the bent tacks to Mr Petersen.

'Where …' I was trying to add *shall I put these* when he indicated, with his chin, a halved wooden wine barrel. It was as if he neither needed nor wanted me to speak in full sentences. Throwing them into the barrel, I smiled at the sound they made and began running my hands through these curling trinkets, revelling in the clinking. Many of them were so bent they formed hooks linked together forming a chain. I held them up, pleased with how they clung to each other when I swung them a little, like a line of fish changing directions, dancers. Glancing over my shoulder, I saw Mr Petersen go to the back of the workshop. I put the bent tacks into my pocket.

Next to me, another barrel was filled to the top with small odd-shaped scraps of leather. I plunged my hand deep among them and pulled one out. I saw in it the shape of a horse's head. Rummaging again, I found two more pieces that looked like the dolphins I'd once seen swimming in the port river. Flattening them out, I moved them around, imagining them diving in and out of the water as the horse stood watching.

'Keep.'

I startled. Mr Petersen was beside me with a note on a small piece of paper. I gathered up my leather playthings, ready to put them back in the barrel.

'Keep,' he said again. His generosity made me feel guilty about the tack chain but I shoved them into my pocket and took the note from him. 'Do you know where McBain's tannery is?' I nodded. I'd been there once with Da when he was delivering hides for Friend Hogan. The smell of the place had made me want to vomit.

'Go there first thing tomorrow and give him this note. Tell him you work for me and are there to collect these,' he said, indicating the note.

Work! I had work! Making for the door, a skip in my step, I turned. Now my words came loud and clear.

'Goodbye. Thank you.'

'No need to thank me as long as you do what you're told.'

I was at the door when he spoke again. 'You can keep the twisted tacks too. But next time, ask.'

Horrified, I blushed and turned and curtsied as I'd seen the Mayfield girls do when they had an important visitor. A laugh exploded from him, showing his brown teeth.

'There's no need for curtsying. And you'll no' want to wear your fancy clothes tomorrow. It's dirty work is this. Don't forget, go to the tanner first thing tomorrow.'

I darted off before he changed his mind.

Both Ma and Fiona were at work still when I got back to their room. I changed into my uniform and folded my Sunday clothes. Leaving them under Ma's bed, I squirmed further and took out the spice tin, quickly putting the treasures I'd taken from Mr Petersen's into it.

The asylum bell rang, summoning me back, along with dozens of others filing back behind the wall, like admonished children, compliant and forlorn. Even though I'd done very little work, I was tired and hungry. I ate my bread and tea and slept without a dream.

***

I rose early again the next morning and went straight to Ma's room. I knocked quietly and Ma pulled me in, checking that no one was watching. Fiona was awake but still in bed.

'I'm to do a job today, at least. Mr Petersen said to not wear fancy clothes. None of my dresses fit anymore. I was thinking that perhaps I should wear Joseph's dungarees that he grew out of. Do you still have them?

'So he's taken you on?' She rummaged under her bed and dragged out what she had: trousers, a calico shirt, and a waistcoat.

I hadn't expected to feel so comfortable in boys' clothes but immediately I put them on I felt confident somehow.

Ma shook her head in resignation. 'They will have to do. Lord knows what people will say of you now.'

Pushing the asylum uniform under her bed, I saw Joseph's tweed cap. I pulled it on in place of my cotton one and tucked my hair into it, pulling it low over my ears. Fiona's eyes widened as she stared at me from over the top of her blanket. I winked at her as I knew Joseph would have. When she laughed, I couldn't help but laugh too, and soon Ma joined in; three women connected by our strange and vulnerable circumstances.

'Make sure Mr Petersen pays you,' Ma said as I left. 'And speak up for yourself.'

***

The tannery was at the edge of the town in an area known as Thebarton. The stench met me from half a mile away and, as I got closer, the ammonia gas made my nose run and my eyes water. It was already a hive of activity. I made my way around three large coppers filled with boiling water, soap, and soda. Two men were throwing a large cow hide into one. Others were washing wool skins in the river that ran nearby, while others were hanging the washed hides on lattice boards to drip. To the far side, racks of hides were hanging out to dry.

'What do you want, laddie?' The tanner said it twice before I realised he was talking to me, mistaking me, understandably, for a boy. I approached him with Mr Petersen's note. He studied it for a time, then set about rolling out several pieces of leather and bundled them together with a belt-like strip to make it easier for me to carry.

'Tell Petersen it's as good a leather as he'll find in the colony. Come all the way from Port Lincoln.'

On my way back to Leigh Street, I saw two girls sitting on a bench outside the Newmarket Inn, talking to a policeman. I recognised them from the asylum. They wore ill-fitting dresses made of red and gold taffeta, low cut so that the girls' breasts bobbed about as they laughed and pretended to polish the policeman's badge.

Noticing me watching, one of them called out. 'What are you gawping at? Never seen a working girl before?'

Rather than walk past them, I stayed on the river side of the road, hurrying on, keen to return to the safety of the shoemaker's. I recognised Mr Jones, the owner of the general store, talking with Mr Petersen when I arrived. He had two pairs of new shoes under his arm. I laid the leather on the table and, hearing them mention the gold escort, I took my time flattening it out, staying within earshot.

'Tolmer and his men brought back the largest load to date. They got through without a hitch this time, travelling along the Coorong to Tailem Town.'

'No trouble with the natives, then?'

'No, they've no need for gold, although there was a mob who came into their camp near Mannum, apparently. There might have been trouble but young Malcolm Macleod was with them. He knew a couple of them it seemed and was able to talk with them using some of their language. He worked out they just wanted some flour and sugar and they left without a fuss.'

I stopped what I was doing, not even pretending to be busy now.

'Aye,' Mr Petersen said. 'I've heard Macleod is working with Tolmer. They say he's a good lad and has a way with the natives.'

'Some say more than that, with the women.' Mr Jones laughed but Mr Petersen shook his head.

'None of our business.'

Noticing me hovering, Mr Petersen said goodbye to his customer and gave me two threepence pieces.

'One for Mr Ennis, one for yourself. Be back here before lunchtime tomorrow.'

***

I'd changed into my uniform when Ma burst through the door.

'What did he say?'

I gave her the threepence and told her I was to go back the next day. She hugged me with tears in her eyes.

'I knew you could do it. I'll keep this hidden with my savings.'

Rummaging under the bed, she found my spice tin. I'd not pushed it back far enough to keep out of her sight.

'What's this?'

'I brought it from Echunga,' I said, grabbing it from her before she could open it. 'Just some silly drawings of mine and Macca's doll.' I tried to keep the quivering from my voice, unsure of what she would do if she found Margaret's letter. I gave it a gentle rattle, hoping to persuade her I was telling the truth.

'Fancy you keeping my old spice tin,' she said, in too good a mood to be suspicious of my actions. 'You can stay here while I go get us a jar of pickled oysters and a fresh loaf. We'll eat then in the park to celebrate. Just don't let Mrs Bartholomew see you.'

As soon as the door closed behind her, I gently prized off the tin's rusted lid. The smell of cinnamon floated to greet me. I drew it in, comforted by the aroma that reminded me of better days at Echunga, when all the family was together.

Lifting the doll and Margaret's letter out, I put the tacks I'd taken the previous day on the bottom covered by the leather, planning to one day make something ornamental out of them to hang on our bare wall.

Holding Macca's doll, or chess piece as he called it, I wondered again why Kiani said he needed it. Did she think it had magical powers, in the same way Ma believed that the cross she now openly wore around her neck would keep the devil away?

'I've never really stopped being a Catholic,' she'd said when I'd asked her about it. 'It's how I was raised. I can't let their ways go. Not even for your father.'

Da said such things were superstitions; he had faith in God alone and had no need for icons to connect him to his saviour. I wanted to believe him, but God did not seem to be doing a great job. I was without a home, the twins were gone from us, Da and Joseph were hundreds of miles away, and Ma was working all hours. Macca was in trouble too, if Kiani was to be believed.

Putting the doll back in the tin, I was about to replace the letter when I realised that years had passed since I'd first tried to read it. Back then it was the notebook I valued but I'd kept it to remind me of the terrible consequences of my theft. A penance, as Ma would say.

I was about to throw it out when I remembered Ma's reaction to it all those years ago. Something about Tottie being accused of stealing and Macca leaving in a hurry. My reading had improved over time, enough to get me by, so perhaps I could now see for myself why she'd been so adamant that I burn it.

Checking to see that Ma was not coming back, I went to where a gap in the curtains allowed enough sunlight in to decipher the now very faded writing.

My dearest Aunt, I write to you about a matter so dear to my heart that I barely know if I should commit the words to paper. But you are my sole confidante. I implore that you not speak to another living soul of what I am about to impart.

I have written to you previously about a young Scotsman, Malcolm Macleod. He is not of our persuasion although he does express great admiration for the way of the Friends with regard to our simple service. He says it is not unlike his own family's style of worship which preferences direct connection with the Almighty, uncluttered with idolatry and papist hierarchy.

Macca had once told me that his family's church, like our Meeting House, had no altar or hierarchy of seating, and how they'd removed the bells from the bell towers, for the tolling of manmade objects was seen as a distraction from true worship. Even music, other than sacred music, was forbidden.

Surprised that Macca had such a significant conversation with Margaret, I read on.

Although two years my junior, he is mature beyond his years, due in part, I am sure, to the fact that, having been driven from his home in the Scottish islands at a young age, he was forced to leave his parents' guidance and spent his formative years among seafaring adults.

A pang of jealousy rose in me now. She knew such personal details about him.

I am drawn to him Aunt, in a way that I feel for no other man. And I do believe that he feels the same for me, for he seeks my company whenever he can and is playful and kind.

My mind raced as I reread the last lines. Could it be true that Macca once felt affection for Margaret? Was it of her that he spoke of when he said he'd once been in love? My head whirred, my emotions crashing like a wave.

I have allowed him small courtesies that, were I not fond of him, and he of me, could be labelled as indiscretions. I allowed him to hold my hand longer than required while he removed a bee sting and, on another occasion, I sat with him, unchaperoned, on the banks of our creek, while he sang a song of love.

No wonder Margaret was so enraged at me when she found the letter was missing from the notebook.

> *Given these very clear indications of his commitment to me, and my allowances to him, you can imagine my horror when he told me he was in love with another.*

My heart raced now. Not Margaret then! I read on, now with a feeling of triumph.

> *And that is not the worst of it, Aunt. A conversation with Friend Stephen Hastings has led me to believe that it is a native woman who has captured his affection!*
> *Oh how I shudder to imagine that the same hand that held mine has also held that of a native woman.*
> *My shame is immense, dear Aunt. I seek your advice and reassurance that I have done no wrong.*

So, it was Ngama then that he referred to. Even while my heart ached for Macca, I felt a soaring hope that one day he would be mine. Along with the hope came a feeling of triumph over Margaret. I knew I should perhaps have felt pity for her, but I could not.

I heard Ma's footsteps on the path so I scanned the last lines. It was something about a carved item and being robbed by a native woman. This must have been what Ma had meant when she'd referred to *poor Tottie*.

'Are you ready, Annese?

I shoved the letter into the tin as she came in the door. 'I'll leave my tin here,' I said, putting it well back under the bed. 'It'll not be safe with me.'

'We'll need to hurry before…' She hesitated. I knew she meant before I had to go back behind the wall.

Taking the bread and oysters, I finished her sentence, saving both of us from having to face the awfulness of my situation just yet. 'Before the sun goes down.'

We found a bench in a quiet corner of the park. Tearing the bread into chunks big enough to hold an oyster or two, we ate quickly. The oyster juice ran down our chins and we laughed as we mopped up our messy faces with more bread. I pushed the revelation of the letter to the back of my mind, enjoying sharing this rare moment of bliss with Ma.

When the bell rang to summons me back to the asylum, I hugged her tightly. 'We'll find somewhere to stay together soon, you'll see.'

That night I dreamt of Macca holding my hand and shouting at Margaret that she must leave us alone. The dream turned into one of forbidden pleasure. I woke to my body aching with desire.

CHAPTER 12

At first, I left for work fearing I'd be told that my time there had come to an end, due either to my quiet ways or because I'd been replaced by a boy. I gave thanks each day I passed out of the gates for having work and that Mr Petersen assigned tasks that didn't require me to talk to customers.

As the days turned to weeks, I relaxed a little more enjoying the routine. Mr Petersen had never commented on my choice of clothes other than shrugging when I'd first appeared in them and muttering something about them being more practical.

Even though he knew of my status as an inmate, it was more than I could face arriving in the baggy grey garb, the symbol of my despair. Sometimes, Ma said it was best I not to use her room and I'd change at a hidden spot near the river. On one such occasion, Mr Petersen had seen me stashing my uniform at the back of the workshop.

'You can change in the small storage room, Laffer. You need feel no shame; many a good person has found themselves needing help, at one time or another.'

He gradually increased my hours and gave me extra on paydays when the work had been especially strenuous. But the coins in Ma's savings box still came nowhere close to what we'd need to find lodgings together.

With each of Tolmer's return trips, a cautious buzz of optimism began filtering throughout the colony. I'd not seen Macca again but Da sent word he'd met up with him and was sending back seven ounces of gold in Ma's name to the Assay Office.

'It's more than we earn in three months,' she said. 'I'll start looking for digs as soon as it arrives.'

That night we celebrated again with a feast of clams and oysters on the riverbank. We ate till our bellies were full and I gathered the courage to ask Ma the question that had been going around in my head.

'Ma, do you think Macca is courting?'

She took her time to answer. 'I don't know. Why do you ask?'

'I am thinking that, some day in the future, I will want to be married and it is Macca who I think will be the man most suited.'

Until the words came from me, I'd not realised this was what was on my mind. But once said, I knew it to be true. I expected Ma to either admonish me for talking nonsense, or simply laugh as if I were a foolish child. But she grew serious, wiped her greasy lips with her arm, and straightened her skirts.

'Macca? Where does this come from? He is too old for you. He was just a boy when we knew him and anyway, I've heard rumours that he's drinking too much these days. That's something he'll not easily leave behind, even for a wife. Anyway, he'll be expecting to be with a woman who…'

I didn't want to hear any more. 'You're wrong. He's expecting to be with me. I know it. He will quit his drinking to marry me.'

Ma shook her head and hugged me again. 'Enough, Annese. You see how innocent you are? You have no knowledge of such things. Let's not talk of this again, child.'

We left the conversation there, but I'd have to prove to her and Da that I was capable of being a wife and a mother. And that Macca was worthy of me.

Not long after this discussion, Mr Jones was at the workshop and I heard him tell Mr Petersen that Macca had left the gold escort.

'He just took off we just took offhile they were at the camp near Mannum and he's not been seen since. He was drinking heavily, they say, and has likely gone native.' He sniggered when he said it.

I tried to stop listening, my heart breaking. I didn't want to believe anything bad about him, but the longer I went without seeing him, the more confused I felt. A blanket of heaviness fell over me.

Luckily, Mr Petersen didn't seem to notice my morose state. In fact, he was giving me more and more difficult tasks, letting me use his blades on cheaper cuts of leather to cut the boot laces to exactly the right length. He'd even shown me how to use a moulding shape, the *last* he called it, to shape a boot.

'You've a good eye for this work, Laffer. You're able to imagine what the finished boot will look like from a flat piece of leather. It's a gift that few have.'

Each day I'd sort through the binned offcuts, retrieving pieces he'd discarded as too small or too damaged. I'd turn each piece this way and that, seeing the possibilities, finding the pieces he could use if he just did things a little differently. I'd draw a shape onto the underside and show him.

'Laffer, you are a treasure,' he said, laughing. 'I've an order for shoes for an upcoming wedding and I was worried that I'd not enough leather for the trimmings. But you may have just solved my problem.'

That day, he doubled my wage.

***

The wedding Mr Petersen referred to was sending the whole town into a spin. The groom had been lucky at the goldfields and it was to be the fanciest wedding yet seen in the colony. With the sudden demand for stylish shoes, Mr Petersen let me take over the making of the everyday farmers' boots. He taught me how to wet the leather and curve it around the last and how to use his many blades, each having a different purpose. He'd call on me to cut the trimmings for the fancier shoes too, knowing my eye for designing was now as good as his own and my fingers were more nimble. Doing this work reminded me of my childhood drawings and it brought me the same joy.

The work kept both of us busy from dawn till dusk and, before I knew it, three months had passed since I'd first entered the asylum, and the stash of coins in Ma's box was almost enough to pay a month's rent on a boarding-house room.

I hadn't seen Macca in all that time and he'd sent no word of his whereabouts. I began to resign myself to Ma's plan for me to stay unmarried, taking comfort in the knowledge that I could make my own living as a shoemaker's assistant.

I was about to leave work one day when Mr Jones came in with a fresh order.

'I'm needing two more pairs of shoes for this blessed wedding,' he said to Mr Petersen. 'A young gentleman and his sister—twins, I believe. They speak with a German accent, although their names would suggest otherwise.'

I was about to change into my uniform but hung back. Twins who spoke with a German accent. Could it be Thomas and Polly?

'The young lady has asked for a Balmoral-style shoe, would you believe? The young man, a bit of a dandy if you ask me, wants boots with pointed toes of all things.'

I moved a little closer to hear more clearly. I could well imagine Thomas being described as a bit of a dandy. Mr Jones noticed my interest and addressed me directly.

'I've a seamstress making the young lady's dress from cloth brought in especially from England. The gentleman's suit is coming ready-made from none other than Bond Street.'

'What is their surname?' I whispered.

'Oh, you do speak,' Mr Jones said, eyeing me up and down. 'Scholz is their name. Thomas and Polly as I recall. Why do you ask?'

Polly and Thomas in Adelaide! I gripped the bench trying to appear calm.

'What is it Annese?'

'Brother and sister. Boarded out,' I managed to say.

Tears welled as guilt and humiliation filled me. I closed my eyes, willing the scrutiny of the two men to finish.

'Strange girl,' Mr Jones harrumphed, before turning away. 'Well, they must be doing well enough, if their orders are anything to go by.'

The men went on to discuss the possibility of gold in the colony and the Government's offer of a reward of £10,000 if enough gold was extracted.

'It's said that Echunga will soon become a goldfield site.'

I was longing to ask more about the Echunga reference but, with the attention turned from me, I quickly gathered my asylum clothes and went to Ma's work dressed in my work clothes.

She met me at the door, waving a letter, a joyous smile on her face. 'Polly and Thomas are coming. They'll be in Adelaide Town for the week before the wedding and they want to meet up with us on the Sunday.'

'Both of us?'

'Yes, of course.' In her jubilation, Ma didn't notice my distress.

'But I'm not allowed…'

She hesitated for only a moment. 'We'll see to that. I'll talk to Father Murphy. I'll not let you miss out on seeing your family. Do you think they've changed much? Will they still…' Ma's hand went to tidy her hair as if they were about to appear at that very moment.

'Of course they've changed. They were children when we last saw them and according to Mr Jones, they'll be wearing the finest clothes and shoes for the wedding.'

Ma's face fell as she looked around. 'Do you think they'll really want to see us or are they just being polite?' I realised she felt just as humiliated by our circumstances as I did. It was my turn to be reassuring. 'Well if they don't, I will give them a good walloping.' I said it with the same accent she'd used to us as children many a time. She laughed then and, for the first time since our fraught discussion about me marrying Macca, I felt her warmth toward me reawakening.

'We must write to your father to tell him. He'll be sad to miss them though.'

I wrote while Ma dictated and we managed to get it finished to send off with the next escort. But it crossed over with his letter, which arrived just a week later. Ma brought it to my work for me to read.

'Dear Kitty and Annese, we are heading home. We've had some success but we're getting less and less gold each day. I fear that we've exhausted our plot, for we've not found anything for the last two weeks. We could move to richer pickings but neither of us fancies the idea. The Chinese are here in large numbers now and there is much unrest about the new tariff.

There is a rumour too that a Mr Chapman believes there's gold near our old home at Echunga. Perhaps our fortune lies closer to home.'

Ma hugged me tight. 'They've found some gold, and they'll be here soon to make good at Mr Chapman's findings.'

I didn't want to contradict her. My reading was that they'd not found enough to justify staying on and were pinning their hopes on something that had not yet happened.

'At least we'll be all together,' I said.

Ma left the letter with me and I reread it, hoping to find a mention of Macca. I longed to know where he was, although my fanciful hopes grew dimmer every day. But it was not from Da's letter I learned of his news. Nor from Ma or Mr Petersen.

It was from Kiani.

CHAPTER 13

They allowed me out of the asylum to attend Mass with Ma, on the excuse that I was preparing for my confirmation. The Sunday after we received Da's letter, I was getting changed back into my asylum clothes when Ma answered the tapping on our door. She stepped back in fright and was about to slam the door shut at seeing Kiani. I could not blame her, for Kiani was wearing a possum-skin coat, her head decorated with feathers.

'Stop, Ma! It's Kiani.'

'How do you know that it's her?' Ma hissed. 'Anyway, she can't come in. Mrs Bartholomew doesn't allow natives.'

'Macca in trouble,' Kiani said, unconcerned it seemed by Ma's comments. 'He needs his doll.'

'What doll?' Ma demanded.

Kiani turned to her and I felt Ma stiffen as she stepped in towards me. 'He said someone will buy our dolls. Macca needs the money.'

'She means the stone doll, Ma. Remember? The one he gave me when he left us.'

'You still have it? After all this time? Where is it?'

'It's…'

'No,' Ma interrupted, whispering now as if Kiani was not still within earshot. 'Don't say it, not while she is here. You can't trust them. Their ways are different.'

She turned to Kiani. 'Thank you for your message. We will get the said item to Mr Macleod.'

I almost laughed at her attempt at sounding grand. But the idea of finding Macca ourselves appealed to me too, but for very different reasons.

'Kiani, where is Macca? I'll take it to him myself.'

Kiani shook her head. 'He a long way. He says the man an English man and will pay him much for them.'

Ma stepped closer. 'How much? Who is this man who will buy it?' she demanded.

Kiani remained silent, staring ahead.

I gently pulled Ma behind me. 'Who is it will buy our dolls, Kiani?'

She held my gaze. I smiled and nodded, trying to reassure her.

'Macca said he is museum man,' she whispered. 'Macca say he pay lots of money. He said we can share it. Three ways.'

I nodded again. 'Okay, come back next Sunday. I need to talk it through with Ma first. I live…' Even saying the words to Kiani brought shame to me.

'The asylum,' she said. There was no judgement in her voice, only compassion in her eyes. 'I will come back. Sunday.'

'Get the doll, Annese,' Ma said as soon as Kiani walked away, an urgency in her voice. 'We can't leave it here now. She'll come back while we're away. I'll take it to Mrs Bartholomew. She'll know if it's worth anything and be able to keep it safe if it is.'

I didn't think Kiani would steal it, but a part of me knew Ma's caution was probably justified. And her idea to have Mrs Bartholomew value it made sense. Pulling the tin from below the bed, I remembered that the letter was on top. If Ma saw it, she might get angry that I hadn't burned it all those years ago. I had been foolish to keep it, for it was evidence of my theft, but now that I'd read it, I wanted to show it to Macca. I wanted him to laugh with me at Margaret's foolishness. I wanted to hear him say that he'd only declared his love for another, to ease himself out of an awkward situation.

I kept the tin in front of me so Ma couldn't see, shuffling the letter to the bottom before handing her the doll. 'Macca says it is a chess piece and that it's made of ivory.'

She turned it over several times.

'You know, I've never really looked at it before, not at the detail. The carving is very complicated. Look at the way it twists and turns. It could well be very valuable, Annese.' She put it into her pocket. 'Mrs Bartholomew will know.'

***

It was a whole week before I saw Ma again. As we walked to church, she reported back about the chess piece.

'Mrs Bartholomew said she should keep the chess piece in her safe until she finds someone who could value it. She said it is almost certainly ivory and that the carving is equal to any she has ever seen. We're not to give it to anyone until we know its worth, certainly not a native.'

'But Kiani is not just any native, Ma. Her and Macca…' I could not think of a word to describe their relationship and the trust I knew they held in each other.

'Mrs Bartholomew said they can't be trusted, even the nice ones,' Ma said, as if reading my thoughts. 'They don't value things like we do. She's given them clothes and food when they've come to the door and they just share it around and are back for more the next week. She said they've no appreciation for art or culture like we do. The chess piece would mean nothing to them. She said Kiani would likely just trade it for tobacco or flour.'

How could I explain that she was wrong? Surely the fact that Kiani still had her carved doll meant she valued it in some way. Ma took my silence as agreement.

'It's sad, Annese, but as Mrs Bartholomew said, the best we can do is make the natives' lives easy until they're all gone.'

I stopped and grabbed her arm. 'Until they are all gone? Is that what we are all hoping for?' My anger drew attention from a couple nearby and clearly shocked Ma.

'Keep your voice down, Annese. It's not what we hope for. It's just what will happen.'

I shook my head, tears now filling my eyes. 'I'm not going to Mass to be with those hypocrites. Tell Father that I am feeling faint.'

I went back to Ma's room and sat looking out the window. But Kiani did not return. I couldn't blame her if she'd been scared off by Ma's suspicious ways but I wanted to tell her it was my decision to keep the doll until I saw Macca. I persuaded myself that she'd probably gone to find Macca by herself, with her chess piece at least.

Weeks passed with no word from Mrs Bartholomew, and when each Sunday brought no sign of Kiani, an uncomfortable sadness crept upon me, a guilty fear. I began to think that maybe Ma was right. Their ways were too different, and I found myself accepting that soon they'd all be gone. It was just what was going to happen. I could do nothing to help Kiani or her people.

My friendship with Kiani had ended. She would not be back.

CHAPTER 14

With money now coming into the colony from the goldfields and more ships docking every day bringing goods and foodstuffs from the old country, a quiet optimism was returning to the colony. Local farmers doubled their orders from the stores. The wedding to which Polly and Thomas had been invited seemed to symbolise everything that people envisaged of the future. A future of plenty and of growth.

Excitement rippled throughout Adelaide Town as the day of the wedding neared. Pastoral families began arriving from as far as Mintaro, Naracoorte, and even New South Wales. Commissioner Tolmer and Captain O'Halloran were invited and it was said they'd attend resplendent in their official uniforms.

Polly sent word to Ma that they were staying with a friend of Mrs Scholz, a Mrs Walther at Klemzig. She invited us to attend for afternoon tea there on Saturday afternoon.

'I've arranged with Mrs Bartholomew to have the time off. Father Murphy has agreed to tell Matron you're being schooled in your catechism in the afternoon. She's a Proddy, so will not know any better.' She gave me one of her conspiratorial smiles. 'One thing you can count on in the Irish. We're good at the blarney. You've just got to get the afternoon off from your work.'

'Afternoon tea,' I exclaimed. 'Who do they think we are? We have nothing grand enough to wear to such a to-do.'

As the day approached, the more anxious Ma became about coming under Polly and Thomas's scrutiny.

'Do you think we should decline?' she said, looking down at her inflamed hands, her voice fraught and desperate. 'I'm sure they are only asking to see us out of duty. What if, at this very moment, they are moaning at having to spend time with us — a domestic and a shoe-maker's assistant.'

I was nervous too, especially about meeting Thomas again, but I knew how important it was that we accept the invitation. 'You've nothing to be ashamed of, Ma. You've worked hard all your life and kept the Lord's commandments. That's all anyone asks. And my circumstances—well, they'll change soon. Surely Polly would not have asked us unless she truly wanted to see us. We shall meet with them with our heads held high.'

I took her hands, reddened beyond her years, in my own. 'We'll mend our Sunday clothes as best we can. And did you not say Mrs Bartholomew has recently replaced her leather gloves because of a tiny tear? Maybe she'll let you have her old ones. I'll patch them with the scraps from my work. I'll have them looking as good as new.'

The Friday before the afternoon tea, I was helping Mr Petersen re-heel a pair of lace-up boots. He caught me looking at them and seemed to know what I was thinking. I'd told him about the reunion in order to get the afternoon off.

'They's your size, Laffer. It'd be a shame if the heels were not well balanced when we return them to their owner. I think maybe you should wear them for a day, to make sure we've got them right.'

The smile on my face was my reply and I stepped towards him to take his hand in thanks, but he'd turned away.

I left work early the next day. It wasn't a laundry day and Mrs Bartholomew gave Ma and me permission to use the laundry to bathe, using the hot water from the copper. The luxury of having enough warm soapy water for us to each have our own bowlful brightened Ma's spirits. We used Mrs Bartholomew's discarded face washers and towels. They'd lost their fluffiness and she'd thrown them out as rags, but to us, they were a luxury.

Ma sang as she washed and dressed, a trick she often used to hide her nervousness. 'Come on, Annese, we'd best hurry. We don't want to be late.'

Pulling on the borrowed boots, I made sure I caught each button with the freshly cut laces. The heels were taller than any I'd worn before. Standing in them, I felt as if I was a different person—someone good.

Ma insisted I wear her bonnet, having borrowed another from a friend. It made me look too old, like a spinster, but I hadn't the heart to say no to her. Linking arms, we sang as we walked to Klemzig, trying to quell the rising panic.

The house was grand but not as intimidating as Mrs Bartholomew's. Polly must have been watching out the window because she threw the door open before we'd even knocked. Her smiling face, plump and slightly freckled, as it had always been, was now framed by a mass of blonde ringlets held in place with a red ribbon. She flung herself into my arms and then into Ma's. We were all awash with tears when Mrs Scholz and her friend, Mrs Walther, joined us. Behind them stood a tall, thin young man and it took me a moment to realise it was Thomas. His stature was like Da's but his thick wiry black hair was Ma's. He parted it well to the side, a fashion I'd seen in a likeness of Prince Albert. He even had the beginnings of a thin moustache.

'For goodness' sake, come in,' he grumbled, barely glancing at Ma or me. 'Do you really want all and sundry watching you?'

Polly, unperturbed by his gruffness, linked arms with us. 'Tea is set up in the garden. Aunt Mathilda has been kind enough to allow us to have guests when we are guests ourselves. Thomas, make yourself useful and let the kitchen staff know that they can serve us now.'

We walked through a hall, past a large stairwell, and onto a veranda that opened into the garden where a table was set with a white linen cloth. Polly insisted that Ma and I sit either side of her. Pink, white, and purple flowers abounded everywhere, climbing over trellises and lining winding paths. A bank of white roses covered one of the fences. The other was hidden by fruit trees, stretching wide, their branches laden with peaches, apricots, and almonds. I could barely stop myself from running to smell their sweet ripeness.

Thomas re-joined us with a friend in tow. Although he'd grown to the height of a man, he still had about him the gangly gait of a boy. He nodded politely to us now.

'Mrs Laffer, Miss Laffer.'

I almost laughed at the formality. 'May I introduce Frederick Scholz.'

'Stop being such a stiff-neck, Thomas,' Polly giggled. 'Frederick is our stepbrother and our cousin,' she said to me. Seeing our confused looks, she hurried on. 'On the Scholz side of the family. It gets very confusing. Or maybe you didn't know? Mother, Mrs Scholz, has re-married to her late husband's brother.'

Her confident manner was no longer that of a child. While the passing years had given me experiences I'd learned how to overcome, they'd filled her and Thomas with an assurance that nothing bad could happen. The world was theirs to enjoy, not to survive, as it was for me and Joseph.

I noticed Frederick smiling adoringly at Polly. His clothes, though well cut, showed signs of wear and tear, his hands ink-stained.

Mrs Scholz poured tea from a large silver pot and insisted we take one of the delicate sandwiches placed on the lowest level of the tiered plates. On the next level were cakes with white icing, and jam tarts at the top. I could see Ma's hands shaking and feared mine were too as I tried to not upturn the entire setting.

Polly was asking about Ma's work. 'I've heard the Bartholomew house is very grand,' she said and then, realising it might be an insult to her hostess, continued, 'but this is said to be the best garden in the colony.'

'And you are working too, Annese?' Mrs Scholz asked. I felt all eyes on me and my words stuck in my throat.

'A… A… a shoemaker's assistant,' I eventually got out. From the corner of my eye, I saw Thomas smirk and was not sure if it was about my work or my clumsy words.

'How intriguing,' Frederick said, a kindness in his voice. 'I thought only men were cobblers. You must be good at what you do.'

His gentleness relaxed me enough to whisper a reply. 'His nephew left for the goldfields. Mr Petersen is happy with my work.'

'Well you'd better prepare to be replaced,' Thomas snapped. 'The Mount Alexander gold is almost finished. Men will soon be flocking back to Adelaide looking for work. You'll have to step aside.'

It was not what he said that upset me, for I knew well enough how tenuous my work was; it was the angry bitterness in his voice, so at odds with the child I'd once known.

'Oh, I'm certain she will be married by then,' Polly said. 'You must have a beau, Annese, you are so pretty.'

'No,' I said, knowing I could never talk about Macca in such company. If they too had heard the rumours about him being with a native woman, they'd be horrified to think I'd even consider him. And sitting here feeling welcomed in such genteel company, I too questioned the sanity of my dreams.

'Well, I am sure that will change,' Mrs Walther was saying. 'You have such lovely eyes and gentle manners. Do you not agree, Frederick?'

I felt a red flush on my neck. The teacup rattled in my hands. I'd not expected, nor did I welcome, any conversations about my looks.

I noticed Thomas watching me closely. 'As chance has it, I met a certain Malcolm Macleod recently. We somehow got talking about Echunga and when I said my former name was Laffer, he said he'd known me as a babe.'

'Oh, that must be the man we know as Macca. He did indeed know you,' Ma said brightly. 'He was friendly with your father and was often at our tent.'

I saw the ripple of embarrassed surprise spread through the group. 'Before we built our hut,' Ma murmured.

'Well, he was worse for the drink when I saw him. Said he was down on his luck having been robbed of a windfall. He was raving somewhat about a chess set or some such. Said he had to get something—from you, Annese.'

'Was he in Adelaide?' The words were out of my mouth, loud and clear before I could stop them. All eyes were on me again, but for quite a different reason.

'Oh, she can speak up then,' Thomas scoffed.

'Thomas, mind your manners,' Mrs Scholz remonstrated.

'No. We were both in Melbourne. Mother,' he said looking at Mrs Scholz, 'took me with her to buy the wedding present. A chap there has imported goods directly from London's Grand Exhibition last year. But I don't suppose you'd know anything about that.'

The last words were aimed firmly at me and I shrivelled beneath his glare.

Mrs Scholz slapped the table. 'Enough. Apologise, Thomas. Annese is your sister. She and your mother deserve your full respect.'

Thomas pushed out from the table. 'Only Polly is my sister, and you my only mother. No true mother would give her children away. No true sister would let it happen.' He strode from the garden and we heard the front door slam.

Ma let out a quiet sob and a silence fell over the group.

'I'll go after him,' Frederick said, giving Polly a look that seemed to say 'again'. Taking Mrs Walther's hand, he continued in his calm and confident manner. 'Perhaps we should leave Mrs Scholz and Polly with their guests.'

'Thomas doesn't mean it,' Mrs Scholz said as they left. 'He's going through a difficult time. It's why I encourage his friendship with Frederick. He is such a steadying influence.'

Ma searched her pockets for a handkerchief. Wiping her tears she turned to Polly.

'Polly, you and Thomas must know, your father and I did everything we could to keep you both. But we were living in a tent at the time and we couldn't feed you all. It was only supposed to be for a short time, the boarding out. But Mrs Scholz came along and… well, we thought it was for the best.' She looked to Mrs Scholz and nodded.

Polly took her hand. 'I know. And because of you and our father, Thomas and I have had a wonderful life. Mother… Mrs Scholz… has always explained your circumstances to us in the kindest way. She's never pretended she was our real mother, although it is how we think of her. But we know that you were the person who brought us into the world and looked after us as best you could in the early years. You too, Annese. Thomas is acting like a spoiled brat at the moment. He'll come good.'

Polly's gentle command of the situation astounded me. Once again I felt like the younger sister. It was hard to believe she was nearly four years younger than me.

We all fell quiet, nothing more could be said in the little time we had left. Eventually, Polly turned the conversation back to the wedding, describing her dress. Mrs Scholz followed her lead and talked of bouquets and bonnets. But my mind could not switch back. Thomas's reaction left me beyond words, as did his reference to Macca saying he needed to see me. I recalled Kiani's request and wondered if the circumstances were related.

A gentle sunset tinged the sky as Ma and I took our leave. Polly linked my arm in hers as we followed the others back through the house.

'Did you see Malcolm Macleod, too?' I asked determined to find out more.

'No. Only Thomas and Frederick went with Mother to Melbourne. Why do you ask? Are you sweet on him?' She pulled me closer and laughed.

She spoke with such confidence and yet she seemed so playful and childish too. Carefree. I wondered if it was money that gave some children the skills to easily manage the adult world.

'Well, are you?'

'No. Well, yes. Well, I don't know.'

Polly collapsed into a fit of giggles. 'I think that means yes. I shall tell Frederick to arrange a meeting if he ever sees him again.'

We caught up with the others. 'What meeting?' Ma asked.

I squeezed Polly's arm hard enough for her to get my message.

'Oh, for us young ones to all get together again before we go home. Annese, you must bring Joseph if he has arrived back too. Thomas would love to see him again—even though he pretends otherwise.'

Our conversation as Ma and I walked home was filled with both joy and sadness. 'You believe me don't you, Annese. We didn't want to give them up.'

'Of course I do. Anyway, we haven't given them up. They are still part of our family.'

We walked on in silence. Nearing Ma's room, I decided to ask her advice, even though I knew her thoughts on the subject.

'Do you think I should try to find Macca? Polly seems to think Frederick could get a message to him.'

Ma shook her head as if the burden of the decision was too much for her on top of what had just occurred. 'It's up to you, Annese. Macca is a complex man. A troubled man, from all accounts. I would once have trusted him completely, but now I am not so sure. But he gave the chess piece to you, not me. You are old enough to make up your own mind now. And make your own mistakes.'

Quickly changing, I walked through the asylum gates just as the bell began ringing. My afternoon in a gentle garden seemed like a dream already. Sitting down amongst women so destroyed in both body and mind by the horrors of their lives, I realised Thomas's childish outburst towards me was nothing. Still full of Mrs Walther's delicacies, I gave my pathetic meal to a young pregnant girl sitting beside me. That night I lay awake for hours wondering how I could find Macca and if I would still feel the same way about him if I did eventually see him. Would the chess piece help him get out of whatever trouble he was in? Maybe if he could get a really good price for it, I could also pay the starting fee required for a place for Ma and me to rent.

CHAPTER 15

"Gold at Echunga." The headline in *The Observer* was on everyone's lips. I joined a crowd gathered around the newspaper stand in Rundle Street, leaning in, trying to hear over the rabble. From what I could gather, Mr Chapman and his son had finally begun panning and within days found enough nuggets to convince the Colonial Secretary, Mr Finniss, that there was gold to be found there. All of a sudden, Echunga was the talk of the town.

Although pleased at the business it was creating, Mr Petersen seemed to be the only person resisting the excitement. 'There'll be boots needed whether there's gold or not. The sooner we finish this order, Laffer, the sooner we get onto the next one.'

He was right, for we received five new orders that day, mostly from men keen to be part of the action so close to home. It was almost dark when we finished for the day and Mr Petersen gave me an extra sixpence for my effort. I hid it from Mr Ennis and would give it to Ma after Mass the following Sunday.

The service was in Latin so I didn't understand a word. I'd learned when I needed to stand and when to kneel and followed Ma's lead as to when to respond and when to stay silent. I found Father Murphy's sermon about God's love for all hard to accept when I knew that Kiani's people were becoming more and more reliant on charity as their land was settled and fenced.

When the collection plate came around, I was angry to see Ma put a few of our precious coins in it, especially when I learned much of it was used to pay for a new painting of Mary while we in the asylum lived in such dire conditions.

'I miss the quietness of the Quaker Meetings,' I said as we walked back towards her room, 'although it felt good to be singing.'

We found a discarded newspaper on the way and sat under a tree to read it. 'It's all about Echunga,' I exclaimed, scanning the first few lines. 'It's a firsthand account by the young Mr Chapman about the gold there.'

'Read it,' she said. I hadn't read out loud since my school days and my stomach tightened a little, even though it was only Ma listening.

Fifty or sixty horsemen began galloping towards us through the stringybark. At their head rode Mr Finniss, my father, Mr Hampton and a body of police. Soon everyone began to wash at once. Kettles, billies, saucepan lids, pannikins and even hats were called into requisition.

'I hope Da and Joseph get home soon before all the claims get taken,' I said. I thought to add Macca but didn't.

***

All my attempts to find out where Macca was had failed. I'd thought of writing to Da but if, as we hoped, he was on his way home, the letter would never find him.

To my surprise, I'd become quite friendly with several of the asylum girls who worked at the tavern. I had a fair idea it wasn't just serving rum that they did, but they were kind enough to me and I knew how hard it was for a single woman to survive, even as the colony began to prosper. When I asked them if they knew any of Tolmer's men, they'd laughed.

'Interested in making a little extra, are you?'

My protests only escalated their laughter, which told me they'd not been serious.

'Is it one of them in particular you're asking after?'

'Malcolm Macleod. He's known as Macca. He's a friend of my parents.'

But my enquiries led nowhere. Whether they didn't know him or weren't willing to say, I never quite knew.

As it turned out, I had no need to write to Da. Six weeks after receiving his last letter, I was in Ma's room getting changed to go to Mass when there was a hefty knock on the door. Ma screamed with delight as she opened it and threw herself into Da's embrace. I hastily shoved my grey uniform under the bed and pulled on my pinafore.

Da turned to me and held me from him, shaking his head, tears in his eyes. I thought at first he'd heard about where I was living. Ma and I had agreed not to tell him or Joseph about my situation. But his smile soon told me it was with pleasure that he observed me.

'My little Annese. You've turned into a young lady while we've been away.' He hugged me and I felt his tears on my cheek.

'Have you heard about the gold find at Echunga?' Ma said, releasing Joseph from her arms.

'We were halfway home when the news came through. We walked day and night to get here.'

Joseph peered around at Ma's cramped living space. 'Have you really both shared this one room?'

Ma and I exchanged a look. She shook her head. 'We're at work most of the time,' she said. 'But never mind us Joseph, tell me of the journey home.'

'I will but not in here. I can barely stand up straight.' It was true; his hair brushed the ceiling.

'We aren't allowed visitors here anyway,' Ma said, shuffling us all from the room and locking the door behind us. Finding the shade of a river gum, we pulled up a couple of large fallen branches to sit on. The pleasure on Ma's face was unmistakable as she settled, her hands in her lap, keen to hear Joseph's account of their travels. Like Ma, Joseph was a natural storyteller. Listening to him, I saw how chiselled his face was and heard how his voice had deepened. I thought about how popular he would be now with all the girls in Echunga.

'Was a dreary day when we packed up our tent, a swag each, and started walking with the last of our findings well hidden.'

Ma and I exchanged glances again. As thrilled as we were that they were home and with us, we both knew the importance of their findings.

'We expected to meet the escort going east and, sure enough, when we got to Wattle Flat, Tolmer was there with his men.'

My heart leapt at the mention of the escort but I knew better than to interrupt. Joseph caught me watching him and winked. Did he know something about Macca?

'The escort men were full of Chapman's news about the possibility of gold at Echunga. Even though they were going the other direction, we decided to lodge most of our findings with the escort, keeping back enough to buy two horses.'

'Two horses!' I gasped. Never had I expected we would own one horse, let alone two. Tears filled my eyes as the reality of the changes their findings would bring dawned upon me. I desperately wanted to know when the gold would arrive but could not ask without divulging the truth about my lodgings. 'Where are they? The horses?'

'At the Diggers Inn stables. We've booked in there for the night already,' Da said. 'Don't get your hopes up, Annese, we'll have to sell them to get money to set up again. We only bought them to get back to Echunga ahead of the crowds.'

'So when will you head down there?' Ma asked.

'Day after tomorrow. Joseph and I will stock up and hire a dray. We'll stake a claim before they're all gone.'

'Leave us again? Already?' Ma bit her top lip, trying to hold back her disappointment.

'We have to,' Joseph said. 'There's already a rush on. Even some of Tolmer's crew left him mid-journey to go there. We have to be in on it, Ma. It'll be the making of us. We can get another couple more tents and live together at the diggings.'

Ma shook her head. 'No. I won't have us living in a tent again. And what about my work here? And Annese's? We can't just leave. No, you two go on and we'll join you when we can afford a hut of some sort.'

Da took her hand. 'It won't be for long, Kitty. We've got more experience than most and there'll be work aplenty at Echunga soon too, for men and women alike. I'll send word as soon as I hear of a position for you. If we strike it lucky, you'll never have to work again.'

'And me? Am I to follow you down there?' Even as I said it, I couldn't decide whether I wanted his answer to be yes or no. I loved my work and how would Macca know where to look for me?

I saw the hesitation in Da's eyes too. 'Yes, if that is what you want, Annese. But I wondered if you might want to stay here.'

Stay in Adelaide on my own? I opened my mouth to protest but it was then that I saw the change in him. A tiredness that was not just about the journey. And his voice seemed different too. Harder somehow, as if resigned to a new truth.

'You are an independent woman now and Adelaide is already bringing you more chances,' he continued.

Independent! More chances! He could not have been further from the truth.

Ma glanced at me and I nodded. We couldn't lie any longer.

'Annese has to find another place to stay. She can't… she isn't allowed to live with me and hasn't for some time.'

All eyes were on me now. In a flood of jumbled words, I told them what had happened. Da's face crumpled and Joseph turned from me, whether in disgust or shock I couldn't tell until he turned back.

'I'll go now and sell the horses,' Da said. 'She'll not spend another night in that place.'

***

Ma and I went to St Thomas's and caught Father Murphy just as he was preparing for Evensong.

'Our circumstances have changed. You can tell the Matron Annese will not be returning. You can take these and give them to another poor soul.'

I handed over the bundle of my uniform and cap and silently prayed that I would never see them again. I prayed too for the poor girl who would wear them next. As they left my hands, the bravery I'd feigned for so long to keep me safe dissolved. My knees began to shake, as relief flooded through me. I crumpled to the ground. A thundercloud within me dispersed into tiny wisps and a white light coursed around me.

***

I shared Ma's bed that night. Joseph arrived early the next morning.

'I've been asking around and was told the Temperance Hotel has some rooms that are suitable for a single woman.'

A single woman. His description of me seemed far removed from how I saw myself. My sixteenth birthday had come and gone but I felt no different than I did at fourteen—except, of course, for my lustful thoughts about Macca, which I kept hidden. And coming from him, the brother who I'd giggled with and teased when he farted, made it all the stranger, for he too had altered so much. I felt as if my world was on the verge of changing completely.

Ma and I visited the Temperance Hotel later that day. She spoke at length with the manager while one of the girls showed me a room. It was twice the size of Ma's room and had one single bed, a double bunk, a washstand, and a small wardrobe. By the time I joined Ma, the decision had been made. I was to move in the following day.

'You'll be on the second floor,' the manager said, 'sharing with two Irish girls.'

We all had dinner at the Diggers Inn and Da handed me the money for a month's rent.

'The bank gave me an advance on the gold that's coming. We didn't have to sell the horses. You can pay me back each pay day. Now tell me about your work. Ma says you are well regarded.'

It was only then that I heard the change. Da no longer used the words of his upbringing. Thou had become you. Was this a conscious decision, to fit it, to become at one with his fellow Australians? Or simply one of the many changes that come with living amongst those who spoke a more contemporary vernacular?

Putting the notes carefully in my pocket, I told him about Mr Petersen, the workshop, and the tasks I'd undertaken. I could see they were impressed, although Joseph had his concerns.

'You've taken a man's job. It might not last long, Annese, now that so many are returning. Do you have a beau?'

I shook my head, avoiding Ma's eyes as thoughts of Macca filled my mind.

'There's no need to be thinking of marriage,' Ma said. 'Better to make her own way than get attached to the wrong man.'

Joseph glanced at me, a questioning look showing he read between Ma's words. I shrugged, hoping to dismiss his concerns.

We talked until they called last drinks and, after a prolonged farewell, Ma and I snuggled together full of thoughts about the future.

CHAPTER 16

My two roommates were there to greet me the next day.

'Good morning, I'm Sarah.'

'And I'm Ellen, welcome to our palace.' She twirled around, laughing.

'You can have the bottom bunk. Ellen prefers the top one so she can lie in bed and spy on people through the curtains.'

Ellen opened the wardrobe. 'This is yours,' she said, pulling out an empty drawer, 'and your dresses can be hung here although there's not much space. I'm afraid I've taken up over half.'

'Only one dress,' I whispered. Pushing myself to make conversation, I asked 'Do you both work?'

'I work here cleaning, and in the kitchen,' Sarah said. 'But I want to train as a milliner as soon as there's an opening.'

'And you, Ellen?'

'Nowhere as yet. The authorities found work for me, but I was dismissed after two days. I didn't know which fork to lay where, so they sent me to make beds. I couldn't get that right either. Not to their standard, they said.'

'Didn't you learn any of that back home?' Sarah asked. 'You must have known they were looking for domestics when you agreed to come.'

'I can do domestic work right enough,' Ellen said, gazing at herself in the mirror, 'just not for the likes of them. Now they're saying they'll send me to a farm to do dairy work, but I won't go. I've seen all the cows I ever want to see in County Kilkenny.'

'You'll be sent back to the Immigration Depot if you can't pay for your room here,' Sarah said.

'Don't worry, I'll pay my way,' Ellen said taking tweezers to her eyebrows. 'There's always one way for a girl to get by.'

I knew what she meant but Ellen did not look like someone who'd do that. The asylum girls who frequented the tavern all had a sadness to them. It occurred to me then that perhaps that was a product, not a prerequisite.

'What work do you do?' Sarah asked.

'Shoemaker's assistant. Leigh Street. With Mr Petersen.'

'You can make me some new boots then,' Ellen laughed. 'Lace-ups that come over my knees. The men like that. And a whip too.'

Sarah gently slapped Ellen's hands, and laughed too, shooting me a sideways glance. 'Don't be so naughty, Ellen. Poor Annese will ask for another room.'

But Ellen took no notice. 'I imagine it's very quiet at your shoemakers with old man Petersen. I've heard tell that even when his wife was alive, he barely spoke to her from one week to the next. A girl I met at the tavern said that when he needed to be bedded, he'd just point to his wifies bodice and grunt.'

They acted out the scene, Sarah as Mr Petersen and Ellen as his wife, and laughed as they pretended to copulate. Although I knew it was wrong to make a mockery of my boss, I couldn't help but laugh with them.

Sarah had already left, and Ellen was asleep, when I dressed in my work clothes the next day. The streets were busy with men returned from the eastern goldfields as I walked to Leigh Street. The newcomers had not seen me before in my strange attire, and I received numerous looks and a few comments suggesting that I was masquerading as a boy.

With so many more people on the streets, Joseph's words about me taking a man's job, so similar to Thomas's but with none of his malice, rang in my ears. I half expected to see Mr Petersen's nephew at the bench when I arrived. But it was just a large stack of orders for work boots that greeted me.

Mr Petersen glanced up. 'No grey uniform?'

'No. My Da is home with his findings. I've found digs at the Temperance Hotel.'

He put down the boot he was working on and smiled as I'd not seen him do before. The relief on his face almost matched mine from the day before. 'Good for you, my girl. Good for you.'

When he bent back to his work, he wiped a tear from his cheek and I smiled too.

Flicking through the orders, one caught my eye.

Malcolm Macleod, size 10. 5 shillings deposit. Remaining payment of 6 shillings upon receipt. Will collect 1st October.

I tried to stay calm but my mouth went dry and my thoughts raced. Macca would be here in just a week.

'Well, come on Laffer, get a hurry on.' Mr Petersen had come to my side and he took Macca's order from me. 'Oh, so that's what's got your attention.'

That day and the days to follow went quickly, with hardly a word passing between us from morning to evening, for we understood without words what the other needed. I was absorbed in stretching an upper onto a sole when I sensed someone standing over me.

'So it's a shoemaker you've become.' My heart jumped at the sound of his Scottish accent. I threw myself into Macca's arms before even taking a proper look at him.

'What's this?' Mr Petersen demanded.

Macca peeled me off him and put his hand out. 'I'm a brother—well, like a brother,' he said. 'Malcolm Macleod. You'll have some boots for me, I hope.'

He looked much older, his beard down to his chest. His face, what I could see of it, was hollowed out. Even his eyes seemed to have dulled.

'Get your friend his boots, Laffer. He looks like he could do with them.'

I glanced at the boots Macca was wearing. They were falling apart and his clothes were no better. What had happened to him? If I had seen him as a stranger in the street, I would have crossed to the other side. I wondered what else had changed.

Mr Petersen's bluntness did not upset Macca. He laughed and my feelings for him flared. I loved that laugh as much as I ever had. Surely, he was still the same person beneath the squalor.

'You're right enough there, Mr Petersen. These have seen things and been places no boots should have to endure.' Turning to me, a sorrowful look on his face now, he lowered his voice a little. 'But I survived. And now I'm back where I belong.'

I heard Mr Petersen grunt behind me and, thinking he was annoyed at me, I went back to my stretching.

'You'll be finishing for the day I expect, Laffer,' he muttered and threw me a shilling coin. 'That's your bonus early. You'll be earning it in the next few weeks right enough. Take your friend for a feed. He looks as though he could use it.'

Thanking him, I tidied my bench and left with Macca. 'The Blenheim does a good lunch of stewed hogget,' I said, resisting the urge to take his hand. 'And they've a lady's lounge.'

'Sounds grand, Annese. And I'm not as skint as I look. I'll get us a beer each.'

Over lunch, he talked of his adventures, although I knew from the way he stopped talking and shuddered every so often there was more to tell.

'So you left the escort?' I prompted after one of the silences.

'Aye, I did. I couldn't hold my tongue any longer. It all came to a head over the way they treated a young Aboriginal man. Freddy, they called him, but his name was Poltpalingada. He'd done two trips with us negotiating with the local people and directing us to waterholes that saved our lives. But Tolmer insisted he not sit with us when we ate. And he was always given the worst of the meat.'

'Did you and Tolmer have a fight about it?'

Macca shook his head. 'It didn't come to that but I knew that my time was up with him. I gave Freddy my rations for the day and left. He had a little English and I enough of his language for him to tell me where his family were living and how to find food and water on the way. They were not far away and, using some words he gave me, I was able to explain what had happened. They welcomed me and I stayed on with them for a time.'

'Our Thomas said he saw you in Melbourne.'

Macca's brow furrowed. 'I do remember meeting him, but I was…' He hesitated.

'The worse for drink?'

He hung his head. 'Is that what Thomas said?'

I nodded, waiting to see his reaction.

'Well, he was right. I'd been drinking way more than was good for me. And gambling. What else did Thomas say?'

'That you told him you'd lost a windfall and you needed something from me. The chess piece.'

Macca grimaced. 'I don't even remember saying that, Annese. The rum is an evil thing. I only drink beer now and even that not often.' He looked long and hard at me as if he didn't know whether or not to share a story.

'So was it the chess piece you were needing?'

'Well yes, but I should never have said that to Thomas. It's yours. I gave it to you. And one to Kiani. One thing you should know though; it could be worth a lot of money. I met a man in Melbourne, sent out here by the British Museum to collect Aboriginal artefacts. I told him about the chess pieces my parents found on the Isle of Lewis and that

I'd been given one and my brother another. When I described them, he could hardly contain himself. He said if they were what I claimed, he'd pay me good money.'

'So is that why you're here? To get them back?'

He shook his head. 'No, not now. They're yours and Kiani's. But to be honest, I did consider it at the time. I'd run up a big debt with some unsavoury characters. It was around that time I met up with Thomas. I wasn't in a good place, Annese.'

'And now?' He wouldn't look at me so I raised his chin. I needed to look into his eyes for the answer.

'I'm okay again now.'

'The money?'

'I went back to whaling for a time and paid off my debts. I don't want to take the chess pieces back. They're in good hands with you and Kiani. My Ma would be happy about that.'

I could see he was telling the truth. I wanted to lighten the mood, to see the old Macca. 'I remember you once telling me how your Ma and Da found them in a sandhill. But I'd thought it just a story you made up. I didn't know they'd ended up in a museum.'

His mood shifted. 'I must admit it's a story few believe, Laffer,' he said, tweaking my nose as he used Mr Petersen's nickname for me.

'But why were they in a sandhill if they're so valuable? And how did your Ma find them?'

'Nobody knows who buried them or why. It was actually my father who found them. He was looking for a place to bury a dead cow and came across an underground chamber. When he saw the wee figures, the dolls as you call them, he was too frightened to touch them; to him, they looked like little devils. When he told Ma, she thought he was delusional from the drink. But he took her to the site and she realised he'd not been drunk. There were dozens of them; all made of walrus ivory, they found out later.'

'So what happened to the rest? Did they sell them?'

'Aye, most of them. Gave one to me and one to my brother when we left. I think my older brother Murdo got some too when he left for Canada along with hundreds of others on the promise of a better life. Ma told us they were for safekeeping, although they didn't exactly keep our family safe.'

'If the museum man you met in Melbourne is right about their value, they should have been paid well for their find.'

He shook his head. 'No, they only got a pittance. Ma thought she got a good price and it did put food in our bellies for a year or so, but from what I can gather, they were sold on not much later for ten times what we got for them.

'I don't remember much about it; I was just a baby. But my brother Murdo told me we were pushed off our croft just a few years later.' His jaw clenched and he shook his head. 'It broke up our family and destroyed my parents. My father died soon after, of a broken heart, Murdo said.'

'Did they not try to sell these two pieces?'

'Murdo said Ma didn't trust anyone enough to ask. She was afeared they'd take them from us. Anyway, there was no stopping them—the landlords. They wanted our land and that was the end of it.'

I would have loved to hear more about his family but a sadness crept over both of us; he, remembering his family, and me recalling the dark months after Polly and Thomas left.

'And now we are doing it to others. The Aboriginal people.' His voice cracked and he shook his head as if trying to get rid of something.

I began to protest but he cut me short. 'Yes. Even you and I are part of it, Annese.' It was like a slap across my face.

'Some say it's the natural order of things, natural selection,' I said clinging onto words I'd heard to ease my pain. 'They say it's the way of things that the strong survive over the weak. That the natives will soon all die because it is the way it must be.'

'No, Laffer,' he said raising his voice as he glared at me. A few people looked in our direction. He continued in subdued tones. 'They are the owners of this country and they are far from weak. Trusting and naïve about our greedy ways perhaps, but not weak. They have lived here for thousands of years. And you and I, all of us are as guilty as anyone by doing nothing to stop the destruction of their ways.'

His jaw stiffened as he swallowed his self-loathing. I could only think to change the subject.

'So what happened to them, the chess pieces?' I whispered.

I was afraid he'd be angry for my obvious diversion but he laughed his sad laugh and wiped his eyes with his sleeve.

'Aye, you're right. It's too hard for me to talk about what we are doing without getting angry and that does no one any good. So yes, let's talk about the chess pieces. That's a safe topic for a genteel dining room.' The bitterness in his voice told me he didn't mean what he said. I waited for him to recover his composure.

'Well, according to the man I spoke to, most are in the museum in London and some in Edinburgh. I could tell he knew he could fetch a very good price for them.'

My mind raced. If I could sell the one that Macca insisted was mine, Ma wouldn't have to go out doing cleaning and laundry every day. We could get some rooms of our own until Da had a cottage built for us at Echunga. I might even be able to make sure it had a tin roof and a room for both Joseph and me.

But Kiani's words came back to me. *Macca needs them… To keep him safe.* I looked at the state of his clothes and the ragged empty look on his face.

'I think you should take them back, Macca, both the one you gave to me and the one Kiani has. They will keep you safe. I'll get mine from Mrs Bartholomew and we'll find Kiani.'

'Why do you think I need to be kept safe?' He laughed as he said it, but still, he waited for an answer.

'It was something Kiani said. She came to see me. She told me that they must both be with you. She said you were in trouble and she would take them to you. But Ma wouldn't let me give her the one I have.' The words rushed from me now with the relief of having someone I could share the story with. 'Ma said she couldn't be trusted. She said…'

'Slow down, Annese. You've lost me. You saw Kiani? How long ago?'

'A few months ago now. She was going to come back the next day but I haven't seen her since.'

Macca's head was in his hands now and a wave of shame flowed through me. 'I'm sorry, Macca. I should have…' I didn't really know what I should have done, but I wanted it to be right between us.

'It's okay, Laffer. Your Ma was probably right not to give it to her, but not for the right reasons. So where is it—your chess piece?'

'Ma's boss, Mrs Bartholomew, insisted we leave it in her safe box.'

He bit his lip and it was some time before he spoke. 'I don't know how Kiani knew I was in trouble but I shouldn't be surprised. Her people have ways of knowing that we don't understand. I remember telling her the same story as I told you about how Ma said they were for my protection. But I didn't think she had enough English at that time to understand. I certainly didn't think she'd remember. I can't believe either of you remembered really. You were both only little.'

'I'll contact Mrs Bartholomew tomorrow and get back the one you gave me.'

'No. As long as you trust her, it's probably in the best place. The man who was going to buy them has gone back to England, and good riddance to him. He said he wanted me to help him buy some Aboriginal artefacts. I thought he would pay for them but when I learned he intended to just take them, I refused to work for him. His attitude reminded me of when my parents were short-changed for the chess pieces.'

'So Kiani didn't find you to give you hers?'

He shook his head as tears gathered in his eyes. 'No, although I heard from one of her family that she was looking for me. I heard too she's been accused of stealing it. That and another trinket. Some story that goes back to when she lived near Echunga.'

A vague memory came to me of Margaret Mayfield's letter. She'd written something about a robbery and I'd assumed it was Tottengarr and that's why she'd been sent away. But what if it had been Kiani?

'Did they say who accused her?'

'No, just that it happened at Echunga. Why? Do you know something about it?'

I couldn't think fast enough. I needed time to work out what to tell him, worried he'd be angry that I'd read Margaret's letter and then lied to her. Worried too because of what it said about him and her.

'No. Nothing,' I lied. 'Did Kiani's family tell you where she is now?'

'No. They were angry and said they didn't trust white men anymore.'

'Can't we just tell whoever has accused her the truth, that the chess piece is hers now?'

He shook his head. 'Probably best not to at this stage. It'll likely be forgotten unless she gets into trouble again. But I think we need to find her. If she did steal the other object, she needs to get rid of it or she'll go to gaol for sure. Her family too maybe.'

The thought of the letter, still in my tin, weighed even more heavily on me now. Not only was it the cause of the twins being taken from us, it was possibly also evidence against Kiani. I needed to read it again to be sure of what it said.

'Macca, I need to tell you something.' But he didn't answer and, at first, I thought he didn't hear me. His whole body was shaking. I'd never seen a man cry like that before. Deeply. In silence.

I should have been sad too. I should have taken his hand and reassured him, but something else swelled in me, something I only later understood.

I was jealous. His passionate tears were not for me. Margaret's words came back to me. *he told me he was in love with another... it is a native woman who has captured his affection!*

'Is it for Ngama you cry? Did you take her as your wife?' He stared at me then, angry and confused. 'I heard stories. I didn't know what to think.'

'I would never lie with an Aboriginal woman. There are some men who do; some with love, most from lust. But even with love, it is not right. We're not a part of their lore. They have rules about who can be together in that way, strict rules about families, just like us. They're not savages.'

He spat the last word out. Its brutal sound spun around me.

'I know, but that is what they're called. It's what everybody says.'

'Well, they're wrong. We could learn so much from them if we only bothered to stop and listen and watch. They understand what this land needs. Look how our crops are failing and our animals starving. If it hadn't been for the gold, who knows what would have happened? We are making such a mess of it.'

He pushed back from the table. 'You will have to choose for yourself what you believe, Annese.'

I grabbed his hand, hoping to stop him from leaving. 'Where will you go now?'

'I don't know. Away. Away from all this hypocrisy.'

'Macca, I have to show you something, a letter.'

But he was gone, leaving me with my shame.

CHAPTER 17

Ma was at work and Fiona was just leaving when I arrived early the next morning before going to my own work. I rummaged under Ma's bed and, finding my tin, took the letter out, careful to not tear it along the thinning fold lines. It was the end of the letter concerning the robbery that I mostly wanted to read as I'd previously skipped over it. But I could not resist rereading Margaret's heartfelt words about Macca.

> *Although two years my junior, he is mature beyond his years, due in part, I am sure, to the fact that, having been driven from his home in the Scottish islands at a young he was forced to leave his parents' guidance and spent his formative years among seafaring adults.*
>
> *I have allowed him small courtesies that, were I not fond of him, and he of me, could be labelled as indiscretions. I allowed him to hold my hand longer than required while he removed a bee sting and, on another occasion, I sat with him, unchaperoned, on the banks of our creek, while he sang a song of love.*

This was the image that had stayed with me since last reading the letter and, despite my dislike of Margaret, I couldn't help but feel sorry for her now. I too would have fallen in love with Macca if it were me with him on the bank. And I too would have hoped that he sang words of love to me.

Given these very clear indications of his commitment to me, and my allowance to him, you can imagine my horror when he told me he was in love with another.

And that is not the worst of it, Aunt. A conversation with Friend Stephen Hastings has led me to believe that it is a native woman who has captured his affection!

Oh how I shudder to imagine that the same hand that held mine has also held that of a native woman. My shame is immense, dear Aunt. I seek your advice and reassurance that I have done no wrong.

I wondered again if it was Ngama he referred to? He had not said to me that he did not love her, only that he'd not lain with her. Putting these thoughts aside I read on, keen to know what Margaret had written about being robbed by a native.

I now move to another matter. I was at my piano one day when a native woman came to the door. She was with a girl of about ten years of age. They asked for flour and sugar. As you know from my previous correspondence, Father has instructed that we must be generous to these poor savages. I myself believe that such charity breeds laziness, but, in accordance with Father's wishes, I agreed and turned to walk to the kitchen.

To my great horror, they followed me into our house.

I remembered Margaret's contempt when Tottengarr assumed she would eat with them. It reminded me of Macca's story too, about Tolmer making the Aboriginal man eat separately from the others. I read on.

The girl went to our mantle and was handling the ornaments we display there. I quickly grabbed several food items, barely taking my eyes from her. I passed the food to them, waving my hands as I did to scare them away. The girl took my offerings and, as she put the items into her woven bag, I noticed in it an object not of their world. I demanded she show it to me. Aunt, it was a thing of strange beauty. An item of intricate carving made of ivory, I think.

I read this section twice and knew then with certainty that it was Ngama and Kiani, not Tottengarr as I'd previously assumed. I knew with a certainty too that the item Margaret had seen was Kiani's chess piece.

I made a grab for it and yelled 'thief' but she moved quickly and rushed out the door, the other one following. They ran to the water tank where the child turned and called out something to me—'yacca', I think—before they disappeared into the bush.

'Yacca.' I said the word out loud. Of course! It was 'Macca' that Kiani had said. She'd been trying to tell Margaret that Macca had given the doll to her. But Margaret had heard 'yacca,' a common enough word used to describe the spiky bushes that grow in abundance around Echunga.

I smiled, thinking of Kiani's courage and quick thinking, and wondered if it would have made the situation better or worse if Margaret had known Macca had given it to her.

I read on, knowing that the next section would address my most important concern. Had Kiani stolen another item from her?

Going back to the mantle, I checked to see if anything was missing but all seemed to be as it had been. But the artefact she carried had clearly been stolen from some poor settler's home. I took matters into my own hands.

I removed from the mantlepiece Mother's much loved china horse, an heirloom she has cherished since a child, and hid it within my pocket.

I gasped. Would Margaret be so cunning?

Several farm hands, having heard my cries, gathered at the door. I instructed them to fetch Father and tell him we'd been robbed of a precious ornament by a native and that they'd already stolen another expensive item from elsewhere.

Anger rose within me. All my old hatred of Margaret joined with my despair for Kiani. In that moment, I hated Margaret with all of my being. I hated her in a way that challenged my upbringing and my faith which called for forgiveness and understanding. I hated her for falsely accusing Kiani. I hated her for dismissing Ma and bringing tragedy to our family. But most of all, I hated all that she represented.

I knew then that, unless I spoke out about the letter I stole, Kiani would always bear the label of thief.

I grappled with the decision I needed to make. I knew any punishment I received if I owned up to theft and deception regarding the letter would be mild compared to what Kiani would face. I was not so concerned about my own status, but my parents relied on the goodwill and support of the Friends. An admission would likely make an enemy of Margaret and her powerful family. Her brothers and brother-in-law were on many important committees. Their influence went beyond the Quaker community now too as they were also related to the Bishop of Adelaide's new wife.

I knew in my heart the right thing to do, but the temptation to rip the letter up and pretend I'd never read it was strong. My mind raced with scenarios that would excuse my decision to destroy the letter. *It was not my fault that the natives were blamed for things they didn't do. I hadn't been the one to take their land from them. If Kiani had been smart, she would never have let Margaret see Macca's doll.*

These thoughts tumbled around within me, pulling me away from thinking about Kiani's predicament. It would be so easy for me to simply let my lie remain hidden and hope that Kiani was never found.

But Macca's words came back to me. *All of us are as guilty as each other.* I understood fully now what he was saying. I could get away with theft and lies. I could conveniently persuade myself that my decision would make no difference. I could simply agree that Kiani's people were a dying race and there was nothing we, the settlers, could do.

I could simply turn away and pretend I wasn't seeing what was happening around us.

The image came to me of Jesus coming between an angry crowd and a woman of sin, demanding only those without sin had the right to judge her. Did I have the courage to be that person?

I thought about seeking guidance from my parents but I already knew their answers would not satisfy me.

As I put the letter away, I came across the newspaper with the article about Mr Chapman's gold find. But it was another story that caught my eye.

Entitled 'The Native Mission at Port Lincoln', it was written by the Lord Bishop of Adelaide, Augustus Short, the one whose wife was related to Margaret. His opening paragraph filled me with fear.

On the first occasion when I visited Port Lincoln in 1849, …
five natives had fallen victim to flour mixed with arsenic, which
they had stolen from a shepherd's hut.

Counting on my fingers, I was relieved to calculate that I had seen Kiani after that date. But what if they were still putting arsenic in flour to stop the natives from stealing it? I knew Kiani would steal flour if it meant staying alive. A terrible image of Kiani lying dead, poisoned, flashed before me. I'd once found a dead possum with its stomach blown up and pink stuff at its mouth. Da said it must have eaten poisoned flour. He'd thrown it on the fire. I could still remember the smell of it.

'Why would anyone spoil good flour?' I'd asked.

'To stop the natives stealing it,' he'd said.

'But if it's poisoned, nobody can use it. They might as well just give it to them.'

Da had laughed a sad laugh and shook his head. 'Out of the mouths of babes.'

Joseph had overheard us and pulled me aside later. 'We poison it so they don't expect something for nothing. They'll just become lazy if we give flour to them.'

'Or do some people just want to kill the natives?'

He'd pushed me away. 'You ask too many questions, Annese.'

I realised now that he didn't mean too many, he meant too dangerous. Despite the dark feeling growing inside me, I read on.

… the Australian Aboriginal possesses not the slightest implements or arts of civilization. They make nothing but a spear or cloak of skins, a small net or mat of grass to hold the roots he digs up, or the opossum skins which he preserves. A few branches torn from the trees form his shelter.

I thought about the time I'd gone to Kiani's family's camp and the wonderful safe feeling I'd had lying in her hut. We'd been living six in a tent at the time and I'd envied her the space and stability of their houses. They were built so soundly and would not have flapped and trembled in the wind as our tent did. I remembered too Ngama's fish catcher and the fact that she kept only enough for her family. And as for the possum coats, Kiani had let me put hers on once, one cold winter's day. I'd pulled it over my thin holey jumper and was warmer than I'd been for months. She'd wanted me to keep it but I knew the walloping I'd get if I appeared with it at home. I wondered if Bishop Short had ever worn a possum coat or been fishing with an Aboriginal person. Maybe if he had, he wouldn't write such things.

I read on.

He owns no superior in his tribe, holds all property in common,
is but a wandering hunter within the limits of a certain territory,

engaged in frequent feuds with neighbouring tribes, treating the wives as slaves.

I read this bit three times. The words *'all property in common'* puzzled me. Did he mean sharing? I'd seen the natives sharing on many occasions. If one of them was given food or clothing, they would not eat it all themselves but distribute it, always to the older people first. Ma once told me how outraged Mrs Bartholomew had been when she saw an old coat of hers being worn by an old man who was the worse for drink. She'd given it to an Aboriginal woman who'd worked in her garden but the woman must have passed it on, shared it. I guess that was what he meant by holding *all property in common*.

'Mrs Bartholomew was the colour of beetroot,' Ma had said, laughing. 'She stamped her foot like an impatient horse.'

'Why was she angry? Perhaps the old man needed it more,' I said, not really seeing the joke. 'That's just Christian isn't it—to share? Isn't that what we want, for the natives to be Christians?'

Ma's smile disappeared and I feared I'd asked a dangerous question again. But she wasn't annoyed; she was fearful.

'It's not as easy as that, Annese. You'll soon learn that there's more than one type of Christian.' At first, I thought she was talking about Quakers, Catholics, Lutherans, and the Church of England, but her voice was sad, as if she'd just been reminded of something. 'And don't you go asking your questions of a stranger. You'll end up in trouble. People already think you odd and some folk don't like those who are different than them, especially if they are making them uncomfortable.'

Turning back to the newspaper, I re-read the last words again *'treating their wives as slaves.'* I knew a little about slaves. The Friends often talked of the work of the Quakers in America, courageously hiding the slaves as they made their way north to freedom. From what I could gather, slaves were black men and women with no rights who worked to make money for the colonists.

But how did this apply to the way our native men treated their women? If it meant they were harsh on their women, well I'd seen plenty of that in white families too. And, other than a lot of shouting sometimes, not so much among the natives. There was a woman who came regularly to Mass with four little children. Her eyes and cheeks were often swollen and bruised. I'd asked Ma why she stayed with her man if he did that to her. Ma said marriage was a sacrament from God and could not be broken.

The only sacrament I knew were the wafers and the wine Ma took at Mass. But how could marriage be a sacrament? I hadn't had time to ask that before Ma said the thing most shocking to me.

'If she leaves him, she'd have to leave her children behind because, by law, they belong to him.'

I'd seen this woman's husband often enough, drunk and shouting of a Friday night. 'But everyone knows he wouldn't look after them. They'd end up taken like….'

I stopped short, but Ma had gone all sad anyway and patted my hand. 'So if you do ever marry, Annese, pick very carefully.'

The next paragraph of the article was filled with words I barely knew.

and, by a tyrannical polygamy, appropriating them to the old men of the tribe, or from time to time relaxing this custom into promiscuous intercourse.

I knew the word intercourse; it was what happened between a married man and his wife. I remembered Macca saying they had lore of their own. Maybe this is what he referred to. I knew of one Irish girl at the asylum who was being forced to marry a man twice her age. Some said he'd raped her and left her with child. I kept reading, wondering if our laws were any better than those the bishop was criticising.

occasionally driven by starvation to practise infanticide

At the asylum, I'd heard women talk about white women leaving their babies in the cold when they were too ashamed or too poor to care for them. They'd talked about a woman, Mary Lee, who was fighting for better support for women so that such practices were no longer needed.

Bishop Short's final words sent a chill through me.

Such is the degraded state of the native Australian, and such the difficulties of taming, educating and Christianising these bond slaves of Satan.

Signed, Augustus Adelaide

My hands trembled. *Bond slaves of Satan.* Could he really be talking about our natives?

Kiani's smiling face came to me, her carefree play and gentle kindness. I thought too of her family camping by the creek at Echunga and heard again the laughter and the gleeful screams of their children. I saw the strong, proud, painted bodies of the men as they gathered for a corroboree dance. I thought too of the Aboriginal people I saw every day here in Adelaide Town as they went about their daily lives, hurting nobody. It was true, the ones in Adelaide seemed sadder than those I'd grown up knowing and there were some who would squabble amongst themselves, sometimes worse for drink. But that was true of many a white person too. So why did the bishop write such hateful words? Why would someone who followed Jesus talk of people with such anger?

A dark despair spread through me like poisoned flood water. If important people, Christian people, really thought like that, who would protect Kiani? If even the bishop thought her people were *bond slaves of Satan*, who would believe Kiani about the chess piece if she was ever found with it?

I knew I had to do something with the letter. But what?

Putting the newspaper away, I vowed to find Macca. Only he would help me ensure Kiani was safe. That night I dreamed Kiani put a baby son into a basket near a river to sleep. When she got there in the morning the baby was gone, and the chess piece was in his place. Kiani screamed and was surrounded by white people who wanted to stone her. I knew I should call out like Jesus did for Mary Magdalene.

But even in my dream, I stayed silent.

CHAPTER 18

Finding Macca turned out to be harder than I'd thought. I wrote to Da asking if he was at Echunga but got no reply. I read every newspaper I could lay my hands on, turning to the court reports, in case he was mentioned, and, with trepidation, scanning the death notices. But found no mention of him. When one of Tolmer's men came into the shop I even asked him if he knew him. He shrugged me off, muttering about being harassed by a girl. Mr Petersen intervened, giving me a stern look, although when the man left, he took a kinder approach.

'You're young yet, Laffer, and Malcolm Macleod is a man with a colourful history. Perhaps you should give up on him.'

But I was not willing to be deterred.

When Ma finally got a letter from Pa, she came to find me at the Temperance.

'He wants me to go to Echunga. Read it out loud, in case I have missed something.'

We were lucky enough to get in early and have already found a small amount of gold, enough to buy a small lot in Echunga Gardens. Joseph and I work from dawn until dusk six days a week at the diggings and, when there's no Meeting to attend, spend the First Day putting up our hut. Macca showed up yesterday and helped us. He said that his mother would be horrified if she knew he'd worked on the Sabbath.

At last. My heart leapt and I put the letter down and started to plan how I could get to Echunga. Ma took the letter from me and began slowly reading it out loud.

The hut is very basic, Kitty, made of slabs Macca cut from the local trees. But we've managed to put on a pitched roof and I bought some redwood offcuts for covering the floor. Imagine, Kitty—no more dirt floors! There are windows too and, when we have enough funds, we'll have glass in them.

I looked up to see tears in Ma's eyes. 'Keep reading, Annese.'

Friend Hogan says you will be welcome to work at the hotel, but he only has work for one at this stage. Annese may get work there later. I think it best she stays in Adelaide for now while she has work and lodgings.
Your ever-loving husband and father
Joshua

I ran his words over in my mind. *I think it best she stays in Adelaide for now.* My heart raced. 'Am I not to come with you, Ma?'

She took the letter from me and stiffened her back as she always did when she had bad news. 'You've good work and lodgings here. We will send for you as soon as we can.'

I wondered if Ma knew that her words echoed those she'd said when the twins left and I feared in that moment that I would never again live under the same roof as my family. But even this thought was overshadowed by my need to see Macca.

'You must promise to find work for me there and send for me as soon as you can.'

Ma gave immediate notice at Mrs Bartholomew's and I helped pack her few things into a large carpetbag.

'I'll keep this,' I said putting the spice tin aside.

'Oh, that reminds me. Mrs Bartholomew says she will keep the chess piece if we want. She gave me this.' She handed me a handwritten notice signed by Mrs Bartholomew.

I hereby acknowledge receipt for safe keeping one ivory chess piece belonging to Annese Laffer.

'You're to present it to her when you want it back.'

As Ma climbed onto Friend Hastings's dray that afternoon, I gave her a letter for Macca.

'Make sure he gets it. It's very important.'

'You've no business writing private letters to a single man, Annese.'

'It's Macca, Ma. It's not a love letter, if that's what you think. It's about the chess piece.'

It wasn't a lie nor was it the whole truth, but she was in a good mood and didn't ask for more information. Waving her goodbye, I returned to the Temperance. Sad as I was at being alone, I could not help but also feel a nervous excitement at what the future held for me. I didn't feel very different from the little girl who'd played in the creek, but now I truly was an independent woman, living apart from my family, with my own income. Even the cloud of Kiani's situation didn't deter me from enjoying the moment.

With Ma gone, I stopped going to St Patrick's and started back at the Meetings in North Adelaide. There were quite a few Friends in the colony now but they still mostly lived near Mount Barker and went to the meetings there, although some would come down the hill on a First Day to boost our numbers. Our sombre gatherings, held mostly in silence, suited me much more than the showy chanting and devotions of the Catholics. The Church of England service was not much different from the Catholic from what I could tell, and ever since I'd read Bishop Short's article about the natives, I knew that I would not fit well with them.

Two weeks after Ma had left, I was brushing and plaiting Sarah's hair when a knock came at the door.

'Mail.'

Ellen collected the letters and passed them all to me without checking who they were for.

'I never get mail,' she said. 'Anyway, I'm off out to have some fun. There's a boat just in and the crew has been paid.' She put on a new bonnet and pinched her cheeks. Her wide smile almost hid the sadness I saw in the way her shoulders held tight, as if she was keeping something inside.

I sorted out my letters and passed Sarah's to her. Nothing from Macca. I'd written to him again because he'd not replied to the letter I sent with Ma. My hope of helping Kiani now seemed like a foolish and childish dream.

I opened the letter from Ma first. It wasn't in her handwriting. She'd possibly asked one of the workers at the Hogan Arms to write for her.

The Hogan Arms taint what it used to be but it's easy work compared to Mrs Bartholomew's. I've been thinking of the twins a lot since being here and wondering how they are. Do you think you could write to them and ask after their welfare? You should ask after Frederick too. He seemed to be a bit keen on you.

I hope you are now quite settled and keeping on at your work. Echunga has very little to offer a single woman. The men here are better suited to the single life.

Your loving Mother.

She didn't mention Macca and I wondered if that was deliberate. She certainly wasn't encouraging me to join them. I found her comment about Frederick strange too, for surely it was Polly that Frederick was keen on.

The other letter was from Joseph and was the longest I'd known him to write.

Dear Annese, Father asked me to write to you as he is keen for you to join us at Echunga and knows that I am more likely than Ma to persuade you, for she thinks your prospects are better in Adelaide.

I, however, agree with Da. I don't like the idea of you being alone in Adelaide. Coming here would not be a step back in time but a positive step forward. Ma could do with some help around the house.

Father and I stay six days at the goldfields, returning to spend First day with Mother. When we can, we attend the Friends Meeting at the Mayfields' house or, if there is no Meeting, we spend the morning making good our home. As always, the afternoon is devoted to prayer and Bible reading.

Our cottage is not the grandest, although we are all very pleased with how cosy it is. We began by lashing together poles made from the local trees. We stripped the bark from them and stood them side by side. Once they were in place, we made daub. It's a mixture of clay and straw. It fills the cracks and, once dry, creates a weatherproof cladding. In time we will whitewash the walls with a mixture of chalk and egg.

While many have settled for a flat roof, Father insisted we top our cottage with a pitched roof, which we will cover with thatch made of local reeds. The floor is made of hardwood offcuts from the local mill. It is warm underfoot and pleasant to the eye.

Reading Joseph's words, I could feel his happiness in what he and Da had achieved. I felt a sisterly pride along with an acute loneliness at being separated from them all.

A new quarry has been cut and some of the town's buildings are now built of stone. Although many families still live in tents, both at the diggings and also in the town, there is no doubt that the goldfields have brought in a new era at Echunga. You would not recognise our old hometown and its surrounds. There are two stores now. One is at the goldfields, which has been named Chapman's Creek, and the other larger one in the town which continues to serve as a Post Office.

I would not be honest if I did not report that the progress has not been all for good. Friend Hogan has requested for a local constable to be based at Echunga to manage the unruly behaviour of both diggers and farmhands, especially when the monthly cattle sales are upon us. So far, this has been rejected due to the allocation that has already been made of mounted constables at the goldfield. Instead, an agreement was reached to build a lock-up, in the form of a lean-to, on the side of the unmanned Police Station.

There is work here for anyone who wants it now, Annese. There is even a boot maker, a Mr Tummerton. He's a saddler too. I spoke to him on First Day just gone. He says he has work enough to keep him going for a year. He is looking for someone, a boy he said, to cut and stretch the hides. I told him of your work with Mr Petersen. He was not too keen on having a girl but I told him you were hard-working and did not speak unless you had to, and that seemed to impress him.

I tried to imagine myself working for anyone other than Mr Petersen. Would this Mr Tummerton understand my quiet way? Would he be as kind and patient as Mr Petersen? I could always go back to working as a cleaner or in the laundry at the Hogan Arms, or maybe the new Wheatsheaf Hotel. But I'd learned so much about making and repairing shoes and boots, the thought of never doing that work again saddened me.

The Mayfields too are looking for domestics but since it is Margaret Mayfield who you would answer to, I am not sure she would consider you. She still mentions the notebook you took, even in company. Her memory is long and her forgiveness short, I fear.

That was certainly an option I did not want. I occasionally saw Margaret up in the town when she was there visiting her sister. I made a point of crossing the road to avoid her. Even knowing the lie she'd told about Kiani, I still felt intimidated by her. And anyway exposing her would mean owning up to my own theft and lie.

Shivering at the thought of one day confronting her, I forced my attention back to Joseph's letter.

Macca is one of three mounted constables at the goldfields. His early work with Tolmer was taken into consideration when he applied for the position and his previous insubordination seems to have been forgiven. Anyway, there are now no natives nearby to distract him.

Distract. Is that how people, even Joseph, understood what Macca had done? As if his stance was a weakness rather than a strong act of justice.

Ma said I must tell you that Macca is no longer the man we once knew. On more than one occasion, I have seen him intoxicated. He rambles on about someone called Kiani, a native girl from what I can gather. He repeats again and again, in a state of despondency, that he feels responsible for her. When I question him, he dismisses me, saying I am better off not knowing. I put his mood down to the drink but there are some who say he is unhinged.

He asked after you once too. He was visiting our hut and was stone-cold sober on that occasion. He spoke of a chess piece. It made no sense to me but Ma seemed to know of it and said it was not for her to discuss. She is quite short with Macca these days. I can only think it is to do with his drinking and his reputation with the natives. It is a shame, for they were once fond of each other, both having the Celtic blood.

Joseph's letter sent my mind buzzing. Why was Macca drinking so heavily? At least he'd asked after me, but only in relation to the chess piece. I knew Ma meant well, trying to steer me in another direction, yet still, I felt a longing for him.

Ma thinks you are better off staying in Adelaide Town at least for now, but Da and I want you with us here. In my opinion, there is no need for you to be living amongst the rabble there. No doubt within the coming years you will be thinking of marrying and, if you choose your husband wisely, will no longer have to worry about working. There are now plenty of young men within the Society of Friends who would understand and even appreciate your silent ways.
You are much missed by us all, dear sister.
Your devoted brother
Joseph.

'Are you alright, Annese?' Sarah asked.
'I'm well enough.'
But Sarah kept watching me. She'd worked out that I needed time to find my words and I trusted her to listen so I went on.
'The men in my family think it's time I go back to Echunga and look for a Quaker husband.' I laughed, trying to hide my anguish but she didn't join me, no doubt seeing through the facade.
We'd talked about marriage and all it meant after we'd attended a meeting at the Women's Temperance Society to hear a young Scottish woman, a Miss Catherine Spence. There'd been a large crowd of mostly women, with a small number of men. I'd never heard anyone, man or

woman, talk with such lively passion. She talked openly of her belief that married women were greatly disadvantaged by the current laws, having no rights over their property or even their children.

I'd recently come to the realisation that the Quakers' ways, where women's opinions had equal weight to those of men, were not how it was in most churches. Miss Spence's speech had me wondering if it would indeed be best for me to stay unwed. With all that I was hearing about Macca, maybe I was better off without him.

I put the letter from Joseph in my tin and was refolding the newspaper I'd kept with Bishop Short's article about Port Lincoln.

'Can I read that?' Sarah asked. 'I need to practise my reading if I'm to get an apprenticeship. I'll read out loud to you, if that's alright.'

I nodded.

'Look, this one is about William Wright, the man they hung for murder.' I knew a little about it as I'd gone to a special meeting of the Friends where we'd written a protest letter to the Governor about the hanging. Our pleas had fallen on deaf ears. On the day of the hanging, we'd held a special Meeting and sat in silence while the horror took place.

'Poor man,' Sarah said. 'Listen to this.'

If the stragglers who arrived in front of the gaol at 7 o'clock entertained the idea that there was to be a late remission, their hopes were dispelled by the hateful spectacle of the gallows, with its rude cord dangling from the beam, and its black drapery fluttering about in the chill wind of the stormy morning.

I shivered at the image of the *black drapery.* The memory of a dead wedgetail eagle Kiani and I had once seen flooded back. A settler had tied it to a fence, its massive wings spread wide, its head hanging sideways. I could still hear Kiani's guttural scream as she fled, leaving me alone with the broken bird.

Nausea threatened to overtake me.

'Are you alright, Annese? You've gone pale. Do you want me to stop reading?'

I shook my head.

The crowd gradually increased, and, if there could be a more disgusting sight than the gallows itself, it was presented by the bulk of the spectators—unwashed loungers, reeking from the night's debauch, or only half recovered from its effects by a hasty hour or two of sleep; women hurrying to the spot as if pressing to join in some ordinary amusement, and some even carrying with them their shivering unweaned infants.

And there were hosts of children; neglected little urchins with pallid countenances and dirty garments. Every purlieu...

I read the word with her. It was one I didn't know.

'*Purlieu.* What does that mean?' Sarah asked.

'I guess it means all sorts.' I took over reading.

Every purlieu of the city's worst locality seemed to have belched forth its inmates and frequenters, and to have assembled them around the frightful structure.

'I'm glad I didn't go,' Sarah said, shuddering, 'though plenty of people I know did. They were probably the "purlieu" and their children, the dirty urchins. You know, Annese, I didn't expect to see any poverty in South Australia. The way they talked about it to us back in Ireland, we thought we were coming to the land of milk and honey. But it's not much better than home, for some at least.'

I thought about telling her of how we were living when the twins were taken, but stopped short and read on.

But there were others too whom we should less have expected to have seen at such a gathering. Of them, we can only say 'De gustibus.'

'That sounds like German. I suppose it means disgusting,' Sarah said. 'It is disgusting isn't it—watching a person be killed, no matter what he's done? I'd get rid of that newspaper if I was you, Annese. It's too sad.'

For a moment, I considered telling her about the article by the bishop, but she was right—we'd had enough sadness. She took the newspaper from me and held my hands.

'There'll always be something to be sad about. You must take your happiness where you can get it, Annese.'

CHAPTER 19

Leaning out of the open window, I tried to rid myself of the dark image of the hanging. I could see Sarah walking east along Hindley Street. The rabble, as Joseph called it, was stirring on the streets below with the usual optimism that filled the town when a supply boat was in. People spilled from the hotels, drays littered vacant blocks, their owners offloading goods onto smaller trolleys. Young boys, excited by the extra money they would earn, scurried to finalise deliveries to the many shops now scattered across Adelaide's square mile.

Joseph was right. Adelaide was changing but he had no need to be concerned for me. Other than work and attendance at the Meeting, I was content to stay at home watching life from my window.

I turned to the west, thankful that the nearby cattle yards were empty. On market days the smell and noise from the adjoining slaughterhouse was a rude reminder of the brutal way the animals ended their days. Standing on the tips of my toes, I could see the nearly completed rail bridge. It had a pedestrian lane so I could soon go to the Meeting house in North Adelaide, without fear of being washed away. For the time being, I would have to use Frome Ford, well known for being frequently flooded. Looming beside the new bridge was the gaol where the hanging had been held. I'd walked past it often enough on my way to the tanner, its imposing walls looming over me, like a haunted castle. I shuddered at the thought of being locked away with no sunshine or grass or trees. At least when I was at the asylum, I had my walks to and from work to enjoy the sun, the wind, and the rain. And now I had the river and the trees and, on my days off, when others would wander through the shops or go to the taverns, I'd instead venture into the bushland that still fringed Adelaide Town and lie on my back watching the clouds and listening to the insects.

I began to daydream about living back in Echunga. I'd be able to roam as far as I liked, waking up every morning to the wind in the trees and a chorus of birds. I could go to the creek and… I shook my head as the thought of the creek reminded me of Kiani and Ngama, and all they had lost forever.

From my window, I could see the sun as it slowly made its way towards the horizon. Clouds, streaky and slow-moving, lit up as the sun's rays turned them into fancy ribbons. Pushing dark thoughts aside, I tried to make sense of everything Joseph had written. Would I be happier back in Echunga once again amongst my own people? Was Ma's idea that I stay in Adelaide her attempt to keep me away from Macca, who seemed to be drinking more and more? And why was he asking about Kiani and the chess piece? Was he in trouble?

I was about to close the window when I heard cries coming from the river below the gaol. Two young lads were running, calling for their father.

'Pa, there's a baby. A baby on the bank.'

I looked around, expecting to see passers-by rallying to help, but a band had just struck up near King William Street and people were flocking towards it. I didn't know what I could do to assist, but I ran down the stairs and arrived at the Newmarket Inn at the same time as their father rushed out of the Inn to meet the boys.

'A baby, wrapped around with reeds,' one of the boys gasped. 'A native baby.' I may have imagined it, but it seemed their father's shoulders dropped with relief when they said 'native'. He showed no signs of being in a hurry now.

'No need for you, Miss,' he said, waving me off. I'd been about to leave, for what use would I be, but something in the way he dismissed me compelled me to follow them, staying several steps behind as the older boy took the lead. The younger one lagged beside me, ashen white and holding his stomach.

'Are you alright?' I asked.

'We was just digging for sand, Miss,' he whimpered. 'I saw it first, its tiny fingers looked to be reaching out to me. Honest, Miss, it was there already. Nothing to do with us. We only saw it once we moved to the new dig spot.'

'Nobody is blaming you,' I said, wondering why he would be worried about being blamed. By the time we caught up with his father and brother, they'd lifted the baby's body clear of the reeds. It was blue and wrinkled. Long dead.

'Just a native boy, but perhaps we'd best get the police anyway.'

Just. But perhaps. Anyway.

The words caught my attention and filled me with dismay.

The father turned to me then, a dark expression on his face. 'What's your name. Miss?'

'Annese Laffer.'

He looked at me more closely. 'You're the quiet one what works for old Petersen. A Quaker.'

I nodded, astounded that I was known to the likes of him.

'Go get the police, Billy,' he said to the lad at my side. 'Make sure you tell them that you had nothing to do with this. You was just collecting sand. We've had enough trouble with the natives.'

The boy seemed frozen to the spot. 'I'll come too,' I said to him.

Turning on me, the father narrowed his eyes. 'Mind you tell them the baby was already dead.'

Reaching North Terrace and out of sight of his father, Billy took my hand. I gave it a soft squeeze and smiled. 'It's not your fault, Billy. Come on, let's hurry.'

We arrived out of breath at the station. 'Baby's body in the river. Dead,' I managed to say as I pointed to where we'd come from. I was relieved to see the urgency with which the Constable responded. Grabbing his helmet, he called for his horse to be brought to him.

'I'll need to talk to you some more, Miss. Meet me back at the place once you've caught your breath. Give the young lady a sweet tea,' he called to his colleague as he left.

'Just water,' I whispered, understanding fully for the first time that I'd become involved in an event that was possibly a crime. I took Billy outside and we sat on the steps. Despite my protestations, a young officer gave us both a heavily sugared tea and a bush biscuit to share.

'You'll have had a shock, I expect.'

I'd taken my first sip when I heard another voice behind me. 'Probably the baby of that native woman who jumped yesterday.'

I held my breath hoping to hear more, but Billy was wriggling about.

'I need to pee, Miss.'

'Shush,' I said, then, realising the opportunity, I set our mugs down and went back inside the station, pointing to where I could see the lavatory out the back. Nudging Billy towards it, I lingered inside, looking towards the street but listening to the conversation behind me.

'She'd been in gaol for a couple of weeks for stealing sugar and was at the asylum ready to be put at the new training place for natives, near Port Lincoln. Poonindie.'

Poonindie. I strained to hear more.

'So how did she come to be jumping off the bridge?'

'Her family visited and brought her baby in one of those woven bags they carry. They were all there when a visitor, a Quaker woman checking on conditions at the asylum, identified her as someone who'd stolen from her years ago and demanded she be charged.'

My pulse began to race. The story was frighteningly familiar.

'She demanded we search the native's bag and sure enough, they found a fancy ornament. The woman said it was the one she'd seen on her and began shouting for us to do our job and check for her report from years ago.'

I shuddered at the memory of Margaret demanding I give her the letter back. I'd heard at the Meetings she'd been nominated to do the checks on the asylum, and given a prayer of thanks that I was no longer there.

'Did you?'

'No, of course not. It was from years back. I told her I couldn't do it right then and that the native was being taken to live at the training school anyway. I thought that would satisfy her, but she'd become irate and grabbed the native woman's arm and took the ornament from her.'

'Blimey. A right fighter then, for a Quaker?'

'As I expected, the native fought back. Before I could stop her, she'd kicked the woman in the shins and made a grab for the ornament, hitting the bossy woman in the face as she did. So she let her go and then started yelling "assault". The native took off like a frightened hare with the baby under her arm.'

The policeman's voice was taking on the lilt of a storyteller and the group laughed at his story. I glanced behind me and was glad that Billy was still in the lavatory.

'She ran towards the river,' he continued, louder now as the others gathered to hear him. 'We thought she'd get away but the ford was flooded over and we soon found her sitting on the riverbank, sodden and wailing.'

The laughter was awkward now. 'And the baby?' one of them asked.

'There was no baby. My guess is it's the one found downriver.'

I sensed their mood change.

'So why are we even considering it a murder? Surely it was an accident?' I could tell from the gentleness of the voice that it was the one who'd brought us the tea.

'The Quaker woman had followed us to the ford. She saw what was happening and said the native should be charged with murder as well. "They do that you know, drown their unwanted children."'

My mind raced. Murder! Did they really think a woman would deliberately drown her baby? If it was Kiani, and I was almost certain now that it was, I knew in my very soul she would never do that.

Billy came running back through the station. Noticing me hovering at the door, the policemen stopped their chatter, exchanging guilty glances.

'How long have you been there?' the older one snapped at me. 'You'd better be off now, Miss. Corporal Dalton needs you to be a witness at the scene.'

Billy took my hand and we made our way back along the river. I had no words for him now, my mind spinning. By the time we got back, the poor wee baby had been wrapped in a towel and placed in a basket strapped to Corporal Dalton's horse. Billy let go of my hand, staying well back. His father was explaining his sons' involvement to the police.

'We was at the exact same spot last evening and the river was at the same height. Tis best time for getting the sand. We sell it to the assay office for the sandbath they give the mixed metals from the diggings. There was no body last night, I swear.'

Seeing that the police were inclined to believe him, the father gained confidence in his account. 'So it's most likely the baby of the mad native woman what escaped from the asylum and jumped in the river. I heard all about it at the Newmarket. Savages they are.'

The corporal heard my gasp and held his hand up to the man to stop him talking, taking me aside.

'Tell me what you saw, Miss...?'

'Laffer. Miss Annese Laffer.' My voice came out as a whisper. Perhaps sensing my fear, he walked me even further upriver.

'Nobody's in trouble, Miss. Just tell me what you heard and saw.'

Taking a deep breath, I spoke slowly, recounting seeing the boys shouting and running. 'The boys' father called out that it was just a native child and I should fetch the police, anyway. He said "anyway" as if...'

My voice cracked as I thought of that poor baby and wondered what might have happened if I'd not come along. Would the man have left it there, hoping to avoid trouble?

Dalton looked up from his notes. 'You did the right thing, Miss Laffer. There's one law for all, that's what our proclamation says, and it's that which I'm employed to enforce.'

He finished writing and thanked me again, taking down my address and place of work. Summoning all my courage, I raised my voice a little.

'The baby's mother. The one who jumped…'

He cursed and then shrugged. 'I guess it will be in the papers soon enough. What did you want to know?'

'Her name? The mother?'

'The native girl? Kitty. They call her Kitty.'

For one moment, relief swept over me. Kitty—not Kiani. It was all a horrible coincidence. But a distant memory crept upon me and I heard as clearly, as if it had been yesterday; a memory of Kiani saying *Kitty*, over and over. I'd thought she was talking about Ma, but I now realised it was perhaps herself she was referring to. She was giving herself a white person's name.

I knew for sure now. It was no coincidence. The native girl was Kiani and the dead baby her child.

'Not murder,' I said.

The vehemence of my statement drew his full attention. 'No one has been charged with murder, at this point. Do you know her, the native girl?'

'Yes. Kiani… Kitty would not murder. I know the Quaker woman too. Margaret Mayfield.'

He checked his notes.

'Yes, Miss Mayfield. She said the woman had robbed her years ago and that she'd an ivory-carved artefact with her at the time. A stolen object, she believed. The native woman had it when she was arrested.'

My fear turned to anger. 'Margaret Mayfield is a liar.'

He jolted at the change in my voice.

'She's lying. I can prove it.'

I hadn't intended to yell but my reaction brought another policeman to his colleague's side.

'Everything all right?'

'Yes,' Dalton said, glancing at me. 'Miss Laffer is just overwrought. But I have her statement already. She can go now.'

'What will happen to Kitty?' I kept my voice calm now, and it worked. The older policeman left us alone.

'If I have my way, she'll be taken to Poonindie on the next boat as originally planned. The further she is from Adelaide, the better for everyone. There should be an inquest into the baby's death. We'll bring her back if there's more serious charges to be answered.'

As I scrambled back up the riverbank, a solitary crow screeched above the gaol and three pelicans winged their way east along the river. A violent shudder went through me, as if the very earth was shaking me. My stomach lurched and I vomited until I could expel no more. My body knew what my mind struggled to believe. If Kiani was charged with murder, she'd have very little chance of proving her innocence.

Now I had to find her.

CHAPTER 20

I slept badly and left late for work. Annoyed at first at being forced to walk around a large group gathered on the pavement, I stopped short when I heard what they were discussing.

'They say she jumped into the river with the baby.

'Held it under.'

'I heard she threw the baby.'

'They took her to the hospital but she refused to stay there. Said the spirits of the dead had not been cleared.'

'Where is she now?' My voice came out raspy but the group seemed keen for me to join in.

'She was taken to the port with some others. They're being sent to Port Lincoln this afternoon on the *Petrel*.'

This afternoon! How would I get there so soon? Leaving the gossipers, I walked towards Leigh Street, slowly now, buying myself time to think. I could walk the eight miles to the port when I finished work but that would mean walking home in the dark. I needed to leave immediately.

I rushed into the workshop. 'I need to take the day off.'

'Do you just?' Mr Petersen grumbled. 'You do remember there's boots and shoes to be finished ready for collection Monday next?'

'I'll work tomorrow to get it done.'

He put down what he was working on. 'You're not in any sort of trouble, are you, Laffer?'

'No. I just need to get to the port. There's someone I need to see before they go away.' I chose my words well, for his face softened.

'Ah, a suitor.'

I didn't want to lie to him so I stayed silent. Picking up his work, he looked at the clock on the wall. 'If you hurry, you'll get a ride with McBain. He goes every Saturday at this time to collect hide.'

I hadn't run—truly ran—since I'd left Echunga, where Joseph and I would have races. Back then, when no one was around, I'd take my dress off and run in my pantaloons. There'd been no need or occasion to run since I'd moved into Adelaide Town and, in my usual attire, it would have been nigh impossible. But I was wearing my work clothes. With no petticoats or frills to impede me, I walked at great speed till I got to the riverbank. Then, after checking to see there was no one around, I ran as fast as I could to the tanners, only stopping to retrieve my cap when it flew from my head.

Mr McBain's horse was already harnessed to the dray when I got there and he greeted me with a wave. 'Don't usually see you on a Saturday, Laffer. And in a hurry, it seems?'

'I need to get to the port,' I puffed, straightening my clothes and tucking my hair into my cap as best I could.

'Do you now? Well, you're just in time. Come on then, you can sit next to me or up back with Toby.'

Thinking Toby was a boy, I thought it best to sit up front. But when I heard an impatient bark and saw the wet muzzle and brown eyes of a sheepdog appearing over the side of the dray, I climbed into the back, letting Toby lick my face as we jolted into action.

It was my first trip to the coast since we'd arrived. Ma and Da said they'd seen enough sea on the journey out to last them a lifetime. I had vague memories of being carried on Da's shoulders as we made our way from our landing spot at Holdfast Bay into Adelaide Town. I recalled how I'd felt seeing Aboriginal people lining the route, sitting in small groups around their fires. It was the first time I'd seen black skin. Ma tried to shield my eyes from their naked bodies, but she soon realised it was impossible with so many of them. Anyway, it wasn't the natives who shocked me. I'd been told about kangaroos, but nothing prepared me for the wonder of seeing them bounding over bushes, then freezing stock-still when someone called out, alert but calm. We'd seen a joey that day too as it clambered, headfirst, into its mother's pouch and, moments later, righted itself to peer out at the strange gaggle of newcomers. I remember how I'd longed to join it, cocooned and safe. Belonging.

Since then, Holdfast Bay had been abandoned as the port. We were heading to the new harbour, officially called Port Adelaide, although most called it Port Misery. There was still only a scattering of houses along the way but no native camps to be seen now. Even the kangaroos stayed well back from the road.

We followed the river for about half a mile, then headed north-west. The road was well-worn and more than twice as wide as any road I'd been on before.

'There was going to be a canal dug along here,' Mr McBain said, as if reading my thoughts. 'Ships were to be brought right up to the city.'

'What happened?'

In my mind, I'd asked the question straight away, but it may have been minutes later, as Mr McBain looked confused.

'To the canal,' I clarified.

He turned to look at me fully and nodded as if he had just remembered something he'd heard about me.

'They decided to build a railway instead. It should be running by the end of the year.'

'Quicker and less trouble no doubt.' My words came easily as I'd heard several of our customers saying this. It helped that Mr McBain was not looking at me as we spoke.

'Aye. And less expensive in the long run.'

The openness of the wooded area that lined our route surprised me, so different was it from Echunga and the hills that surrounded Adelaide in the other direction. At first, I thought the hundreds of sheep I saw were wandering quite freely but I then saw fences enclosing large tracts of land. The area they grazed was dusty and brown, after a long dry spell. They seemed to be eating stones. A number of trees, mostly eucalypts and wattles, still lined the edges of the cleared land but I could see hundreds of stumps, ugly reminders of the trees cut down. Some of the stumps were so wide I couldn't begin to imagine how old the trees had been; survivors until we settlers had arrived with our love of buildings and wool. I wondered where the possums and koalas that had once lived in them had gone.

As the woodland fell away, the soil became sandy and covered with what looked like a juicy plant I'd seen before. A small group of native women were filling their baskets with it, and looked up as we passed, watchful, it seemed, until they were sure we would not stop. Several ducks flew overhead as the road drew towards the inlet where bushes with roots like angry spears grew from the mud.

'Mangroves,' Mr McBain said, 'God's guardsmen.'

At one stage we got so close to these mangroves that I could see dozens of tiny silver fish swimming through the twisted roots. A cloud of mosquitos hovered. Frogs croaked.

Ahead, I could see a cluster of masts bobbing and swaying. I remembered hearing that the Aboriginal people had thought the ships were rafts carrying upright trees when they'd first seen them. I wondered what they understood about them now with the estuary filled with dozens of vessels of all sizes bringing goods they could never have dreamed of. How strange they must think us.

As we got closer, the enormity of the task I'd undertaken became clear. I'd expected to have to search only two or three ships to find Kiani. Instead, there must have been close to twenty clippers jostling for position along the wharf. I gasped, causing Mr McBain to turn to me.

'Looking for someone in particular, Laffer?'

'Yes. She's on the *Petrel*. Port Lincoln.'

'You're in luck. It's the *Petrel* I'm looking for too. It's bringing my hides over. Is she coming or going?'

'Going. Poonindie.'

He stared at me. 'Are you looking for a native woman?'

I nodded but knew I would never be able to explain my mission. 'Archdeacon Mathew Hale.' I recited the name I'd read, hoping to sound informed about what I was doing.

This time he nodded.

'Mr Hale spoke at the service on Sunday about his plans for the place. A training school.'

I nodded.

He pulled up at a hotel stabling yard and threw a coin to a boy to mind the dray.

'Come with me,' he said. 'I'll take you to the *Petrel*.'

I clambered down and we headed to the harbour edge, Toby running alongside us, yapping joyously, his tail wagging so hard that his whole bottom end swayed.

Six ships were berthed against the wharf, with another five sat mid-harbour. Their masts stretched like giant spindles toward the sky. Scattered around them, like chickens waiting to be fed, were at least twenty smaller craft, creating an atmosphere of chaotic optimism.

Two of the ships were being loaded, the others unloaded. Barrels and crates were carried or thrown by men yelling commands in words I rarely heard, except on market days or late at night.

A boy with a trolley carrying crates of screeching chickens pushed past us. A small flock of sheep was being guided down a gangplank, greeted by two boys and a black-and-white sheepdog who corralled them into a makeshift pen. Mr McBain grabbed hold of Toby, who wanted to lend a hand.

Mesmerised by the skill with which the dog managed the sheep, I was nearly bowled over by a runaway barrel.

'Out the way, lad,' a weathered man yelled at me, then seeing my hair, which had fallen loose again, mumbled, 'Well I never! Seen everything now. No matter, you'd better keep clear, be you lad or lassie.'

Mr McBain gently pulled me to him. 'You'd better stay close, Laffer. Don't want Mr Petersen accusing me of not looking out for you.'

I was glad of the comfort it brought as he led me by the elbow to the quieter end of the dock where four smaller boats were berthed.

'That's the *Petrel* there and if I'm not mistaken, that's Hale himself and his good wife.'

Approaching us were a man and woman, both well-dressed as if they'd just stepped out of the theatre. I thought them to be father and daughter.

'Good morning, Mr Hale, Mrs Hale.' Mr McBain nodded to the couple and then extended his hand to the gentleman. 'Archie McBain. We met at the service last Sunday and I heard you speak at the public meeting last month too.'

'Ah, McBain, of course,' the gentleman said. 'We spoke of a distant relative we have in common, if I'm not mistaken.'

'The same. And this is Miss Laffer. She works for Mr Petersen, the cobbler. Her people are Quakers.'

I'd been introduced to well-to-do people before and knew enough to give a small curtsy. Mrs Hale laughed and took my hands in hers. 'There's no need for that, Miss Laffer. We've no time for airs and graces and I can see by your rather unconventional attire that you may be likewise at odds with formality.'

'Work clothes. Easier...'

She gazed at me, waiting for me to finish and when I didn't, she smiled. 'We're all the same in God's eyes, Miss Laffer. That's what brought us to the colony in the first place.'

'So what business have you at the port on such a glorious day?' she asked Mr McBain.

'I'm loading skins that came in yesterday from Port Lincoln on the *Petrel*.'

'The very boat we are going back on,' Mr Hale said. 'But with a rather different cargo. We're taking six poor souls to safety at our training school at Poonindie. They would have been gaoled otherwise or thrown back onto the street.'

'Kiani. Kitty.' Her name burst from me, startling the others. The men exchanged glances but Mrs Hale was quick to answer.

'Yes, one of them is called Kitty, and also Kiani I believe. She…'

She stopped, no doubt wondering what I knew about the baby.

'She has recently had an accident and lost a child,' Mr Hale stepped in. 'She broke her arm in the accident as well. We've known her for some time. She went to our Kintore Street school for a while.'

He turned to Mr McBain. 'She's very bright, speaks quite good English, and, given some time to recover, will soon be very employable. Are you looking for a domestic servant by any chance?'

Mr McBain laughed. 'No. My wife and I manage well enough. It's Miss Laffer who seeks her out.'

Mrs Hale watched me closely. 'Do you know her, Miss Laffer?'

'Friends. From Echunga.'

A gravelly voice called from behind us. 'McBain, you'd better collect your hides before some other bastard claims them.'

Mrs Hale lowered her eyes at the language but looked at me from under her lashes, raised her eyebrows a little, and smiled ever so slightly.

'I've got to go, Laffer,' Mr McBain said. 'I'll be loaded and ready to leave in an hour. If you want a lift back, meet me in front of the Admiral Hotel. If I'm not outside, Toby will be. Send him in to find me.'

Although I didn't know Mr McBain very well, I felt a pang of trepidation as he and Toby walked away, and almost ran to join them. But Mrs Hale linked arms with me. 'Come, we'll go to the *Petrel*. The new girls were taken on board this morning. I am sure Kitty will be glad to see a friendly face.'

I was flooded with relief to see Kiani was on the ship's deck, surrounded by a group of ten women and a few children. As we walked up the gangplank, the children scurried to their mothers' sides. I was about to wave to Kiani but drew back. The devastation on her face told me she was no longer the Kiani I knew.

'Kitty,' Mrs Hale called. She didn't look up until we were standing beside her.

'Kiani, it's me, Annese. *Yerki*.' Hearing the name she had given me all those years before, she scrambled to her feet, wincing with the pain in her arm.

'Take me to my baby,' she begged. 'He needs smoking. Release his spirit.' She began beating her chest as if trying to pound out the pain.

Mrs Hale tried to calm her. 'Your baby is gone,' she said slowly and gently. 'The man must look at his body. The coroner.'

Kiani grabbed my hand and pulled at me. 'Annese, no man. No look.'

The foolishness of my actions hit me when I realised I had no plan as to how I could help her.

'I must return my baby to Country. Peramangk,' she said again. 'Please, Annese.'

An overwhelming weight of helplessness filled me. What a stupid thing I'd done. I couldn't help her; I could barely look at her.

She let go of my hand and pushed past me, making for the gangplank. It was only then that I noticed the policeman on the wharf. He stepped in her way, preventing her from disembarking. I saw her look into the sliver of water between the boat and the wharf, a gap so narrow she would surely have broken another limb if she'd jumped.

She sank to her knees, broken. Three women surrounded her now, some crooning, some wailing as they gathered her up.

I turned to Mrs Hale. 'Why is the policeman here? Can she not leave?'

'No, she can't. One of the conditions of her release was that she come with us to Poonindie. From what I can gather from Mr Hale, it's not just sugar she was guilty of stealing, you know. And there may be more serious charges. She's lucky to have been released into our care.'

'But she is innocent.'

'Annese, I know you mean well but the best thing you can do for her is let her come with us. Poonindie is the safest place for her now.'

I could see she truly believed what she was saying, but I could only think about the Kiani I first knew, and realised beyond doubt that her only safe place had long been destroyed.

Mr Hale came up to us. 'Say your goodbyes, Miss Laffer. If you care to write to us, we will let you know how Kitty is doing. They all take some time to settle in and Kitty has more than most to contend with. But she will soon realise she is in the right place.'

'Maybe you could even come to visit yourself one day,' Mrs Hale said, giving my hand a final squeeze. 'We are encouraging as many as we can to see the work we are doing. Although I suggest you bring a man with you—your father or a brother perhaps. It's a hard trip for a woman alone.'

'Visitors disembark now or stay the distance,' a crew member called out.

I didn't want to intrude on the circle of women around Kiani and knew that nothing I could do or say would make any sense to her. I walked away, only turning back when I was far enough for my tears to not be seen. I waved to the Hales as Kiani disappeared below deck. Above, a gull called, plaintive and bereft.

'Write to us,' Mrs Hale called as the boat pulled away from the wharf. 'Write to us, Annese.'

I managed to lift from my despair and wave goodbye. I envied Mrs Hale's freedom. Married to a man who was at least trying to make a difference. Was it him or his power that she'd married? Would I too be better equipped to make a difference if I had such a man in my life? Could Macca ever be a man of Mr Hale's influence?

Somehow, through a fog of helplessness and despondency, I found the Admiral Hotel. Toby greeted me with the innocent joy only a dog can express. I wished in that moment that I too was ignorant of the tyranny of being human, a tyranny made so much greater because I knew how much worse life was for some than others. My life had been both blessed and forever scarred from knowing Kiani. I now knew the guilt that Macca knew, and wished with every fibre of my being that he was here now to share my pain.

The dray was filled with stinking skins so I sat alongside Mr McBain. Once or twice he tried to make conversation but he soon recognised my sombre mood. Instead, he quietly sang songs about the highlands and glens of his homeland. The words washed over me like a balm, and we were soon in front of the Temperance.

'Mind how you go now, Miss Laffer. Remember, you canna change what the Lord has set down. Your friend is in good hands with the Hales. Get to bed early and all will be right in the morning.'

Passing the kitchen I realised how hungry I was, having not eaten since breakfast. But I couldn't even face going to fix myself anything. Relieved that Ellen and Sarah were out, I remembered where Ellen kept her sweets. I took two, promising myself to replace them. Although it was only late afternoon, I put on my night dress, planning to feign having a stomach upset if the girls came back. I was about to go to bed when I remembered I still had the newspaper article about Poonindie under my bed. I retrieved it.

Poonindie, on the River Tod, was proclaimed a native reserve, exempting it thereby from sale to private individuals. It includes a small run for 3,000 sheep.

3,000? That did not seem small at all to me. I read on.

Fear of being put to death by the wild natives, according to the prevailing custom among the native tribes, is thought a sufficient restraint upon the Adelaide schoolchildren to prevent them from leaving the station. Various duties of farming and sheep- and cattle-herding for the young men, and domestic duties for the women, offers the best means of training these young people to the habits and duties of civilised life.

I had to reread this section to realise that when it said wild natives, it meant the Port Lincoln Aboriginal people, not those who were being taken to this Poonindie place. The Adelaide schoolchildren were those who, like Kiani, had attended the Kintore Street school for native children that Mrs Hale spoke of.

The Archdeacon had first to gain their affection. His simple, kind, firm, Christian earnestness, teaching, controlling, reproving, governing, in short, with enlightened charity, these children of the bush, has at length been blessed with a considerable degree of success.

I knew now that the Archdeacon was Mr Hale. He did indeed seem both kind and firm and a small ray of hope grew within me. Was it possible that Kiani would benefit from being at Poonindie?

Many young adult natives, who would have belonged to the most degraded portion of the human family, are now clothed and in their right minds, sitting at the feet of Jesus, and intelligently worshipping through Him, their Heavenly Father.

Let us look at the present results, under the heads of civilisation, moral training, and Christian attainments. We find eleven married couples decently clothed, clean in their persons, keeping their own huts and clothes in order, and much attached to each other, in place of the promiscuous unchastity and the brutal degradation of the native women in their wild state.

I felt relieved to think of Kiani with her hut but I could not reconcile the Kiani I knew with the words, *brutal degradation.* My mind tumbled in upon itself and once again I longed to talk to Macca,

> *Not far off is a small native camp, and the contrast between these two groups would convince any candid observer of the truth for which the Archdeacon has always and steadily contended, viz., that the aborigines are not only entitled to our Christian regard but are capable, under God's blessing, of being brought out of darkness into light, from the power of Satan unto God.*

I'd heard the words *out of the darkness into light* often enough at Meetings, but I would not believe Kiani was under the power of Satan, nor that God would exclude her.

I climbed into bed, exhausted from all I'd seen and read. As I pulled the covers over my head, sleep mercifully took the horror of the day from me.

CHAPTER 21

Just four weeks after my trip to the port, I received a letter from Da.

Although your mother and I are not in total agreement, we have come to the conclusion that we must stay together as a family. You are to give Mr Petersen a week's notice and join us in Echunga. Mr Tummerton is keen to meet you with a view to starting work with him if you prove your worth.

I gave notice that day at the Temperance and at work.

***

The hardest part about leaving Adelaide Town was saying goodbye to Mr Petersen. We'd shared hours together, mostly in silence, but we both knew how fond we were of each other.

'You'd better take this,' he said, passing me a brand-new knife. 'Mind you keep that Mr Tummerton up to the standard I've trained you to.'

I had no words for him, choked as I was with emotion. I squeezed his knobbled hands and took one last look at the workshop that had provided me with safety, food in my belly, and the sense that I, Annese Laffer, was a woman of worth.

Da arranged for Stephen Hastings to take me to Echunga. His dray was fully loaded, so I sat beside him. At Glen Osmond, I turned as we began our ascent on the road to Crafers. Behind us lay the neatly defined squares of Adelaide, a regularity that hid the complexity of life there. I wondered if Echunga would still hold the simple charm it had when I was young. Turning to look ahead, I could see the road had been widened since I'd made the journey in the other direction and was strangely relieved that the impenetrable mass of trees, full of hidden mystery, still lined our route. I wondered if Kiani's family now lived within the eucalypts and stringybarks, sheltering among the rocky outcrops.

The memory of her at Port Adelaide stayed with me, bringing with it a despondency with no solace. Even the Meetings failed to alleviate the darkness. Their commitment to the 'brotherhood of man' and 'Christian fellowship' rang hollow. They offered no solutions, just a quiet acceptance of the inevitable. My hopes lay with Macca alone.

The road had us winding over rugged brows. The immense yawning gorges on both sides, filled with gigantic trees reaching to the sky, set my heart soaring. How I had missed the elevation of my soul that only the natural world could bring. The yellow baubles of the wattles massed into a welcoming golden corridor. Reaching the summit, we turned towards the Onkaparinga River, passing through several established hamlets that had not existed when I left. Each had two or three cottages and a shop, and were surrounded by small paddocks totally cleared of bush. Evidence of a bush fire could be seen in the bright green shoots against blackened trunks, celebrating a determination to live where whole swathes of vegetation had been ravaged. I knew that some plants needed fire to burst their seed pods and remembered Macca once telling Da about the Aboriginal way of controlled burning.

'They wait for just the right weather and wind direction, burning inwards to keep control. They burn to clear some of the undergrowth to create better conditions to hunt kangaroo. It helps prevent bushfires too. Their fire creates, not destroys.'

With thoughts of Macca never far away now, I unhooked a velvet bag Ellen and Sarah had given me as a parting gift. The size of a small hand, it was made of cherry red velvet and embroidered with tiny shells. A plaited cord encased the edges, joining at the top to form a loop to hook onto the button on my waistband. I laid it on my lap and carefully took the chess piece from its soft cocoon, shielding it from Friend Hastings.

I'd collected it from Mrs Bartholomew's the day before I left.

'Mind you take care of that wee doll,' she said. 'I expect it's worth more than you think, although you might have to go back to the Motherland to find anyone who wants to pay for it. I can't see anyone here appreciating its value.'

Putting it back alongside Margaret's letter, I re-hooked the pocket bag safely to my waist and felt a surge of excitement, even though I was leaving behind good friends and a good income. Knowing that by nightfall I could be in Macca's arms brought a fluttering in my breast, hopeful that with his help I could find a way to prove Kiani's innocence. Even though we'd parted abruptly and we'd never done more than hold hands, I believed with my whole being that we were destined to be together. I had much sadness to share with him, but I trusted that he would know the way to free Kiani and bring her back to…

It was here I stumbled, for where did she belong now?

Perhaps hearing my sigh, Friend Stephen glanced at me. 'Your Ma says she might set up a shop at the goldfields soon. She's done wonders in the town at Mr Miley's store. You know she's recently been approved to handle the post too?'

When I responded with only a nod, he laughed. 'I see Adelaide Town hasn't loosened your tongue, Annese. Hope Tummerton realises who he's taking on.'

We left the main track and entered a narrow road, a trip I'd made many times. At first, I thought Friend Hastings had taken a wrong turn. The landscape seemed different, as if it had been pulled into another shape. I looked for the usual turning point on the road: a huge tree that Da had said was over four hundred years old. But it was gone, its massive stump an ugly reminder of all it had been. Swathes of bushland that had lined the roadside were gone too.

'We still need to use the old bridge,' Stephen said as we approached the creek. 'The new one will be completed soon. Can't come soon enough for me. It'll save us three miles. They're calling it Hastings Bridge, for my brother.' He laughed, a mean laugh, at a joke I did not understand. I remembered hearing that same laugh many years ago. It was a laugh that held bitter words, unspoken.

Soon I could see the Hogan Arms. It took all my effort to remain seated and ladylike, for I wanted to jump from the dray and run to where I knew our hut had been built. But I restrained myself. It was not just the landscape that had been forced to change.

Ma was the first to appear as we pulled up, wiping her tears with her pinafore as she pulled me into her arms. Soon I was in Da's embrace, with Joseph standing behind him, a sheepish, pleased look on his face.

'There's tea in the pot, cheese muffins, and some freshly baked scones with jam and today's cream.' Remembering her manners, Ma turned to Friend Hastings. 'Will you stay too?'

'No, no. Tis a time for family.'

The hut was bigger than I'd expected. Da and Joseph had done a fine job of the daub and one wall had already been whitewashed. The table, made from a roughly-planed slab of red gum, was big enough for us all to sit around with a stool each. Ma had set it with the doilies she'd been given as a wedding present. The silver cruet set Da had brought from Chichester sat in the middle amongst the overflowing pots of jam and cream. It was the first time we'd ever shared such fine food as a family in our own home and I gave silent thanks that the years of hunger were behind us.

'I'll put your bag by your bed,' Joseph said, pulling aside a curtain to reveal a bed covered with a colourful patchwork quilt.

I looked around and could see no other bed.

'But where do you all sleep?'

'There's a lean-to at the back,' Da said. 'Ma and I will have that till I go back to the diggings after First Day. Joseph prefers his tent, or so he says.' He smiled at Joseph and I realised that my homecoming was not without its complications.

'We can sort out who sleeps where in the long term soon enough,' Ma said. 'We all wanted you to have the inside bed for your first couple of nights, to help you settle back in. Now, come on, eat. I don't want any of this food left over.'

As we tucked into the supper, I was bombarded with a dozen questions. They wanted to hear all about the Temperance Hotel, Ellen and Sarah, Mr Petersen, and the news from the Adelaide Meetings.

'Did you get to see Polly and Thomas again?' Joseph asked.

I shook my head, wiping scone crumbs from my mouth. 'No. Polly writes sometimes, but they've not been back in Adelaide Town since the wedding. They're doing fine. Polly is getting quite a reputation for her piano playing it seems. She's been invited to parties right across the Barossa Valley. Thomas continues his studies and has recently travelled to Melbourne again for business with Mr Scholz.'

'And that nice young man, Frederick. Any news of him?' Ma continued to pour the tea as she asked, but I knew what she was hoping to hear.

'No, no news of him.'

I allowed what I thought was enough time to pass before I asked after Macca. Even so, I noticed a prolonged silence before Da answered.

'He's engaged to be married. To Margaret Mayfield.'

My cup clattered into the saucer. 'Engaged to Margaret?'

'It's all very sudden,' Ma said. 'None of us knew they were even courting.' She exchanged a glance with Da, who nodded.

'We can only assume she's with child.'

'His child? Is he sure?'

'Enough, Annese.' Da's anger was like a slap. 'You need to respect his choices.'

A silence fell between us as I tried to control my tears. Da and Joseph made excuses to go outside and Ma began to clear the supper things, but I could not rouse myself to help her.

'I know you're sweet on Macca, but you mustn't let this upset you. Time moves things along. You'll see, there'll be someone else for you soon enough. And if there isn't, it is not the end of the world.

'Anyway, Macca may not be the man you think him. We were all worried about him before Margaret helped him. Thanks to her, he's been staying off the grog of late.'

'Where does he stay?' I demanded. They were not going to keep me from him.

Ma shook her head and sighed. 'He's usually at the diggings, although of late the Mayfields have been putting him up at Fairfield. Margaret insists that he attend Bible readings there twice a week.'

My blood rose again. 'Insists! Who is she to insist he do anything? She's a liar, Ma. How dare she put herself above him.' My shouting drew Da's attention and he looked up from his work in the garden.

'Keep your voice down, Annese,' Ma said. 'There's no need to let your disappointment turn to anger. What are you thinking, calling Margaret Mayfield a liar?'

'She is. She doesn't deserve him. It's all in that letter. You remember—the one in that notebook I… I found.'

Ma looked confused. 'That was a long time ago. That letter is gone surely. You burned it, didn't you? Anyway, it was all a misunderstanding. Water under the bridge and best left at that.'

'There was no misunderstanding, Ma. I took that notebook. I kept the letter and you read it. Don't you remember? I didn't burn it and now I can do good with it.'

Ma sighed. 'It was all so long ago, Annese. I have no recollection of what was in the letter, other than some girlish anguish. Let it lie. No matter what you think you know, Macca is doing the right thing by Margaret, as she did by him. Now come on, let's not ruin your first night home. There'll be no more blaming or calling people liars. We all do the best we can with what the good Lord gives us. Go wash up and call me when you're ready for bed. We'll pray together for God's guidance.'

I knew I should have told her right there and then that the letter lay in my red bag, like a menacing missive. But I knew she was determined to let the matter slide. And the mention of bed was more powerful than my anger, as it made me realise how exhausted I was. As I undressed, I resolved to take the chess piece and the letter to Macca in the morning and together, we could plan what to do to save Kiani.

***

The goldfields were a little over two miles from the town. I set off as soon as the kookaburras woke me at dawn, taking one of the left-over cheese dumplings with me to break my fast. Buttoned to my waist was the red bag with the chess piece and Margaret's letter.

At first, the track was well worn and made for easy walking but the previous night's revelations weighed heavily on me. *Was the child his? Was it possible that Macca actually loved Margaret for helping him, or would the letter prove to him the folly of what he was doing?*

Consumed in my thoughts, I must have missed a turning for I found myself with no path ahead, just a tangle of bush. Annoyed at myself, I was about to retrace my steps when a raven screeched overhead and the familiar sounds and smells of the bush filled me, reminding me how small and vulnerable I was. My concerns and demands were nothing compared with the cacophony of all that surrounded me.

The eucalypts exuded their healing balm, the bees, drunk from the wattle pollen, sent out a reverberating hum. The disquiet within me eased as I gave myself permission to be unsure. Unsure of what to do, unsure of how to save Kiani, unsure of what Macca I would find.

Closing my eyes, I remembered the child I'd once been. A child connected to her surroundings, at one with the bush. Had it been only my childhood innocence that had allowed me to escape the here-and-now and join with the wonders of the world around me? Or was nature still part of me and me of it? Could I regain the joy I'd once felt as my body became one with Country?

I resumed walking and soon heard voices and a thumping noise. Through a small clearing in the bush, I could see a cluster of diggers already at their work. Off to the side, two horses were tethered and a man stood shirtless and bootless tending to them.

Macca.

I'd not seen him without a shirt for many years. His broad shoulders were testimony to years of hard physical work. Testimony to the fact that he was now a man and I a woman who desired him. I pushed these thoughts aside and approached the site.

He startled as I approached, making a grab for his shirt. The relief at seeing him undid all my resolve to restrain my emotions. I flew into his arms, sobbing out all my fears.

'Hey, what's this little one?' he said peeling me away. 'Am I so bedraggled to make you this sad?' His laugh, always slow and laconic, was tinged with tiredness. Putting his shirt on he ran his hand through his hair, a look of strained resignation on his face.

'What brings you here? It is not a place for a woman alone.'

The words flowed from me like water from a dam. The relief at having an ally swept me along.

'We need to save Kiani. Margaret Mayfield falsely accused her of theft and then, when her baby drowned, she accused her of murder. She has been sent away to Poonindie, near Port Lincoln. She is not free anymore, Macca. But this is proof of her innocence and of Margaret's lies.' I pulled the letter from my pocket-bag and thrust it towards him.

Macca's brow furrowed as he glanced at the letter and then back at me. 'Slow down. Blimey, you sure are quick off the mark for someone who used hardly to talk. Come and sit down. The billy has just boiled.'

He brushed off a log lying beside a slowly burning fire and washed out two tin mugs before filling them with tea.

I began over as soon as he sat beside me. 'The letter…'

'A letter. Yes, I see, but let's just finish our tea.'

I sipped and waited.

'Now,' he said draining his mug. 'Start from the beginning.'

I told my story, slowly this time, while he kept his silence. 'So you see you cannot marry Margaret now,' I finished. 'Not only did she lie about the stolen china horse but now she's accused Kiani of killing her own child. She is the reason Kiani is being held at that place against her will.'

He took the letter from me and read it through several times. His hands began to shake and he glanced at a flask beside the campfire before responding.

'I understand you think that the letter would clear Kiani of any wrongdoing regarding the chess pieces, but I can't see what I can do. Not now that I am…'

I didn't let him finish. 'You can show the Adelaide police the letter and tell them that Kiani has the chess piece with your blessing. They will contact Archdeacon Hale and tell him to send her back to her family.'

He stood and stepped away, shaking his head and handing the letter back to me. 'Sorry, Annese, but I can't do what you ask. I owe Margaret too much. I can't incriminate the woman I am about to marry. And besides, where do you think Kiani would go if she came back? To Adelaide, where Aboriginal people have to beg for food? Back here to Echunga, where our sheep have overtaken her land and destroyed her food and water?'

I saw in his eyes the same despair and powerlessness I'd felt. My hopes crumbled.

'We can't do nothing, Macca. Doing nothing is worse than all the rest put together.'

A young man strode to where we sat. 'You coming, Macca?'

Without looking around, Macca waved him off. 'I'll catch you up.' As the man walked off, Macca sat again and took my hands in his. I could smell the rum on him now. 'I can't help, Annese.'

I pulled my hands from his and stood. 'Can't or won't?'

Before he could answer, I asked the question that had been burning inside me.

'Is it yours? Margaret's baby?' The bitterness I felt for him in that moment twisted every syllable.

He tried to take my hands again but I snatched them away. 'There is no baby Annese. I know that is what people are saying, but we have not been together in that way.'

'So, why would you protect her and not Kiani?' I felt as if I'd been ripped apart.

'I made a promise to Margaret, and that's that. There is much you don't know.'

'Macca.' The call, more urgent now, came from the young man.

'I have to go. We'll talk again soon.'

He pulled on his boots, pinned his police badge to his shirt, and donned his helmet, offering me his hand as he mounted his horse.

'I'll take you as far as the crossroads.'

Humiliated. Betrayed. Rejected. I turned from him.

'I'll walk.'

'As you please.' He swung his horse around but turned back to me. 'I will think on all you have told me, Annese. But I can't see that there is anything we can do. Not now. The die is cast for Kiani and her family and thousands like them across this so-called great country. Maybe Poonindie is the best place she can be.'

He'd caught up with his colleague by the time I remembered the chess piece. I took it out and felt like dashing it to the ground. But its strange little face stared up at me and Kiani's words resounded in my ears. *It will keep him safe.* At that moment, I was not so sure I wanted

Macca to be safe, but I put it back into the bag, planning to give it to him for good the next time I saw him.

***

Walking back to Echunga, my heart heavy, my limbs like lead weights, the journey seemed much longer than the one there. The sun had fully risen and, although the morning chill was still in the air, it brought flickering warmth through the trees. I'd reached the crossroads when I saw Joseph running towards me.

'So this is where you are? Our parents are beside themselves with worry, although Ma seemed to know where you would be.'

I shrugged and kept walking. He fell in beside me.

'Macca is a good man, Annese, but he's a drinker too. He might be sober now but it takes a strong man to give it up when he's as far gone as Macca was.'

I shrugged. 'Margaret Mayfield will be the one that will need to worry about that now.'

'I expect so. Look, there's something else you need to know.' I kept on walking but he grabbed my arm and stopped me midstride. 'Macca tried to take his life, Annese. Margaret saved him. She saw him in the flooding creek, stones in his pockets. She talked to him until he came out.'

'Macca tried to kill himself?' I wanted to not believe him but I recalled the sadness I'd seen in Macca's eyes so many times. The despair when he talked about Kiani and her people. I thought too of the flask and smell of rum. Was he truly such a broken man?

'You must accept it. Macca is now tied to Margaret.'

We stood looking at each other as his words sank in. I could not accept that they were bound to each other but I knew now that my belief in Macca's love for me was misplaced. If he loved me, he would never have attempted to end his life.

I hugged Joseph. We'd fought so often as children, but he'd always been there to protect me.

'I'm due at the diggings,' he said, releasing me. 'Go directly home now, won't you?'

Upended, torn apart, I'd walked half the way home. Kiani's desperate plea, *I must return my baby to Country,* filled me like lead. As I sank to the ground weeping, I was overwhelmed by the magnificence of a wedge-tailed eagle so close I could have touched him and his flailing, glorious wings. He seemed to enfold me as he slowly, laboriously, rose from the ground. I closed my eyes and gave myself to him and we glided majestically into his airy kingdom to freedom above the treetops. Together, we carried Kiani's deep sorrow away from the tortures of the cruel world.

Her truth had to be told. She had to be free.

CHAPTER 22

Unlike most people, Mr Tummerton didn't try to hide his surprise when I first met him, despite the fact I was wearing Joseph's trousers and waistcoat pulled over my cotton shirt. Sarah had cut my hair to just above shoulder length and I'd curled what was left of it into a bun at the back of my head, covering it with a boy's cap.

'Miss Laffer, I assume? Your brother told me you were not like all the other girls. Someone with a mind of her own, he said.'

I nodded, afraid that he might send me away. 'If you mean my clothes, I can go home and change, but trousers make it easier to get about a workshop,' I said. I could have added that dressing like a boy gave me a feeling of freedom, a freedom I'd not previously realised I lacked, but I didn't think he would understand that.

'As long as you can follow orders while you're here, you can dress as you wish.'

I was about to simply nod but I'd resolved to at least try to overcome my usual reticence to talk. 'I will do that. I have much still to learn from you. I know about shoemaking, but the saddlery you do here is another thing altogether.'

'It certainly is. Harder on the hands but, in my opinion, more rewarding. But all in good time. Now, what shall I call you?'

'Mr Petersen took to calling me Laffer, which suited both of us. I'd be happy if you did the same.'

'Well then, Laffer, there's a hide hanging on the fence that needs flattening. My boy, Tommy, will help you with it.'

I looked around. I hadn't seen a boy when I'd come in and didn't know Mr Tummerton already had an assistant.

'He stays outside mostly. His choice, not mine. You'll find him next to the tank, I dare say.'

The cement rainwater tank was adjacent to the stable. Beside it, a light-skinned native boy was whittling a thin branch. He jumped to his feet as I approached. 'Mr Tummerton said you're to help me with a hide,' I told him.

He pointed to where it hung and together we carried it into the workshop, Tommy quickly returning outside to his spear-making once it was laid on the workbench.

'You've probably heard the rumours about Tommy,' Mr Tummerton said. 'So, I might as well set the record straight from the start. He's my son and there's no shame in that. His mother and I have made a life together and she keeps house for me.'

I'd heard no rumours. Maybe my parents considered it too sensitive a topic to discuss with me, or perhaps they knew I wouldn't be offended by the arrangement. I recalled Macca's insistence that such arrangements were mostly injurious to Aboriginal people, but Mr Tummerton seemed to hold Tommy and his mother with high respect.

But my thoughts were not only about the rights or wrongs of his situation, for they'd quickly turned to Kiani. I wondered if Tommy's mother might know where Kiani's family was now. Perhaps I could ask her what she thought was the best thing to do for her.

'Petersen says you're handy at making use of offcuts. There's a pile of them by the door you can sort into sizes. And while you're at it, I need to mend these boots. Find a piece of about the same colour, big enough to recap them.'

Even though it had only been a couple of weeks since I'd left my Adelaide work, I realised how much I'd missed the smells and rhythms of a workshop. Three partly made saddles lay on a large worktable. Behind them was a wall covered with reins and halters—some new, others well worn. Metal bits and buckles were sorted into type and size in wooden boxes pushed against the wall. Mr Tummerton was clearly a more orderly worker than Mr Petersen, who'd enjoyed the chaos of his workshop.

I soon found a suitable offcut for the mending job and was surprised when Mr Tummerton gave me the damaged boot.

'Show me what you can do, Laffer. Cut it to shape.' I took my time orienting and cutting the leather. I must have pleased him, for he gave me another task, this time mending a saddle bag.

'Don't need to be too fussy on how it looks. So long as it holds together.'

The task took me most of the day and my fingers were red with the sewing it entailed, but Mr Tummerton nodded his approval at the finished item.

'Not bad for a girlie,' he said. 'Come back tomorrow. There's plenty more for you to do. I'll pay you weekly.'

I looked for Tommy when I washed my hands at the tank, but he'd gone. As I walked home, back aching and hands throbbing, a joyful feeling that was rare to me of late swept over me. Concentrating on my tasks all day had pushed all thoughts of Macca and Kiani from my mind. I allowed myself to enjoy the sense of release, at least for the time being.

Our hut was empty when I got home. Joseph and Da were still at the diggings and Ma was at the store. Pulling my boots off at the door, I managed to eat some cheese on a bread roll before lying fully dressed on the bed. I'd intended to simply rest my back, but I must have fallen asleep for I didn't hear Ma come in, and only woke when she gently shook me.

'Come, lass, you'd better eat your supper.'

We chatted about our work as we ate and I asked her about Tommy and his mother.

'I don't know much more than you. They came to the town as a family while we were away. By the time I got here, the gossip had died down. People had got used to the idea, I guess. The boy's mother is rarely seen in the town. They live out towards Meadows. She and the boy come and go a bit, from what I know.'

I longed to talk to her concerning what Joseph had told me about Margaret stopping Macca from taking his own life, but I knew it was not for me to tell, so I couched it another way.

'How was Macca when he first came back here to live?'

I saw that she was about to scold me for asking about him, but she likely saw the genuine concern on my face. 'He was drinking heavily. I'd never seen him so mournful. We've not seen much of him since he told us of his betrothal.'

That night I insisted on sleeping in the lean-to. 'I prefer it out there. I can see the stars from the hammock.'

As I settled, my thoughts turned to Macca again. I remembered how he'd been all that time ago when he'd left the tea house angry over the way others were prepared to accept the fact that Kiani's people would eventually disappear. Had it been that which had led him into such a desperate act?

I tried to convince myself that my past thoughts of marrying him were just a childish fantasy, for in truth he'd never given me a sign that it was what he wanted. But even as these thoughts went around in my head, I felt a longing for him, or at least for the Macca I once knew; the kind and fun-loving Macca.

***

With each day passing, Mr Tummerton gave me more responsibilities. I stuck mostly to shoemaking, although sometimes tried my hand at saddlery. Most of our work came from the goldfields, with an occasional dress boot or shoe order for formal occasions. I was given the job of organising the orders too and noticed one requesting a pair of dress shoes for Margaret.

I'd managed to avoid her since returning to Echunga, seeing her only at Meetings, where I kept my distance. Macca had been with her on several occasions and I couldn't help but feel for the awkwardness he so obviously felt being there with her and her family, though I had to admit he looked very handsome in the genteel clothes he wore on those occasions. He'd put on weight and looked the better for it. On one occasion, he and Margaret had begun to approach me but I'd walked away, pretending not to have seen them. It was still too painful for me to see him with her.

I was at work, concentrating on a tricky boot, when I heard Margaret talking to Mr Tummerton. I tried to hide, but I could see her searching for me.

'Oh, there you are, Annese. I heard that you work as a cobbler's boy. I must say you look the part.'

When I didn't reply, she came towards me. 'Malcolm says you have become a delightful young woman, but you look more like a lad to me.'

So rarely did I hear Macca referred to as Malcolm it took some time for me to understand who she was talking about. 'He's not seen me of late in my work clothes. If he had, I am sure he might say the same. Although I'm not sure why he would speak of me at all.'

'Oh, he only spoke of you in passing, Annese. You have no doubt heard that our wedding is approaching. There's fifty coming from Adelaide. We will put some of them up at our place and others will stay with Friend Sanders and Friend Hogan.'

As she spoke, a vision of Kiani pleading with me at the port almost loosened my tongue with anger. But I knew that, no matter what I said, Margaret was about to marry the only man I would ever love and nothing would stop that. I just wanted the conversation to end.

'I am sure it will be a fine affair, Margaret.'

Behind her, Mr Tummerton began hammering, creating enough noise to cover our conversation as she stepped within inches of me and laid her hand on my arm, squeezing it so I could not retreat.

'Do not come between us, Annese. Malcolm is marrying me. I know you took my letter. If you ever reveal its contents, I will besmirch your and your family's names.'

I heard the determination in her voice, but in her eyes, I saw fear. I was unsure if Macca told her I still had the letter or if she was guessing.

'I don't know what you're talking about, Margaret.'

She dug her fingers sharply into my arm, before releasing me and turning away. She was almost at the door when I blurted my words out.

'Has Macca mentioned the young native girl, Kiani—someone we both know?'

She stopped and smiled weakly at Mr Tummerton, who'd put down his hammer and was watching us. I should have backed off, hidden my head in my work, but the fear in Margaret's eyes spurred me on.

'She was caught taking sugar, just enough to fill her belly, but has now been accused of a much more serious crime. A crime she did not commit. She's been taken to a place called Poonindie. Away from all she knows. Away from family, from friends. Has he told you of her, Margaret?'

A fierce silence fell across the workshop. Her burning glare convinced me she'd made the connection with her letter. I stared back. I felt the power shift.

She came close to me again and hissed into my ear. 'He has mentioned no such thing. You are a liar, Annese.'

I flinched but stood my ground. My heart raced as she walked out of the workshop, her shoes tucked tightly under her arm. I half expected Mr Tummerton to tell me to leave and not return, but, to my great relief, he simply resumed his hammering. It was another hour, during our lunch break, before he approached me.

My heart raced, waiting for him to reprimand me. 'What do you know about Poonindie?'

Relieved, I rushed to answer. 'Not much. I've read about it in the newspaper. I met Mr and Mrs Hale. An Aboriginal girl I know has been sent there.'

'Malcolm Macleod, Macca, knows of her too, you say?'

'Yes. We used to see her and her sister at the creek.'

He nodded then and seemed to be turning something over in his mind.

'I met Macca when I worked for Tolmer at one stage. I was the saddler for the police. He always struck me as someone who would make his mark one day. One way or another.'

'Do you know anything about Poonindie?' I ventured to ask.

He gazed at me for some time as if assessing my motives. 'Some of my wife's people have been sent there too. Hale, the man who runs it with his wife, seems kind enough, but…'

I waited. He observed me for some time before recommencing. 'But her people are pining away there. They miss their Country. They miss their own ways.'

'And your wife, does she not miss her own ways?'

'Yes, of course. But still, she stays with me. She says it is safer.'

'Safer?'

He shrugged. His sadness and resignation reminded me of Macca's. 'I expect one day she'll leave and take Tommy with her.'

Outside a crow called. Mr Tummerton sighed.

'We have it in common, our sadness,' I said. 'Macca too.'

He nodded, resuming his work. 'There's plenty like us, Laffer, if you look hard enough, but none of us knows what to do about it. Maybe Hale has got the right idea at Poonindie. Treat them kindly and teach them how to work in our world until all their old ways are gone.'

I could tell neither of us believed what he said, but we left our thoughts unspoken.

CHAPTER 23

The saddlery side of the work gradually took over more of my time. It was harder on my hands, but I grew stronger as I learned how to cut through the thicker hides, thankful that I'd inherited Ma's strong arms.

'We're a nuggety lot. It's the Irish in us,' she'd say.

My shoulders had broadened with the lifting I had to do, and people became used to seeing me in my work trousers. I heard them call me tomboy, a term I wore with pride, although I knew it wasn't always said as a compliment. I still had to wear my pinafore outside of work, and I resented how many tasks were made awkward by it. I was wrestling with the length of it, trying to squat on the stool to milk our cow one morning, when Macca came to visit. Da was shovelling manure onto the garden but put down his shovel to place the billy over the outside fire. Macca had brought a week-old copy of *The Observer* and he and Da were discussing the rising price of meat and wool when Da pointed to another article.

'It says here they're having great success with the native training mission near Port Lincoln. They've even got some of them playing the flute.'

I stopped the milking at the mention of the Port Lincoln mission but kept my distance. I'd still not spoken to anyone other than Macca about my hopes of finding Kiani.

'Aye, I've read it,' Macca said, glancing at me. 'But is it a success, playing our instruments instead of their own? Or have we just defeated them? My reading of the article is that Hale deeply regrets the wrongs we have brought upon the natives.'

He took the newspaper from Da, glanced at me, and read aloud.

Their contact with civilisation seems but to have destroyed their original independence, without conferring upon them any compensatory advantages.

'So is Hale against what we are trying to set up here—a colony free of religious persecution; a colony established by free men and women, not convicts?'

'I can't speak for him, but I think he at least can see clearly what the consequences have been for the Aboriginal people and is trying to give them a hope of surviving.'

Macca turned to where I skulked in the shadows. 'But perhaps we should ask Annese. After all, she's met Mr and Mrs Hale.'

I stepped forward then and picked up the paper.

'When did you meet them?' Da demanded.

'Tell him, Annese. Tell him what you told me.' It was only then that I realised that his words were a little slurred, his gaze unsteady.

'I met them when I went with the tanner to collect hides.' It wasn't a lie, just a half-truth. 'They seemed very nice,' I finished lamely, willing Macca to stay quiet about the real purpose of my visit, for I knew it would upset Da.

'Still the sly one,' Macca said quietly, before raising his voice a little. 'But do you think it is right, Annese, that we take the land from the original owners, then keep them hundreds of miles from where they lived happy and free?'

'No, I don't, but I don't know what else there is to be done.'

Da looked at me with both suspicion and admiration. 'Has Tummerton been filling your head—him with his native woman and son?'

I could not help but laugh at the irony. 'No, Da. You have. And all the other Friends. Ever since I was born. *Love your neighbour as yourself* and *whatever you wish that others would do to you, do also to them, for this is the Law of the Prophets.* That's what you've always taught me.'

Macca laughed and shook his head with pure admiration. 'She's got you there, Joshua.' He put his hand in his pocket, reaching for his flask, but changed his mind. 'She's wiser than both of us,' he said.

Da emptied his mug of tea. 'I wish I had the answer, Annese. All I know is that we can't go back to Chichester. I have to provide for you, Ma, and Joseph. I have to live off this land now. I couldn't leave Polly and Thomas either.'

I hugged his drooping shoulders. 'You do your best, Da. It's just that I can't bear to see what we have done to them. I'm not like others,' I said, turning to Macca, 'who are all too keen to cast the first stone or even outright lie to justify what we are doing.'

He stared back at me as if through a clearing fog, before reaching for his flask. But instead of taking a swig, he emptied it out.

'Have you got the chess piece, Annese?'

Surprised at his change of mood, I nodded.

'Good. Keep it safe. We will need it. You're right, Annese, we can't do nothing.'

***

When Da went to bed that night, I picked up the newspaper and crept closer to the fire to read it.

> *Archdeacon Hale speaks in warm terms of the natives located at the Training Institution, some of whom are making good progress as flute-players, whilst others are manifesting in different ways. He talks of their advancing intelligence and their taste for the truly elevating pursuits of civilised life.*
>
> *Their contact with civilisation seems but to destroy their original independence without conferring upon them any compensatory advantages. The abuses, rather than the benefits of civilised life, are what the coloured races are most apt to learn. Their powers of hardihood and self-reliance are sapped.*

Yes, that was it. Kiani and her family, once hardy and self-reliant, had been sapped like a dying tree. I shuddered and read on.

Neither Government blankets and flour, nor clerical care and teaching, will ever give them a permanent name and place in the land. Yet by kindness, their hardships may be mitigated, and the charity of civilised usages may atone for some of the evils which civilisation has brought in its train.

I read the article twice, trying to take in all it was saying. Mr Hale seemed to see the damage we were doing so clearly, but instead of being angry, he thought we should just try to be *kind* to lessen the impact.

Kindness? Was sending Kiani to Poonindie kindness? Was taking away her language and ceremonies kindness? Was keeping the body of her drowned baby from her kindness?

Macca's parting words filled me with hope that he had a solution. As I tried to sleep, I remembered the freedom Mrs Hale had enjoyed, and wondered again if marriage would open up my world too or just make me an outcast if it was Macca I married.

***

I'd expected Macca to come back to me with a plan but, when weeks passed without seeing him, my hopes of helping Kiani dwindled again. He'd not been with the Mayfields at the Meetings recently and, when Da said he'd heard that he'd gone somewhere to 'dry out', I wondered if it had just been the drink talking that day.

As much as I wanted to help Kiani, the pleasure and ease of my life began to overtake my anger. Work and home duties kept me busy and I found myself enjoying the gentle rhythm of a life free of distress. Ma was running the store and the Post Office, Da and Joseph had some work with Mr Hastings and spent as much time as they could at the goldfield, where they were having more success than most. We could now afford some luxuries—we'd replaced our leaking bathtub with an anodised tub bought off a gentleman returning to England, and all but Joseph now had a horsehair mattress.

In my spare time, I'd arranged with Mr Sanders to borrow his horse and would ride along the trails used to move sheep and cattle between properties. I'd gone out to the goldfields a couple of times to see if I could see Macca, but to no avail. Mostly I went along the creek, enjoying the freedom and the sounds and smell of the bush.

My improved riding skills came in handy when one day Mr Tummerton received an urgent request for a pair of boots to be delivered to the goldfields.

'Everybody wants things straight away,' he complained. 'Can you ride a horse, Laffer?'

'I ride well enough,' I replied, 'if it's a quiet horse.'

'You can take Bessy. She's quiet enough, but take Tommy with you just in case. He's good with horses and his horse will keep Bessy from bolting if she spooks.'

Tommy appeared after tea break with two horses saddled and ready to go. 'This is yours, Miss,' he said, giving me the reins. Bessy hung her head and nuzzled me.

We headed off, with the boots wrapped in an old newspaper and a name written on a tag. Tommy took the lead as planned and we rode in silence, although on two occasions he stopped, pointing out a mob of kangaroos and later an echidna sliding into the bush.

'Animal plenty scared, Miss.'

'I won't hurt them.'

'Not of you, Miss. The horses. They think they are monsters come to take their Country.'

'Then they're afraid of the wrong thing,' I said.

When we arrived at the goldfields, Tommy took the horses to the creek while I sought out Da and Joseph. Around me, I could see dozens of shafts, each being worked by two or three men. To the north, two hundred or so tents were clustered together. I could see several women there, hanging washing, and cooking over outdoor fires. A store was being built near the tents to provide essential supplies to the makeshift town.

Spotting Da, I asked him where to find the owner of the boots. He looked at the tag and pointed to a man a few yards away. 'Mr F. Scholz. That'll be the young man over there. Did you notice he has the same name as the twins go by now? Coincidence, I guess. There are plenty of Scholz over here now.'

I hadn't even looked at the tag until then.

'Not sure that new boots are going to help him much though,' Da continued, smiling to himself at some joke.

The man was barefooted and covered in dust and grime. 'Thank you, lad,' he said, taking the bundle from me. 'These are badly needed. My old pair fell apart yesterday and I've no others with me.'

I'd decided not to correct people when they called me lad due to the way I dressed. I didn't mind and being set straight caused them embarrassment. It was only as he began to unwrap the boots that I recognised him as Frederick, Thomas's stepbrother.

Gathering the words to ask him about Polly and Thomas, I lingered and he looked up with a questioning smile. I took off my cap and loosened my hair from the bun. Ma had stopped me from cutting it and it was almost mid-back length again. I saw the recognition in his wide smile.

'I know you. Polly and Thomas's sister. Annese. Annese Laffer. You've changed since we last met.' His eyes swept over me briefly before he straightened himself up. 'I'm Frederick Scholz. Do you remember me?' he asked.

'Yes. When Thomas lost his temper.' I glanced at Da, worried that I should not be alone talking to this man, but he'd begun working again.

Frederick laughed. 'Yes. He's still a firebrand but he has a good heart for all his bluster. Well, I must say this is a pleasant surprise.'

We stood smiling at each other, me in my boyish work clothes, he looking like an out-of-place failed digger.

'What are you doing here?' we asked each other simultaneously and then laughed.

'You go first,' he said.

Something about his calm demeanour helped my words flow. 'I live back in Echunga now and work for the cobbler. My father and brother have a claim just over there.'

'Laffer! Yes, of course. You must be Joshua's daughter. I didn't make the connection.'

His dishevelled appearance made it easy to feel confident in his company. 'Do you have contact with the twins? Polly and I write every so often. I think Thomas is still angry at me.'

'I don't see Polly very often.' I heard a sadness creep into his voice before he brightened. 'But Thomas and I are in regular contact.'

A silence fell between us. 'As to what I am doing here,' he said, realising my awkwardness, 'well, I'm trying my hand to make a fortune like everyone else, I expect. There's not much work coming my way in Adelaide and I'm not keen on going to Melbourne. But I'm quickly finding out that gold mining is harder than it looks, so I'm not sure how long I'll be here.'

As we spoke, Da called out something but it got lost in the noise of the site. Frederick and I both waved to him, but he continued to watch us. Joseph was pouring water from a half wine barrel into the top of the sorting cradle, which Da began slowly rocking.

'You'd better go and explain why I'm talking to you. It is good to see you, Annese. You've grown up since I saw you at my aunt's.' His eyes stayed on me longer than was usual. They seemed to hold many questions.

'Yes, I best be off,' I said, but as I was about to walk away, an impulse made me turn back. 'I'll get Da to invite you to our place. We're all keen to hear news of Polly and Thomas.'

'I'd like that.'

Seeing me coming to rejoin them, Da waved to Frederick again. Tommy was still waiting nearby with our horses, and another three horses were tethered at the police camp with two constables tending them.

'If it's Macca you hope to see,' Da said as I came to his side, 'you're out of luck. He was here yesterday but has gone to Fairfield to see his fiancée.'

'It's no business of mine where he is. Are they not married yet?' My voice gave away my annoyance at having been caught out seeking him.

'No. The wedding has been put back. What were you talking to young Frederick about?'

I explained the connection with Thomas and Polly, and that Ma and I had met him when they were in Adelaide for the wedding. 'He'd like to visit with us in Echunga. Will you invite him? I think Ma would enjoy seeing him again.'

'Ah yes,' Da said, looking over to where Frederick was now back at his work. 'I remember your mother telling me about a handsome young man who was a nephew of Mrs Scholz or some such. I'll invite him to come to us after the Meeting, not this First Day but the next.'

'Perhaps you should ask Macca too. He'd be good company for Frederick.'

'I can do that, and Margaret too, of course.'

No one had mentioned the obvious discord between Margaret and me, although I knew it was common knowledge within our community that we avoided each other. I knew Da was doing the right thing, but the idea of Margaret being in our humble hut bothered me. I didn't want to give her any grounds to sneer at us. I tried to think of a way to have Macca invited without her but came up with nothing.

'Have your Ma get in extra supplies,' Da continued. 'In fact, tell her to ask the butcher for a whole hogget. We might as well make it a celebration all round.'

'A celebration of what?'

Da dug into his pocket and held out a nugget the size of an almond. The glee was written across his face. 'Now keep that to yourself. Let me be the one to tell Ma. Maybe at last our luck is turning.'

CHAPTER 24

As the day of our celebration lunch dawned, not even the thought of Margaret being at our cottage dampened my excitement. It was a mild early summer's day with a gentle breeze, so we'd set the table up outside and covered it with the linen tablecloth Ma had brought with her from Ireland. She'd washed and ironed it, but it still had several stains. Placing a bunch of wildflowers over the worst of the markings, I covered the rest with napkins and plates.

We could do nothing about our mismatched cutlery, so I drew up some place markers to make sure that Margaret had the best ones. Even though Frederick had known grandeur much greater than her, I believed that he would not mind our simple ways.

I'd written to Sarah and Ellen and told them about the celebration. Ellen had insisted on sending me one of her crinoline dresses. Recalling her flamboyant style, I'd worried about her choice of dress. But when it arrived shortly before the big day, I'd fallen in love with it. Its pretty floral pattern with various shades of blue against a white background was both subdued and striking. The pattern of bell-shaped flowers and serrated leaves was big enough to be distinctive without being bold. It was the finest dress I'd ever held and I couldn't imagine wearing it.

'You will,' Ma said as she helped me put it on. 'How often does a girl like you get the opportunity to wear such a dress? We've company coming and I won't have you drooping about in your pinafore when you've got such a fine dress at your disposal.'

I pulled it over my head and Ma guided it over the corset and the wire frame she'd borrowed. The frame extended the skirt into a ridiculous width and the high neckline cut into my chin. I opened a button to make it bearable. Ellen had included a note informing me that the sleeves were pagoda style and were all the fashion at the moment. Not used to wearing a frame, I brushed against everything as I passed and the sleeves made doing anything constructive almost impossible. But, even without a mirror, I could feel the flattering effects of the sloping shoulders and puckered waistline and, for the first time ever, I felt the feminine allure that comes with dressing to please.

Margaret and Macca arrived in a trap pulled by a lively pony. I'd been imagining their arrival all morning, trying to prepare myself for the surge of jealousy I knew I would feel. But nothing came close to keeping back my emotions as she leaned on his shoulders for support and he held her by the waist, lowering her to the ground.

I rushed inside and watched through the window until I felt able to talk to them.

Her dress, made of the finest strawberry-pink cotton, had delicate lace at the sleeves and neckline. Her bonnet was tied with a glossy wide ribbon. I'd never thought her pretty, but dressed as she was, I could see how men found her attractive.

Ma greeted them and showed Margaret to her place at the table. 'Annese, fetch Margaret a glass of lemonade,' she instructed, calling me outside. 'Macca, would you like a wine from Friend Hogan's vineyard?'

'No, I'll be drinking lemonade too.'

I noticed how lined his skin was now, evidence of many hours in the sun but also, no doubt, of too much drinking.

Frederick arrived soon after them. His horse, a bay mare at least sixteen hands high, had been carefully groomed for the occasion. He'd been to the barber since I'd last seen him. His beard and moustache were neatly trimmed and his hair cut short, revealing the rich blue of his eyes. Macca, on the other hand, still wore his beard and hair long, although his clothes were those of a gentleman. He wore a tartan waistcoat beneath the jacket that he soon discarded. The bow tied at his neck looked quite silly on him and, when he pulled at it, Margaret slapped his hand as if he were a child.

Joseph helped Ma carry the meat and vegetables outside and Da took his place at the head of the table, saying a prayer of thanks before carving. I'd planned to sit as far from Margaret as possible but Macca swapped his card insisting that he be alongside Joseph and Frederick. Margaret's protests to him fell on deaf ears.

'You've put on a fine spread, Mrs Laffer,' Frederick said as the plates were passed to Da for a generous helping of hogget each. 'I shall tell Polly and Thomas when I see them next.'

'Do you see them often?' Ma asked.

'Only Thomas. He's living in Adelaide now to complete his studies. He's contracted to Mr Bagot and will begin his law degree when he turns sixteen.'

'A lawyer! Can you imagine, Annese?' Ma exclaimed turning to me. 'Our Thomas, a lawyer.'

Beside me, Margaret quietly scoffed. Macca glanced at me and his jaw tightened.

'Thomas tells me Polly is quite the belle of the Barossa,' Frederick continued.

'That Mrs Scholz has done a fine job raising them,' Margaret said smiling. 'Sometimes things turn out for the best.'

Was she expecting thanks for them being taken? Did she not know the heartache her actions had caused? As if reading my thunderous thoughts, Da changed the conversation and a discussion ensued, speculating as to who was making money at the diggings, and who was not.

'There's no telling,' Joseph said. 'Folk are keen to talk about other people's fortunes, or misfortunes, but won't be drawn on their own.'

He was right. Da had stayed quiet about his recent luck and, even now, a day to celebrate his find, he steered the talk in another direction.

'They tell me that young Thomas Hardy has planted vines on the banks of the Torrens at Bankside.'

'He has,' Frederick chipped in. 'He's a hard worker and will probably make a go of it. But you won't get better than this wine of Hogan's,' he said, raising his glass in a salute to Da. 'It's made from the vines Mr Hastings planted is it not?'

'Yes, Friend Hogan acquired them when Friend Hastings went bankrupt.'

'Are you not enjoying your wine, Annese?' Frederick nodded towards my glass from which I'd barely sipped.

I flushed, uncomfortable with his attention. 'I know nothing about wine.'

'Perhaps you should ask Malcolm. He has sampled plenty.' The barb in Margaret's voice was unmistakable.

'As you know, Margaret, I am not drinking nowadays,' Macca retorted.

An awkward silence fell across the table before Macca continued, trying to soften the tension he and Margaret were causing. 'I am sure we can rely on Frederick's opinion though. The wines from the local vines are certainly sought after, even in the mother country. They are thought to be some of the best.'

Joseph, who had clearly been enjoying the wine, stood and raised his glass. 'I would like to toast the soon-to-be-wed couple.'

Macca's fist clenched around his lemonade. Margaret glared at him. Ma caught me looking at them and opened her eyes wide, willing me to stay silent.

'Yes, good health to you both,' Ma said quickly. 'Now who would like dessert? Apple and rhubarb crumble.'

A burst of conversation sprung up around the table about the apples being grown at the Adelaide Hills settlement of Lenswood and the best time to plant rhubarb. Macca stood to help Ma clear the plates.

'Will you stay on as special constable after your marriage, Macca?' I heard her ask him.

'No,' Margaret answered for him. 'Father has offered us a house in Adelaide.'

I took the plates from Macca, for they were clattering in his shaking hands.

'I will need to find work there first though,' he said to Ma as he pulled his tie off and loosened his shirt collar. 'I will not be happy until I do. In fact, I'm going to Port Lincoln next week to meet a man who needs an agent in Adelaide to handle his wool sales. He gets terribly seasick it seems, and can't face making the journey on a regular basis.'

'Port Lincoln. Next week?' My question could have been heard as simply a part of the conversation, but I'd obviously asked with more enthusiasm than I should, for all eyes turned to me.

'Do you know it?' Frederick asked me. 'They say it is the most beautiful harbour.'

I caught Macca's eye and decided to continue. 'I know a little of it. I understand that some of our Aboriginal people have been taken there to a place called Poonindie. They are training them to be servants, although some would say slaves.'

A ripple of discomfort went around the table.

'Annese does not agree with their methods,' Da said, hoping no doubt to smooth any disquiet. 'She has a point, I must say, for it seems they do not live there as free people. And when they are sent out to work, they're often not paid. Our Society of Friends has fought hard to end slavery in the Americas and yet it is hard to see the difference with our own actions here in South Australia.'

'And what do you say about the situation, Margaret?' Macca asked, the bitterness in his voice unmistakable.

'You know well my thoughts, Malcolm. I do not believe anything can come of trying to train them. They are savages and will always revert to their old ways.'

The friction between them reverberated around the table. Ma returned to relieve me of the plates.

'That's enough talk about a subject that none of us truly knows much about,' she said in a slightly raised voice. 'Joseph, will you play us a tune on your tin whistle? Annese, come inside and help me please.'

The sounds of an Irish air followed us into the cottage. Macca came behind with two plates we'd missed.

'I'll get the trap ready for our return trip,' he called out to Margaret, passing the plates to Ma and nodding at me behind Ma's back towards where the horses were tethered. When Ma went back to the table, I snuck to where Macca stood by the horses behind the hut.

'There's no time to lose. I need the chess piece. I'm going to try and find Kiani when I'm in Port Lincoln. If I take yours, the Hales will hopefully believe that the one she has is hers, given to her by me. Without it, they won't believe me. They'll dismiss me as having gone soft on the natives.'

He'd hitched the trap by the time I returned with the chess piece wrapped in Margaret's letter.

'Take the letter too. It's proof that Kiani didn't steal the china horse either.'

Macca hesitated. 'I'll take it but, you need to know, it will be a last resort. I don't want to incriminate Margaret.'

I looked over my shoulder to make sure we were still alone. 'Are you truly obliged to marry her? Joseph told me what she did for you. But I do not see that as a reason to marry against your wishes.'

He looked deep into my eyes. 'I made a promise, Annese, and I'll honour it. I'm sorry. I wish it were different.'

It was the nearest he'd come to declaring his feelings for me, only to say he could never be mine. I leant towards him and rested my head on his shoulder. He pulled me closer before gently pushing me away.

'I'm sorry, Annese.'

Joseph appeared at the side of the hut. 'Annese,' he snapped.

I stepped back, embarrassed and ashamed. But Macca stood tall. 'What is it, Joseph?'

'Annese, Ma says you're to bring Margaret's things.'

'Be careful, Annese,' he hissed as he followed me into the hut. 'You of all people know that Margaret is a formidable enemy.'

Margaret was talking to Ma when I passed her her bonnet. She met my strained smile with a scowl. 'Thank you, Annese. I think I have all that is mine now.'

Turning to my parents, she thanked them for the invitation. 'Come, Malcolm,' she said, waiting to be helped into the trap. 'What has kept you?'

She smiled at me, superior and falsely magnanimous. 'Thank you for your generous hospitality too, Annese. I will see you all at the next Meeting, by which time I will be Mrs Macleod.'

***

I didn't expect to see Macca before he left for Port Lincoln. I'd spent many hours since the celebration lunch, mulling over what had happened between us but, more significantly, how wretched he was. I tried to convince myself that he was doing the right thing by Margaret, but I could not get the sheer misery of it all out of my mind. When he came to Mr Tummerton's workshop two days later, I was both elated and terrified that his plans to go to Port Lincoln might have been cancelled.

'Ah, Macca, good to see you again. Thank you for coming in,' Mr Tummerton greeted him. 'I hear you're off to Port Lincoln the day after tomorrow?' They shook hands like long acquaintances. Macca caught my eye and nodded a greeting.

'I am. I'm meeting with one of the pastoralists over there. He needs an agent in Adelaide and I have applied for the position. He wants me to see his run before he takes me on. What are you needing?'

'I've this fancy saddlebag to send over for Mrs Hale,' he said, indicating the new moleskin bag I'd seen him working on. 'I don't trust those ruffians that call themselves sailors to take care of it. Would you consider taking it to her?'

'Mrs Hale? At Poonindie?' I asked.

'The very same.'

Macca shook his head slightly, willing me to stay quiet.

'Don't worry, Macleod. Laffer has told me about your mutual friend who's been taken there.'

Macca's face relaxed. 'I'm glad, for that will save me explaining a lot.' He turned to me now. 'Annese does not know it yet, but I've come to ask her a favour and it would mean you releasing her from her work for a week.'

Mr Tummerton came to my side. 'Go on?'

'Annese, I think it would be best if it is you who approaches the Hales about Kiani. I came to see if you would consider coming with me.'

The idea of going anywhere with Macca filled me with delight, but all the reasons I could not say 'yes' crowded in upon me.

'I can't. I've my work. I can't let Mr Tummerton down. We're very busy. Besides, Da would never let me.'

Mr Tummerton was studying Macca closely. 'It seems as if Mr Macleod has a plan to help your friend, Laffer. You have my blessing, at least if it will help relieve the dire situation we have cast the first people into. Hear him out.'

He withdrew to the other side of the workshop and began packaging up the saddle. Macca stepped closer to me. 'I know it is a big request, Annese. But it is all I can think of. We can't do nothing.'

'But how could I travel alone with a man engaged to another woman? Margaret would not allow it and neither will my parents.'

Macca's eyes clouded over. 'Margaret won't have a say in it, Annese. She has ended our engagement.'

I could see his pain, but my heart beat so strongly it was all I could do to control myself. I wanted to fling myself into his arms.

'I am…' I knew I should say I was sorry, but we both knew that would be untrue. 'I think you have made the right decision, Macca.'

He shook his head. 'It was her decision. The night after we left your place, I drank a whole bottle of rum. She flew into a rage and ended it. She said I was not worthy of her, and she is right.'

A dozen thoughts flashed through my head. Why had he resorted to drink once again, now that he was free of his obligations? Was he taking work in Adelaide to avoid Margaret and her family? But I didn't get the chance to ask—Macca was still needing an answer from me.

'So will you come if we can clear it with your parents?'

My mind swam again with all the reasons I should say no, but I could not suppress the excitement growing within me. The urgency in his voice thrilled me.

Through the confusion of emotions came Mr Tummerton's voice from the other side of the workshop.

'I know it is none of my business but, for what it's worth, Laffer, I've met plenty of women in my travels who've broken with old rules. Some even disguise themselves as boys or men to do it. You've got a head start on that account.'

Both men looked at me now and it took several seconds before I understood what they were thinking. Standing there in my trousers and cap, I knew I could easily pass as a boy, a deceit that would resolve at least half of my concerns. A deceit that excited me beyond reasoning and filled me with courage and determination.

'Perhaps you could tell your parents you are needing to go to Adelaide for a week for Mr Tummerton, and that I have offered to accompany you there.'

I looked at my boss and could see that he was on board with the plan. 'You could run a few errands for me while you are there, so it wouldn't be a complete lie. Sometimes rules have to be bent—at least the rules that keep people downtrodden.'

I wasn't sure if he was talking about me or Kiani.

Macca grabbed my hands. 'What do you say, Laffer? Will you be my young male travel companion?'

I could no longer contain my smile. 'We will clear Kiani's name once and for all and bring her back to her family where she belongs.'

∞

CHAPTER 25

It took some talking to convince my parents to let me go to Adelaide with Macca.

'Mr Tummerton wants me to learn how to make cordovan shoes from Mr Petersen. He's never done them, and it's what the well-to-do men are wanting these days.' It was what Mr Tummerton and I had agreed we'd tell everyone. 'And Macca is going to Adelaide tomorrow on his way to Port Lincoln. He can be my escort.'

'Where will you stay while in Adelaide?' Da asked.

'If I can't get a bed at the Temperance, I'm sure Sarah or Ellen will share theirs.'

Ma's gaze held mine longer than normal. 'And you say it is only an escort that you are wanting, Annese? We know that he's broken with Margaret.'

I feigned anger at her question, even though I'd expected it. 'Macca and I are not romantically involved, if that's what you mean. He would not harm me. He's a family friend, isn't he?'

Joseph didn't say a word while the decision was being made but drew me aside after. 'You don't fool me with the "family friend" comment, Annese. I saw you and Macca embrace.'

'That was nothing, Joseph. It was like giving you a hug. Like this.' I stood on my toes to embrace him, hoping my teasing would put him off track.

He pulled away. 'Promise me you'll not let this courting progress while you're away. I'm still concerned about his drinking.'

I didn't let on to Joseph but he'd raised my biggest concern. I'd tried to dispel it but it hovered like a dark cloud. I'd be relying on Macca to protect me and keep my identity a secret. If he started drinking while we were away, all our plans, such as they were, would fall apart. I knew he wouldn't deliberately hurt me, but I wanted more reassurance than that. I resolved to talk to him about it before we left Adelaide. If he couldn't reassure me, at least I had friends there to fall back on.

***

We left Echunga before dawn the next day, Macca riding a horse he'd bought the day before, with me on Bessy.

'Stable her near the Temperance. Bring her back when you return next week,' Mr Tummerton said, giving me a shilling. 'And here's your next week's wages in advance.' I took it from him and squeezed his hand.

'I can't tell you how much I appreciate your support.'

'Well, we can't all turn a blind eye to what is happening.'

Macca and I rode in comfortable silence. My initial surge of excited energy waned and I was soon lulled into a dreamlike state by the intoxicating smell of eucalypt and the muscular rhythm of Bessy beneath me. I could hear the low buzz of insects and felt as if the bush opened just enough to let us through and closed shut behind us when we had passed, as if we were being swept into another world unfettered by rules and expectations. A world where I was in control and at one with nature. I became again the child who'd lain for hours among the insects and lizards, unafraid and unaware. A world where I wasn't judged as strange or different. I became the person I'd been when Kiani and I had learned to care for each other; two girls from separate worlds who trusted one another.

Macca's voice jolted me back to the present. 'We'll stop here and give the horses a break.'

I was surprised we were already near Crafers, from where we would make our descent. As Macca placed the carefully wrapped saddlebag for Mrs Hale onto the ground and tethered the horses, I retrieved the bread and cheese Ma had packed in a hessian bag. She'd put in a knife too. The bread was already hardened but I was ravenous. Cutting a chunk of each for myself, I tested the blade as I passed the rest of the cheese to Macca and held up the knife.

'You can use this to cut my hair off.'

His eyes widened. 'Are you sure?'

I nodded. 'It'll give me away otherwise. With it short, I'll easily pass as a boy even without my cap. My shirt is baggy enough.' I noticed Macca's eyes go to my small breasts and a sharp thrill rushed through me before I pushed it aside.

'What about when we get back? How will you explain your short hair?'

'By that time, Kiani will be cleared and free to live as she pleases. Being judged because of my hair is a small price to pay. Besides, people already think me strange.'

'Who thinks you strange?'

I thought he was just being kind but I saw genuine surprise on his face. 'Margaret Mayfield, for one.'

Macca lowered his head. 'I know you think badly of her, Annese, but I still owe her a great debt.'

I nodded, unsure what to say.

'She has her own demons too, you know. We all do.'

'Demons she fights sleeping safely in her own home while, because of her false accusations, Kiani is held in a place without her family. Margaret has to pay for what she has done, Macca.'

'You don't have to convince me that she did the wrong thing, Annese. But haven't we all at times? I'm sure we can get Kiani's name cleared by showing the authorities your chess piece. We don't have to drag Margaret into it.'

'And the murder charge?' My voice trembled.

'From what I can gather, the police are not interested in following up on how the baby died.'

His casual account of the situation enraged me. 'Because he was only an Aboriginal baby you mean?' I flung the accusation at him, as tears of frustration filled my eyes, the image of the lifeless body of Kiani's baby before me. An urge to lash out rose from deep within. But at who?

He reached over and took the knife from me.

'I didn't say I agreed with their lack of action, but yes, because of that. I know how you feel, Annese. I feel it too. Every moment of every day. Ever …'

'Since Ngama?'

Tears filled his eyes. 'Yes, and that was only the beginning. But one thing I've learned, it's that getting angry doesn't help. It just led me to drinking until finally…'

I waited.

'Until finally I didn't want to be here anymore.'

I sensed it was my chance to ask about his drinking and the day Margaret saved him, but he leant over and cupped my face in his hands as if he were holding something precious, before kissing me on the cheek and loosening my hair. I looked into his eyes. All my reservations vanished. I trusted in him. I loved him.

'Come on, let's get this hair off, if that is truly what you want.'

The pain as the knife hacked at my hair turned my anger about Kiani and her baby into a formidable determination. Together, Macca and I would help Kiani clear her name. But I knew now it would be me alone who would bring Margaret to justice.

***

It was dark by the time we stabled the horses. Macca did all the talking and I kept my head lowered. We'd agreed that he would call me Laffer and, if asked, we'd say I was Joseph. I did look like him in this guise, although much shorter. But folk in Adelaide didn't know Joseph and using his name helped me find ways to act out the character I was pretending to be.

'What about my voice? It's not very masculine.'

Macca laughed. 'Well, you're pretty good at saying nothing. And if anyone asks—I'll say you're a late bloomer.'

Our plan worked. Both the stable hand and the publican who served us supper ignored me. I quickly began to experience how different it felt to be living as a boy. The men around us freely used coarse language and joked with Macca about his drinking, as if it were a source of great amusement; as if, amongst these men at least, he was admired for what I saw as his weakness. Although I didn't like the way they almost worshipped alcohol, there was an ease, an openness, about being amongst men as an equal that felt powerful.

'I'll have to find somewhere else to stay,' I said to Macca, finishing my stew and potatoes. 'I can't stay at the Temperance Hotel looking like this.'

'You can share my room if you want. It's what would be expected. Taking a separate room would attract unwanted attention.

'If that's alright with you,' he added, seeing my hesitation.

I nodded and reminded myself that he would never hurt me.

Our bellies full, we agreed to an early night. The room had a single bed only. Macca insisted I take it. I'd often dreamed of the day when I would share Macca's bed but this was not how I'd imagined it.

'I've spent plenty of nights sleeping on a floor. Now, you get yourself sorted. I've some business to see to.'

I knew he was allowing me the privacy of undressing alone, but I worried a little about what his business entailed. Would it involve alcohol? I'd been asleep for about an hour when he stumbled against the washstand as he tried to creep into the room. I could smell the rum. I rolled over and peered from beneath the covers.

'Sorry, Laffer,' he whispered, his voice unsteady as he took his boots off and settled, fully clothed, under the window where I'd put a rug and a pillow.

'Goodnight, my love,' he muttered, before his soft snores filled the room.

I smiled, wondering if he'd said 'my love' by mistake, his brain addled by the drink. I knew most people would think what I was doing was dangerous and morally wrong. But all I could feel was joy. Joy to be sharing his room. Joy to be actually doing something about clearing Kiani's name. But mostly joy at being my own person, free, at least for a time, of all the heavy restrictions and expectations of the daughter of a Quaker.

***

We left early to avoid the other patrons. Macca set off walking at such a pace I had to almost run to keep up. I was greatly relieved when we were offered a lift halfway to the port.

'Take the back, lad,' Macca said to me as he climbed up front. I hoisted myself up, once again rejoicing in the freedom and independence wearing trousers gave me. Macca turned to watch my efforts and winked as I clumsily righted myself, sitting on our luggage, legs apart as he'd told me to do. It felt strange after years of being trained to keep them together; only when shelling peas or doing other chores that needed a lap did girls sit in this way, even under multiple layers of clothes. Up front, the men chatted about the recent buildings along the route and a new type of football.

'It sounds like Gaelic football,' Macca said.

'So they say. A mixture of that and something the natives play called mangarook. The hybrid version started at some posh school in Melbourne—something for the toffs to do in the off-season from cricket.

But it spread to the poorer areas and a couple of us were brought over here to teach others how to play it. I stayed on.'

As they discussed the various rules and skills, I listened with admiration at how easily Macca spoke to a complete stranger and wondered if I would ever be as confident.

'Where are you and the lad off to?'

'Port Lincoln. I've got a meeting with one of the pastoralists over there.'

'And the young man?'

'He's the son of a friend, come to keep me company and learn a little about how other settlers are doing things.'

The lies flowed from him with such ease that I wondered, for a fleeting moment, if he would lie to me as easily if he needed to. But I quickly dismissed the doubt. I had to trust him.

It was much quieter at the port than it had been on my previous visit, and we quickly found our schooner, the *Emu*, loaded and ready to leave. Macca spoke to the captain and we were no sooner on board than we set off.

The nausea began as soon as we left the sheltered waters of the gulf. Even though the sea was relatively calm, the constancy of the rocking set my stomach churning. I couldn't stand and vomited twice, much to the amusement of the crew. Would they have reacted differently if they knew I was female? Would Macca have come to my aid? He did bring me some water but the thought of swallowing anything had me heaving again. Lying down only made it worse, so I spent the afternoon propped against a barrel of rum. When night eventually came, the nausea eased and I rolled out my blanket alongside Macca's. He'd claimed a space for us near the back of the boat away from the crew. I fell asleep quickly, exhausted by the day's events.

When I woke, my stomach had mostly settled and I spent the morning clinging to whatever held me upright, dodging the crew as they adjusted the mighty sails that drove us westward. Several pods of dolphins swam alongside us, and seabirds too seemed to want to know who we were. We disembarked at Boston Bay just after noon the following day. After Macca arranged to get the use of a cart and one horse, we went to the Lincoln, the only hotel in town, where he persuaded me to drink a glass of beer and lime with a mutton sandwich. It worked a treat on my rumbling stomach.

***

His meeting with Mr Partridge was scheduled for the late afternoon. We'd agreed I wouldn't go with him. The fewer people I had close contact with, the better.

'I'll just stay in the room.'

'No, best not. You'll attract attention. It's a fine day and no self-respecting boy would spend it holed up in a stuffy hotel room. I've heard there's great views from Winters Hill.' He pointed to the north at the only significant hill to be seen.

'It's a bit of a climb but you'll make it. My meeting is out that way so I can drop you off at the base and pick you up there in about four hours.'

The thought of being on my own in a strange vicinity filled me with dread. 'What am I supposed to do if I come across anyone?'

'Just nod hello. Keep to yourself and keep walking. Can you whistle? That would be normal for a lad who's enjoying his own company.'

I hadn't tried to whistle for years, although I'd been told I was quite good at it when I was young. Joseph whistled often at his work but it was frowned upon for a girl. Just another new thing for me to try out.

It only took us twenty minutes to reach the drop-off point.

'Take care, Laffer,' Macca said. 'See you here in four hours, or maybe less.'

As I watched him disappear around the bend, a ripple of excitement ran through me. Not since I was a child had I been so totally alone with nothing to do but enjoy my own company. I ran my hands through my short hair and my body trembled with anticipation. If I was standing there as Annese, dressed in crinoline, a restricting corset, and fashionable heels, I'd have good reason to be afraid but, as Joseph, the threats became possibilities; obstacles more like challenges.

The climb was harder than I'd imagined and my whistling soon turned to puffing. But with no one else around, I took my cap off, loosened my shirt, and rolled up my sleeves. The cooling breeze ran over me, arousing a feeling I'd long forgotten. A memory came to me of watching Kiani and her family, naked and laughing when a cool wind ended a hot summer's day. How I'd envied her then.

Did she ever laugh now? Was she allowed to run naked through the bush? My longing to see her again was overshadowed by the enormity of what Macca and I were hoping to achieve. We were two people with no power, no influence, going against a justice system and the Church. But Macca had the chess piece and I the letter. Surely truth would prevail.

The trees surrounding me were not much higher than a tall man, their slender trunks fanning out from the stony soil; the undergrowth dense and tangled. A narrow path led upwards, whether cleared by humans or animals, I knew not. Hundreds of bushes weighed down by white bottlebrush flowers dotted the area. Blackened yaccas pointed to heaven. Strange clumps of fibrous material, maybe roots or small dead branches, were propped against tree trunks forming a shelter for a small animal or perhaps a frightened child. Lining the path, skinny yellow finger-like stems of succulents reached towards me as if warning me to stay alert. All around, the disarray of dull green and grey, a clutter of the living and the dead, reminded me I was a visitor only to this place. I did not truly belong.

Close by, a sudden rustle in the litter of leaves spurred me to keep moving to where the bush thinned and the path widened.

Reaching the summit, I relaxed, as if I'd passed a test of both physical endurance and courage. I took in the beauty of the views over the harbour and outlying islands. I could see the *Emu* still lying in Boston

Bay and watched as several other boats came into the harbour. Sitting on an outcrop of granite, I wondered if this place, named Winters Hill by some white man, was also meaningful to the local Aboriginal people. I tried to imagine what they would have thought, watching from here as strange ships came into their world.

I lay back. My heartbeat slowed. I drew deeper breaths, each one filling my whole body now. The warmth of the smooth boulders entered me. A gentle breeze swirled around me. I felt as if I was being rocked. My eyes closed, heavy, weighted. My body moulded into the granite that held me. A slow chanting filled the air. I felt the movement of bodies circling me, feet stamping, kicking up dust. My heaviness dissolved. I floated out of myself and hovered above my body. The chanting turned to whispers; a calling without words from ancestors long passed, holders of wisdom. I felt Kiani alongside me.

The screech of a seagull pulled me back. I scrambled to my feet, the whispering now a profound silence. I was alone. The ground around me hard, unbroken.

And yet, I was covered with dust. Kiani.

CHAPTER 26

Brushing the dust from me, still puzzled as to where it had come from, I was surprised to see the sun was already almost halfway to the horizon. My strange out-of-body experience had lasted at least an hour and left me both exhausted and, somehow, rejuvenated. I began my descent.

Macca arrived at the junction soon after I did, a relieved smile on his face.

'I'm pleased to see you, lass. I shouldn't have let you go up there on your own. Mr Partridge told me that a small group of Aboriginal people, some with firearms, have been shooting cattle and threatening stockmen.'

'Well, I'm neither of those,' I said, climbing next to him. 'What else did he tell you about them?'

'He says they seem to know the bush as well as the local people, even though they're not from around here, and nobody can catch them. There's been a plea to Tolmer for more police to be sent over.'

I wanted to tell him about my dreamlike encounter and the calling from Kiani, but I couldn't find the words to describe my experience.

'So how did it go with Mr Partridge?'

'Good. He's taking me on. I'll be based in Adelaide and be responsible for getting his stock from Port Adelaide to the market where I'll negotiate the best price.

I worked hard to hide my disappointment that he would not be living in Echunga. 'I'm happy for you, Macca. Is it good money?'

'I'll get a wage and a percentage of the profit. He says I've got the right attitude to the work and should make more than I am now. It'll be a relief to finally leave the police work behind me.'

I began to imagine us both living in Adelaide. Perhaps I could get work with Mr Petersen again and, when we were able to marry, we could rent our own cottage. It was a while before I put my own plans aside and came back to thinking about what else he'd said.

'Do you believe what Mr Partridge said about the armed natives?'

'Yes, sadly I do. It was only a matter of time before they started using our weapons against us. What did surprise me was that he says the leader is a woman, a half-caste as he called her. They call her the Amazon, after another woman doing the same in van Diemen's Land. He said her father is an ex-convict who'd been on Flinders Island off van Diemen's Land. They say it was him who taught her and her brother how to use a gun. I wonder if it is the same woman I met when she was a child on Thistle Island. You knew her too didn't you?'

I recalled my encounter with Tottengarr at the Mayfields'. The idea of her using a gun was not at odds with what I'd seen of her.

'The Mayfields had a part-Aboriginal girl working there for a while. She had an Irish father and spoke English. She said she'd been taken from her family, along with her brother, and left alone at Cape Jarvis. She asked me where *kurra murka* was because she wanted to get back there to her parents. So why would she be over here?'

Macca shrugged. 'There's been so much displacement of the Aboriginal people I couldn't say for sure.'

'She was not at all shy with Margaret and even talked back to her. The Mayfields sent her up to the school in Adelaide. Maybe the authorities sent her to Port Lincoln like they did Kiani.'

We'd reach a section of the track that was well-worn and on limestone. Macca gave the horses a hurry on.

'Anyway,' he said, 'I'm glad you're safe, Laffer. It seems there's lots of conflict happening over here, although Partridge says the Aboriginal people at Poonindie are law-abiding. He seems to think Hale is doing a good job of keeping them, and everyone else, safe.'

'Did you tell him about Kiani?'

'No. Best keep that to ourselves.'

Pulling up in front of the Lincoln Hotel, I jumped to the ground.

'I'll return the cart and then go for a drink,' Macca said. 'You can come if you want but it might be better for you to go to the room now. I'll get them to send up dinner to you.'

I considered going with him to make sure he only had a couple of drinks, but keeping up my cover in the company of a number of men would be difficult. Anyway, I needed to get my thoughts around the enormity of what we were about to do the following day. We hadn't really made any specific plans and, now we were so close, I realised I had no idea what we were going to say.

If Macca was right, and the charge of murder had never been taken seriously, maybe all we needed to do was get Kiani to make a statement that we could sign. Surely the Hales would be happy to let her go once they saw our chess piece? But what if they wanted more proof? Was I ready to go against Macca's wishes and show them the letter?

Exhausted and ravenous from the day's activities, I ate my meal of stew with relish. Macca was still not back when, with a full stomach, fatigue overtook me. This room had two beds so I took the one furthest from the door. As the voices coming from the bar got louder, I tried to reassure myself that Macca was only drinking a couple.

I fell into a restless sleep, waking when I heard him knock on the locked door.

'I canna find my key, Annese. Let me in, lassie.'

I rushed to the door and pulled him in, looking up the corridor in fear he'd been heard saying my name. It was empty. I locked the door behind us.

'You're a good lass, Annese. Too good for me, that's for sure.' His words slid from him in a slur as he wobbled, trying to take off his boots.

He was drunk. Steaming drunk. My disappointment in him turned to anger. How dare he do this to me? He knew how much I was relying on him for my very safety and, right then, I wouldn't trust him to look after a puppy.

'Sorry. Sorry, Annese.' He slapped his hand onto my shoulder, his head wobbling.

I pushed his hand away.

'Quite right,' he said, making a feeble attempt to straighten up. 'You are much too good for me. Find someone else, Annese.'

An empty pain filled me as I watched him, devoid of dignity; a caricature of the man I loved and wanted. Anger and sadness swirled within me. I wanted to hit him. I wanted to hug him.

'Get to bed, Macca. Sleep it off. And stop calling me Annese. I'm Laffer.'

He fell onto his bed, his legs hanging over the edge. I stood looking at him, a war of feelings pulling at me. The man whom I'd admired since I was a child, reduced to a helpless mess. My stomach gripped and despair rose within me.

Loud voices outside our door, men joking as they went to their beds, reminded me of the precariousness of my situation. Along with the painful disappointment was a renewed fear for my safety. Macca was all that stood between me and exposure. Or something worse. Now, he lay unconscious. Incapable.

I was on my own.

The smell of stale rum and tobacco filled the room, stifling me. I wedged a chair under the doorknob, heaved Macca's legs onto the bed, and began taking his boots off. He pushed me away.

'Leave me, I'm no good.' His words came out like a muddy stream.

Waiting until I heard his grunting snores, I took his other boot off before curling up under my covers. I watched as his face relaxed into a quiet sleep and wondered what would make a man, a good man, treat himself with such contempt.

***

Macca was up before I woke. As he washed and shaved, he showed no signs of suffering from his drinking and was softly whistling as he went about his ablutions. Was it possible he had no idea of his actions and what they meant to me?

Seeing me awake he smiled. 'Morning, Laffer. Just give me a minute and I'll leave you the room to yourself. Meet me in the dining room. I've paid for breakfast for us both.'

Relief flooded through me like an incoming tide. The old Macca, the real Macca, was back. My heart turned and the desperation of my love for him drove away my fears. I'd panicked, overreacted, my sheltered upbringing at fault. Ellen once told me that all men needed to drink to excess sometimes. It was the only way they released their emotions, she'd said.

The dining room was crowded with men. A few glanced at me as I sought out Macca. He signalled for a plate of eggs and bread to be brought to me as I poured tea from the large pot on the table.

'You were in fine form last night, Macca,' one of the men sitting opposite us said, laughing. 'Good thing that fiancée of yours wasn't here to see.' The men within earshot all laughed, as if at some private joke.

I glanced at Macca but he smiled and shook his head, avoiding eye contact.

'She'd have a man's balls for breakfast, I reckon.' The table exploded with laughter. Macca's fist clenched, although he continued smiling.

'You'd better hope that baby is yours, Macca. Don't want to be raising another man's bastard.'

I waited for Macca to set the record straight; to point out they'd been taken in by malicious gossip. I waited for him to tell them that the engagement was off. But he kept his silence.

Even though I hated Margaret Mayfield in a way I'd never hated anyone else in my life, hearing these men talking about her like this brought me so close to tears. I pretended to have a coughing fit, excused myself from the table, and went outside.

How could men talk like that, so full of disdain? I thought men were supposed to respect women. I thought men protected women. But worse, how could Macca sit there and let this happen? From below the window, I heard the crude remarks continue until finally, Macca responded.

'That's enough, gentlemen.' His raised voice stopped their banter. 'If you must know, Miss Mayfield and I have parted ways. I don't know what you're saying about a baby but whatever you've heard is wrong. Margaret Mayfield is a woman of the highest standards.'

The room stayed quiet for minutes before a rumble of conversation resumed. Despite my hunger, I couldn't bear to go back inside so I was pleased when Macca joined me with a sandwich of my eggs and bread. I ate it in silence, my mind too full of all that had happened for me to talk. Macca, too, was silent in his anger.

After I finished my food, we walked to the stables where a man was harnessing a horse to a two-person buggy.

'You stay here, Laffer. I'll collect our luggage and Mrs Hales's saddlebag.'

'Have it back by the day after tomorrow,' the stableman said to me, adjusting one of the straps. 'Where is it you're going?'

'Poonindie.' My voice came out crackly. I hadn't spoken all morning.

He looked up, curious. 'What's your business there?'

My mind raced. 'Collecting one of the natives. An Adelaide gentleman and his wife need a domestic.' Macca and I had at one time discussed this as a potential scenario if we were questioned.

He seemed to be examining me. 'Laffer is it you said? I knew Laffers once. Came out with them on the *Eden* in 1838.'

My heart jumped. It was the ship we'd come out on.

'Quakers, if I recall. Good people.'

He continued to watch me as I grappled for what to say.

'That's right,' Macca said, coming up behind me. 'Young Laffer here is the eldest son of that very family. I'm a family friend. Come along lad, we need to get going if we're to be back on time.'

'Give my regards to Mr and Mrs Hale. They're doing a fine job of keeping that lot there and making them civilised. They come into town to church sometimes. Well behaved, clean and polite. More than I can say of the local natives. There's killings every day round here, one way or another.'

'Killings?' The word escaped from me.

'Aye. Sheep and cattle mostly. There's a small mob have got hold of a gun and know how to use it. One of them a woman, some say. We've extra police arriving soon to see to them. The sooner they're caught and strung up the better.'

My shock must have shown on my face.

'I know you Quakers are against it, but I say an eye for an eye. That's what the Bible teaches,' the man said as he walked away.

I looked to Macca to protest but he was busying himself with the horse, his jaw set tight.

'Be back by noon tomorrow. No later,' the man called over his shoulder.

***

We were soon climbing out of the bay area. I caught a glimpse of the *Emu* being loaded at the harbour, readying for departure. We passed the point where Macca had dropped me the day before. The road narrowed and we became surrounded by thick bushland. Other than the horses clopping and the rattle of our cart, we travelled in silence; the final leg of our journey to find Kiani. There was no turning back now.

I looked at the map Macca had borrowed from the publican. The only towns marked were Port Lincoln and Tumby, to the north-east.

'How far is it to Poonindie?' I asked.

'Not far.'

Macca was less cheery than he'd been earlier and I could see his hands shook a little.

'Who are we going to say wants Kiani as a domestic?'

Macca shrugged.

'I think it should be the Mayfields,' I continued. 'They're wealthy enough and, even if the Hales know them, they won't know that you're not engaged to Margaret anymore. By the time they find out we're lying, we'll be long gone.'

Macca turned to me and laughed, a tired bitter laugh. 'Yes, let's do just that.' I wondered if the earlier goading by the men had taken a toll on his commitment to what we were doing. I knew it was not a good time but I decided to broach the subject of the letter anyway.

'If that doesn't convince them, we may have to show them the letter. We can say that Maragret feels guilty now and asked you to come to remedy the situation.'

His jaw tightened. 'I don't think we'll need the letter, Annese. It shows Margaret in a bad light. I don't want that. Anyway, it was written a long time ago. All I have to do is show them your chess piece. That will prove Kiani's innocence.'

'Have you still got feelings for Margaret?'

'Feelings, yes. Do I love her? No.'

'Why were those men so awful about her? Do they know her?'

'One thing you'll learn one day Annese, is that men, many of them anyway, are not very respectful of women. Contemptuous, in fact. Women don't understand that, because they don't normally hear it. They say horrible things when women aren't around. Going about as a boy, you're getting a peek into another world.'

'But Da and Joseph…?'

'Your Da's not the norm. He's one of a kind and Joseph is following him, from what I can see. It's why I admire them. And your Ma, of course.'

'And you. Are you different from most men?'

The image of him lying helpless and degraded on his bed flashed before me, and with it the memory of my fear and vulnerability.

'Me. Well, I don't talk about women in that way but, I'm as bad as any man alive. That's why I left Margaret. She's too good for me.'

His words, the same as he'd said to me in his drunken stupor the night before, hit me like a slap.

'And me. Am I too good for you?'

He turned to me. 'Annese, you are far and away too good for me. You always will be.'

We continued in silence as the track narrowed and we lost sight of the coast. I couldn't hold my silence any longer.

'Isn't it me who should decide if you are good enough for me?'

He scoffed but his smile this time was warm. 'Well then, go ahead. Am I?'

It was my opportunity. 'It's just your drinking, Macca. I don't like seeing you drunk. I want to spend my life with you, the real Macca. Give up the drinking and we can be as we should be.'

'You're right, it is the drink. I have tried, you know, and been clear of it for months at a time. You don't understand how hard it is and why would you?'

It was some time before he spoke again. 'You will find someone one day who will give you what you need. I'll never be the man you deserve.'

If I could have turned back then, I would have. I wanted to run until my lungs burst to get away from the pain of his words. But instead, I sat silent and still, allowing the agony to fill me. I closed my eyes like I did at the Meetings and listened for God's words.

They didn't come. I tried to think of Kiani and her misery but even her pain could not tear me from my own. Was my commitment to her just a way to be with Macca? If I could not be with him forever, should I even be here?

My swirling self-doubt was interrupted when Macca pulled the cart to a stop as an emu, the largest I'd ever seen, appeared in front of us.

Its feathers quivered with anticipation as it stared at me. Challenging me to answer my own questions. I stared back, knowing the answers were right before me.

As quickly as it had appeared it left, rocking its spindly legs into action, crashing into the bush and out of sight. Macca flicked the reins and we went over a small rise.

'Poonindie,' Macca said pointing into the far distance.

'Poonindie,' I repeated. I'm not sure what I'd expected but I was taken back by the extent of the community and the semblance of organisation. Unlike in Port Lincoln where people came and went and our presence was easily explained away, we were about to come under close scrutiny. Our venture was reaching its most critical and vulnerable stage. If we weren't successful, Kiani's chance to prove her innocence would be lost.

I had to keep going for, in truth, I had no other option. I knew too I had to say the words that hounded me.

'I love you, Macca. It is for you to decide between me and the alcohol.'

He turned and looked deep into my eyes as if searching for an answer. I felt the power shift between us. 'But for now, we must find Kiani, together,' I continued. 'I just ask that you stay sober, at least until she is safe.'

'On that, we can agree,' Macca said flicking the horse into a trot.

***

As we drew closer, I could make out two large buildings some distance from a circle of small ones, each enclosed by its own fence. Alongside this circle of cottages was a walled garden. A group of Aboriginal women wearing white people's clothing stood up from their labours as we neared. I looked into their faces but did not recognise any as Kiani.

Mrs Hale came to greet us. So relieved was I to see her, I raised my hand to wave as if to a friend, before pulling it back.

'Perhaps best if I do all the talking,' Macca said quietly as she approached.

'Good morning. We're not expecting visitors. Are you lost?' Her words were kind but distrustful.

'If this is Poonindie, then we're not lost. We've come to deliver a saddlebag from Mr Tummerton and to collect a girl called Kitty for Mr Mayfield.'

Mrs Hale looked from him to me and back again. 'This is highly unusual, Mr...?'

'Macleod. Malcolm Macleod. And this is Joseph Laffer.'

'Well, Mr Macleod, I am expecting the saddlebag but you'd better speak to my husband about the other matter. We do have a Kitty here but we know nothing of a request from Mr Mayfield. Is that the gentleman from the Mount Barker region?'

As she spoke, she gazed at me. I turned away pretending to be surveying the surrounds. 'Joseph Laffer, you say. I met a Miss Laffer once. Very briefly.'

I knew that she would soon remember that I, as Annese, had also been looking for Kiani.

'My sister, Mrs Hale. It was her who recommended Kitty to the Mayfields.'

She was staring at me now. 'You're very like your sister, Joseph.'

I looked away and shrugged.

'Come then,' she said. 'Mr Hale is at the school.'

We followed her as she strode towards one of the larger buildings and waited outside until she came out with her husband. He looked us over carefully as she introduced us.

'Mathew, this is Malcolm Macleod and Joseph Laffer.'

Mr Hale first shook Macca's hand then extended his hand to me. I stumbled and timidly put my hand forward. Macca laughed. 'Joseph is a Quaker and has not been much among others.' The explanation seemed to satisfy the curious looks on the Hales's faces.

'They've come to collect Kitty,' Mrs Hale said. 'They say she's been requested as a domestic by a Mr Robert Mayfield. Have we been notified?'

'Mr Robert Mayfield, you say? Of Mount Barker?'

'The same,' Macca replied. 'I am betrothed to Margaret, his daughter.' Once again, I noticed how easily the lies rolled from him. 'He sent us to ask after her welfare and to request that she be released into our care.'

Mr Hale looked at his wife and sighed. 'Well if it were up to us, we would be glad for her to have gainful employment. She is one of our star pupils. But she has a court matter outstanding. We would need to hear from the Aboriginal Protector or even the police first.'

My hopes plummeted but Macca reached into his pocket. 'That is precisely why it is I who has been sent. I am to be family of the Mayfields and I'm a sworn constable. I will accompany her to see the Protector to get her clearance, of course.' In his hand was the badge that he wore on the goldfields. Mr Hale looked from the badge to Macca.

'Macleod, you say. The same name as…'

Just as I saw a glimmer of recollection, a familiar voice pierced the air. 'Macca. Annese.'

CHAPTER 27

Kiani walked quickly towards us. Her grey dress brushed the ground, its voluminous sleeves gathered at the wrist ballooning out from her shoulders, giving the false impression that she had a rounded physique. Around her neck, a large ruffled collar almost hid her smile.

Macca held up his hand in greeting and raised his voice. 'It's not Annese, Kitty. It's her brother, Joseph. You remember Joseph.'

Kiani was at our side now. I'd been haunted for so long by her desperate look onboard the *Petrel*, to see her smiling now brought me such joy I almost gave myself away. I longed to embrace her but instead, I doffed my cap.

She looked from me to Macca and back again. I could tell she was not fooled and was quick to understand our situation. 'Yes. Joseph. Not Annese.'

'It seems you are both well known to her, Mr Macleod,' Mrs Hale said, a hesitancy in her voice.

'We both met Kitty—Kiani as she was then—at Echunga. It is where her family lived before they were forced to move. She and Annese, Joseph's sister, played together as children.'

Kiani stepped closer to us. 'You take me back to Country. Back to family. My community.' It was not a question but a demand.

Mr Hale stepped forward. 'Go back to work, Kitty. I will come and see you once we've finished talking.'

Kitty obeyed but not before catching my eye. 'Go back. Catch fish together.'

'Come,' Mr Hale said, ushering us towards the larger of the two stone cottages. 'We can discuss this over a cup of tea and scones.' As we walked, he took great pride in pointing out the fenced garden.

'The women are doing a wonderful job digging the soil and planting. We're almost self-sufficient for vegetables. The men built the fence to keep out native animals, under instructions from me of course. But the kangaroos simply jump over it and we've had to shoot several already.'

'Charlie, a newcomer, built the fence,' Mrs Hale said. 'This one, Tottie, is his sister,' she said, nodding towards a tall Aboriginal woman who'd been dusting in the room as we entered. Her hair was cut short and she put on her bonnet but kept her eyes down, leaving the room in a hurry.

'We're keeping her close by,' Mrs Hale said in a lowered voice. 'She and Charlie disappear occasionally and we think…'

'Thank you, Sabina,' Mr Hale interrupted. 'Our guests don't want to hear all that. Now, what is it Mr Mayfield needs? If it is a domestic, there are many here to choose from.'

'He did ask for Kitty. Maybe because his home is on her land.' I could tell from the edginess in Macca's voice that he did not like Mr Hale.

Mr Hale raised his eyebrows. 'That's as may be, but as I said, Kitty has court issues to be resolved. And although she is one of our best, she's become restless of late. She may not be appropriate. She has…'

Mrs Hale picked up the conversation. 'Charlie and his sister just turned up here one day. Kitty is very attached to his sister and now we believe Charlie and Kitty have been together.'

It had not occurred to me that Kiani would have a new family. Our plans had only been for her. I tried to catch Macca's eye, but he didn't take his attention off Mr Hale who'd moved away from us a little and stood with his hands behind his back. I sensed that he and his wife had disagreed about what to do about Kitty and Charlie.

'We encourage the women to marry men from within our Poonindie people,' Mrs Hale continued without looking at Mr Hale, 'although we leave it to them to choose, of course. Kitty and Charlie are well matched although he is half-caste. He has an Aboriginal mother and an Irish father. He has perfect English, although he chooses not to use it most of the time. Mathew is trying to sort out with the Protector what to do about it all. Would there be work for Charlie too with the Mayfields?' Mrs Hale asked. 'We can't split them, Mathew.'

'I am sure there would be,' I said. All eyes turned to me and I feared that my voice was too high and tried to lower it. 'They asked my Da just last week if he wanted to leave the goldfields to help in the dairy. They've taken on more cows and need milkers to supply the diggers. He said they're desperate for workers.'

I saw a brief smile on Macca's face before he regained his formal expression.

'Well that would be fortunate,' Mr Hale said. 'Other than occasionally disappearing, Charlie is as good a dairy man as we have here. So your father works for Mr Mayfield, Joseph?"

I could feel Mrs Hale looking at me and felt so intimidated by her attention that I couldn't answer. Macca jumped in.

'Laffer. We call Joseph, Laffer. He rarely uses his Christian name nowadays.'

'Yes, he does,' I said recovering. 'There and on the local gold site.'

When the tall Aboriginal woman brought in a tray of tea and scones, Mrs Hale helped her arrange them on a table. It was only when she was about to leave that I fully saw her face.

'Tottengarr?' Her name leapt from me.

She scowled at me. 'No. Tottie now. Not Tottengarr.' She left the room in a hurry again. I watched through the window as she ran to the huts.

'Do you know Tottie, too?' Mrs Hale asked me quietly, as Mr Hale continued talking to Macca.

'No, I must have been mistaken,' I muttered, but Mrs Hale continued to scrutinise me.

'We don't use their native names,' Mr Hale was explaining to Macca. 'If they are to gain employment and reach a state of civilisation, and that is the purpose of Poonindie, they need to have Christianised names. Their own are too hard for the potential employers to remember.'

He motioned for us all to take a seat. 'Returning to the question at hand. I am not sure of all the details of the police order but, apparently, Kitty was caught stealing sugar and has subsequently been identified regarding an old crime. That one was much more serious. She apparently broke into a settler's home and stole valuables. She was found with one of them. No other valuables were found.'

It was clear they were unaware of who had laid the accusation.

'She insisted that the valuable piece was hers,' Mrs Hale said, 'and would not part with it. It was while the police were trying to take it off her that she ran and the horrible event with her baby occurred.' She turned to me. 'I am sure your sister mentioned that to you, Joseph. She was very concerned for Kitty and came to find her at Port Adelaide on the day we left.'

I had to respond but was fearful that I'd become emotional. I drew in a deep breath and tried to mimic Joseph. 'All I know is that my sister said Kitty told her the baby had been swept from her arms and drowned.' I could hear my voice wobble and once again Mrs Hale's eyes were fixed on me.

To my great relief, Macca took up the story. 'Yes, we are aware of the accusation that she'd deliberately drowned the child, but at this stage that charge is not being pursued.' He spoke with authority. Mrs Hale seemed to readily accept his information but her husband remained wary.

'That gives us great relief,' Mrs Hale said, 'for we cannot reconcile the notion that Kitty would do such a horrible thing. She mourned her baby for weeks, in her traditional way, unable to speak for quite some time.'

I couldn't stop my eyes from tearing up as the horrid memory of Kitty's desperate pleas came back to me.

'Your sister,' Mrs Hale said with emphasis, 'would have told you of that, Joseph.' I met her gaze and now knew with certainty that she'd guessed my true identity.

'Yes, she wanted to come herself but our father would not allow her.'

'Yes. I see your… her dilemma. As a girl, she could not come.'

I nodded. 'That's correct. She could not come, as a girl.'

Macca stood, commanding the attention to be drawn from me. 'Mr Hale, there was another reason I was chosen for this particular escort. I have with me evidence that Kitty is innocent of the theft.'

'Evidence? What is the evidence, Mr Macleod?' Mr Hale asked.

Macca took the chess piece from his bag. 'I brought this with me from Scotland and another one very similar. I gave this one to Annese Laffer and the other to Kiani. They are ivory chess pieces.'

Mr Hale took the chess piece from Macca and turned it over several times, before handing it to his wife.

'Friend Mayfield is a good Quaker,' Macca continued. 'He asked that I take Kitty to Adelaide where we will see justice done and then bring her to Echunga when she is cleared.'

Mr Hale now looked at Macca with intense suspicion. 'From memory, this chess piece, as you call it, fits the description of what they found on Kitty at the time. It's very valuable, I would think. Ivory you say? How is it that you came by these antiquities, Mr Macleod? I assume you are not a wealthy man.'

I saw a twitch at the corner of Macca's mouth and knew that the barely hidden accusation of theft had not gone unnoticed by him. He raised his voice, speaking not with his usual Scottish accent but one just slightly more akin to the English tone of the Hales.

'My mother gave it to me and another to my brother when we went to sea.' Mrs Hale was about to pass the chess piece back to Macca when

Mr Hale reached over and took it from her. He turned it over several times before looking up.

'And was your mother a wealthy woman?' Mr Hale asked, his question obviously mocking Macca. Macca stiffened and I saw his fist clench.

'Macca's Ma found them in a sandhill,' I blurted. 'They belonged to her and then to Macca. He gave one to me and another to Kiani!'

Mrs Hale drew in a sharp breath. I realised my mistake. 'To my sister, that is.'

'A sandhill! What nonsense.' Mr Hale stood, unaware of my mistake but clearly angered now by Macca's seemingly unbelievable story. 'I have little confidence in you or your claim, Mr Macleod.'

Mrs Hale came to my side as he continued to raise his voice, his face red with indignation.

'I seem to recall now that you are a man with a reputation as a hard drinker,' Mr Hale continued, striding further from Macca, the chess piece firmly in his grasp. 'If you'd ever owned anything so valuable, I imagine it would have been sold long ago.'

The two men stood face to face now. Macca's voice remained dangerously calm. 'You are right to say I've had my demons. That is precisely why I gave my treasures away. But that is all in the past. If you are unwilling to believe me, then at least give the chess piece back to Laffer, for his sister. In the meantime, we will collect Kiani as arranged.'

'I will give it back when you prove to me that it is yours. And as for taking Kitty with you, I will approve nothing of the sort until I have received advice directly from the Protector.'

'You have no right to keep it.' Macca grabbed hold of his forearm; his other fist clenched. I gasped, terrified of what Macca might do. I'd never seen him so angry.

Mrs Hale came between them, speaking in a voice calm and commanding. 'We must settle this reasonably, gentlemen. I will not have you setting a bad example for our population. Put the item in a safe

place, Mathew. Mr Macleod, go and wait by the horses please. Ann…
Joseph, you can come with me.'

Macca turned to me and I nodded. He pushed past Mr Hale as he left, mumbling 'pompous English'. Placing a guiding hand on my shoulder, Mrs Hale escorted me to the kitchen. I knew Joseph would have shaken her off, but my heart was racing and I felt nothing but kindness from her, a kindness I was desperately needing. Glancing over my shoulder, I saw Mr Hale open a drawer in the dining room sideboard.

***

The kitchen was empty. Mrs Hale closed the door behind us and took my hands.

'I know it is you, Annese. Why are you travelling as a boy? Are you safe with this Mr Macleod?'

Her warmth eroded my defences. Was I safe? Here in Mrs Hale's kitchen, with its familiar smells of baked bread and cinnamon, I yearned only for my mother's arms and my father's reassuring voice. I was about to tell her everything, when Kiani burst into the room, Tottengarr at her side.

'What is the meaning of this?' Mrs Hale snapped.

Tottengarr spoke for them, her English as clear as any, for it was, as I now remembered, one of the languages she'd spoken from birth.

'Mr Macca is a good man. He helps our people. This one,' she said, pointing at me, 'knows the truth.'

'We leave with them,' Kiani said. 'You must let us go, Mrs Hale. Me and Charlie must go back to my family. I must see where they put my baby. That Margaret Mayfield, she is no good.'

'She is a liar,' Tottengarr joined in. 'She said Kiani let her baby go on purpose. It was an accident, Mrs Hale.'

Mrs Hale frowned, trying to understand. 'What has Margaret Mayfield got to do with your charges? I thought it was her family who want a domestic and asked for Kitty?'

Through the window, I could see Macca pacing up and down like a tormented animal. I made my decision and gave her the letter, watching as she read it.

'And you are sure Annese that this was written by Margaret Mayfield?'

I looked from her to Kiani. My resolve to protect Margaret dissolved. I wanted the truth to be told. I wanted Margaret's lies to be exposed.

'Yes. It was in Margaret's notebook. It proves Kiani is innocent of the thefts. It proves Margaret's true character.'

Mrs Hale reread the letter and shook her head. 'And the baby? What has Miss Mayfield to do with Kitty's baby?'

'It was her who accused Kiani of murder. I heard the policemen talking about her the day the baby drowned.'

She turned from us. We waited for her answer, three women at her mercy.

Folding the letter, she gave it back to me. 'I can see you all believe in what you are saying, but the letter is hardly evidence unless Miss Mayfield admits that she wrote it. At the moment, it is just an anonymous letter. For all I know, you could have written it yourself, Annese.'

My heart sank and I saw Kiani's hopeful eyes turn again to despair.

'There is too much at stake for me to decide,' Mrs Hale continued. 'I must seek my husband's guidance. We will have an answer for you all tomorrow. Kitty and Tottie, go back to your huts and stay there. Annese, you will stay with us tonight. Mr Macleod can remain until the morning. He can sleep in the stable.'

Kiani and Tottengarr looked at me as they left the room, Kiani with sadness, Tottengarr with a challenging fierceness. Was I strong enough to stand with them? I remembered the haunting whispers I'd heard on Winters Hill.

I waited until they'd left before I spoke again. 'Mrs Hale, please do not tell Mr Hale I am not Joseph. My family must not know until I can explain my actions to them.'

She hesitated before answering. 'Do you feel safe with this Mr Macleod, Annese?

'Yes,' I answered. 'I am safe with him.' I prayed that it was true. 'I have known him all my life. He is a good friend of my family. He is trying to do the right thing for Kiani. For her people.'

She frowned as if struggling to understand all that had happened. 'I can see that, Annese. But I have learned the hard way that it is not always possible. Mr Macleod will need to learn ways to help that don't involve deceit.'

I understood her but knew that for Macca there was no safe way. But this was not what Mrs Hale needed to hear. 'You are right. I will go and talk to him now. I can calm him down.'

She nodded. I was about to go outside when I turned to her. 'And Mrs Hale…?'

She knew what I was asking. 'Yes, you are Joseph. Go to speak to Macleod before I change my mind.'

***

I walked towards the huts where Macca sat amongst a large gathering sitting in the dirt silently, contemplative, reminding me of the Quaker Meetings. A power radiated from them, a power I neither knew nor understood. I hung back until Macca noticed me and came to where I stood.

'Mrs Hale saw through my disguise,' I rushed to tell him. 'I've shown her the letter. She said it's not real evidence. I'm sorry, Macca.'

He shook his head and sighed. 'It's of no matter now, Annese. Our troubles have gone beyond that. Don't you see, they pretend to be on Kiani's side but in the end, they will always do what the Protector says. Kiani and I are leaving tonight. Charlie and Tottengarr will come too. Kiani will only be safe once she is away from all of them.'

'But we have only two horses. And how will we pay for all their fares?'

He laid his hands gently on my shoulders. 'Not you, Annese, just me. You must stay here. We will walk and find Charlie and Tottengarr's family. It is too far and too dangerous for you. The Hales will look after you. They'll get you back to Adelaide. Mr Hale will not be at all surprised that I've abandoned you. He already thinks me a low-class scoundrel.'

I heard the bitterness in his voice and saw again the anger in his eyes.

'No,' I said, brushing his hands from me. 'I'm coming with you.'

He shook his head. 'You have done your part. It's over for you. Leave it to me now.'

Done my part? Did he still not know the other reason I was with him?

'No, I am coming too. I love you, Macca. I want to stay with you, always.' The words flowed from me now like an old river, calm and determined. I had his promise to not drink. I had to trust that.

He closed his eyes and, after what seemed like a lifetime, threw back his head and laughed. It was the laugh of the old Macca. 'I love you too, Annese Laffer. I've fought hard against it for I fear I will only bring you harm. But love you I do.'

We embraced with our eyes only, knowing we were being watched.

'So I can come with you?'

He swallowed his smile and shook his head. 'It will be a very tough walk. There are no tracks where we are going and there'll be no going back.'

'I'm sure I can do it. I need to be with you.'

'Have you truly thought this through? Your family might disown you. The other Quakers too.'

'My family will understand as long as you do the right thing by me, Macca. That means no more drinking. You have to promise me.'

He closed his eyes and drew a deep breath. 'I promise,' he said. 'As soon as we get back to Echunga, I'll ask your father for your hand. We will be husband and wife.'

As if they heard our vows, the women began tapping their sticks and chanting. Their sounds swirled around us, rising from the ground into the air, wrapping us in a sacred veil. I felt my heart lift, blood coursing through me. In that moment we were married, in spirit if not in law.

CHAPTER 28

'We will leave at midnight,' Macca said, not even facing me now so that it looked as if we were both listening to the women chanting. 'North to Tumby. It's a full moon and Tottengarr and Charlie know a way without using the road.'

'I'll sneak out just before twelve. If either of the Hales wakes up, I'll say I'm going outside to the lavvy. But what about our chess piece?'

'We'll have to leave it behind.'

'But it's our evidence. That and the letter. We have to clear Kiani's name.'

Macca shook his head. 'Kiani will have to stay away from Adelaide for a while and avoid everybody in authority. We must take her to live with Charlie and Tottengarr's family. That is their custom.'

'And the chess piece?'

He shrugged. 'It's yours and it may be valuable. Hale had no right to accuse me of theft. If you think you can get it, then do so.'

I squeezed his hand and returned to the house, his declaration of love for me overshadowing any trepidation I'd previously felt. Whatever the future held for me, I could face it if we were together.

Mrs Hale greeted me at the door. As I'd expected, she'd been watching. I pushed my joy away, feigning sadness. She showed me to the guest room. 'I've decided to keep your secret, Annese. I told my husband you're feeling poorly. Kiani and her people need friends like you and Mr Macleod. People who will take risks to change the way they're treated.'

'Does your husband not agree?'

She sighed as if this was a question she too needed answering. 'He does in principle. But he has obligations to the Bishop and the Protector. *His* hands are tied but mine are not. I pray to the good Lord,' she said, glancing at the heavens, 'that I don't live to regret this decision.'

Guilt stabbed at me as I said goodnight to her. She'd been kind and it would have been so much easier for me to become the Annese she wanted me to be. I could have sunk into a deep, trouble-free sleep, knowing I would soon be safe with my family. But I knew too that if I walked away from the man I loved, and betrayed the trust of Kiani, my choice would haunt me for the rest of my life.

I waited until the moon rose above the tree line before pulling on my trousers. The guest room was at the back of the house, giving me easy access to the yard through a back door. But first I had to retrieve the chess piece.

Creeping past the dining table, my boots slung over my shoulder, I located the drawer I'd seen Mr Hale open. It stayed firmly shut. Locked. Looking around for an implement I could use to pry it open, I noticed a pegboard holding half a dozen keys. Only one of them was small enough for the drawer. Hearing a soft groan from the adjacent bedroom, I froze until I again heard snoring. I slipped the key into the drawer, my heart pounding as the lock released. Using both hands, I eased it open. Shadows prevented me from seeing clearly but I soon felt the solid coolness of the chess piece, the ancient grooves of its carvings whispering to me through the centuries. *Protect me and I will in turn protect you.* A shiver ran through me. Could the past break through time? Do our ancestors reach out and guide us?

With no time to make sense of what had just happened, I slipped the chess piece into my bag, checking as I did that the letter was still there. Locking the drawer and replacing the key, I crept from the room.

I knew it wasn't theft but still, I could not help but feel deceitful. I said a silent prayer that Mrs Hale not be punished because of my action.

Outside, the crisp night air filled me with anticipation of what was to come. I could hear a murmur of voices from the huts as I approached. Macca was waiting, his saddlebag by his side. Kiani, Charlie, and Tottengarr wore only the barest coverings. Each carried a reed bag and Charlie carried three spears of different sizes. Tottengarr's bag was larger than the others, similar to ones I'd seen the Echunga men carrying when they went hunting.

I was about to put my boots on when Kiani tapped me on the shoulder and shook her head. She smiled secretively, just as she had when we'd hidden from Ngama, or crept up on Macca and tickled him with a long stem of grass. She smiled as if no time had passed since we were innocent children. I smiled back for, in truth, no time had passed; we were seeds, picked up by the wind and blown to this strange place for this strange encounter.

We moved off, Charlie and Kiani in the lead, followed by Macca and me, with Tottengarr bringing up the rear. Once we were well hidden within the bush and out of earshot, Macca and I sat on a fallen log and put on our boots. He pulled me to him and we embraced. My body thrilled at his touch and my heart filled with excitement. At being with him, yes, but more, much more, with excitement for the venture before me, elation in the knowledge that I was doing something. Taking action. No longer doing nothing. I understood that all those years of watching and waiting, of seeing my world through different eyes had prepared me for what I had now embarked upon.

Tottengarr went deeper into the bush but re-joined us a little up the track. I'd fallen behind and she came beside me, a branch wrapped in her Poonindie pinafore, protruding from her bag.

'You came a long way from home, Miss Annese. Away from bossy Miss Margaret.' She walked ahead a little, wriggling her bottom, mimicking Margaret, just as she had that day at the clothesline. 'Mr Macca your man?'

'Yes, my man.' The words tasted good.

'You will tell police Kiani is not a thief and that she did not kill her baby. And tell them Margaret Mayfield a liar.' Like me, Tottengarr wanted Margaret punished.

'I will do what I can.'

'Kiani will live with our family now.'

'At *kurra murka*.'

Tottengarr stopped short. 'You remember?'

'Of course. I looked it up after you told me about it. It's on the peninsula that looks like a leg.'

'Narungga Country. That way.' She pointed to the east. 'But there is water between us. If we find a boat we can go across or we will have big walk that way.' She pointed north. 'Then back south and towards the sea on the other side of the leg. Are you strong enough to do all that? Macca could maybe get a boat for you at Tumby.'

I'd heard nothing about a boat at Tumby and I wondered if this was Tottengarr's idea or Macca's.

'No, I'll stay with Macca. You have brought your Christian clothes?' I asked, pointing to the wrapping around the branch.

'To hide this.' She reached over her shoulder and unwrapped a musket.

'Do you need that?' I asked.

She laughed, seeing the horror on my face. 'Only for killing kangaroo, I hope. Easier than boomerang.'

'Do you know how to use it?' I asked.

'My father taught us when we were children.'

'I heard about a group led by a woman who was shooting sheep and cattle. Was that you? They're bringing over more police to hunt her down.'

She laughed again. 'Best you don't know the answer to that, Miss Annese.'

We walked on together in silence but I was soon struggling to keep up with her long-legged strides and fell behind. The group stopped, waiting for me to catch up, and then slowed their pace.

We'd been heading north for a few hours when Macca suggested we all take a rest. I'd kept two small loaves from the dinner Mrs Hale had sent in to me the previous night. Macca, Tottengarr, and Charlie went into the bush to find food while Kiani and I built a fire.

'You came and found me, Annese. Now I get back to my family.'

'Do you know where they are?'

'I will find them. My mother and aunties and uncles. My brothers too. My baby needs to learn our Peramangk ways.' She patted her belly and I understood. She was pregnant again.

'Macca says you need to stay out of Adelaide. He says you might be in even more trouble now, for leaving Poonindie without permission.'

'Macca good man but he's speaking like a white man. I don't need white man permission. I don't want to always hide and be afraid.' She grabbed me by the hand. 'I need tell police I didn't steal the doll. I didn't take anything from Margaret. You show police your doll and the letter. They believe you. Tell them I did not do the other thing either. My baby slipped and drowned. I need to send my baby to ancestors.' She stared off into the distance and a cloud passed over her.

'I saw him, Kiani,' I whispered. 'Your baby, the day they found him.'

It took a moment for her to understand what I was saying. 'You saw my baby? He was peaceful?'

'Yes, Kiani. As peaceful as a sleeping possum. The river looked after him and wrapped him around with reeds of love and carried him to the bank.'

'Then you believe me? I not hurt him.'

'Of course I believe you, Kiani.'

'You his aunty now, Annese. We go together and find where they put his body. We tell the ancestors to look after him.' She began humming then, a crooning of sorrow and goodbye. I joined in and felt her music deep within me. Healing. Soothing.

***

Tottengarr and Charlie returned, accompanied by two other Aboriginal men. They carried a large goanna lizard, which they threw onto the red coals. As the smoke curled, Charlie spoke to them, using hand language too.

'Did you learn anything?' Macca asked Charlie.

'Boat at Tumby going to Adelaide but Port Lincoln first.'

Macca shook his head. 'No good. There will be people there waiting to send you all back to Poonindie. We'll keep on walking to *kurra murka*.'

We waited in silence, each of us lost in our thoughts until Charlie hauled the lizard from the ashes and began to peel away its leathery skin, revealing flesh, pink and succulent, greasy and pungent. Tottengarr passed around berries as sweet as Mr Hastings's red grapes. When we finished, Macca drew me aside.

'You must go on the boat, Annese. You need to get back to your family.'

Alarm filled me. 'Will you come too?'

'No, I'll be recognised as soon as I step ashore at Port Lincoln. The Hales will have alerted the police there. You can wear Tottengarr's clothes. I'll tell the boatmen you're my pregnant wife and have to get to Adelaide. No one will be looking for a pregnant woman but stay on board at Port Lincoln, just in case.'

As much as I wanted to say no, I could see the sense in what he was saying. I was already struggling and the walk ahead of us was at least five days. I would be a burden on them. But what about my promises to Kiani? Could I meet with the police alone?

'I'll walk with the others to *kurra murka*,' Macca continued. 'There are not many settlers where we're going but if we come across any, I'll say I'm escorting them on behalf of the Protector. I'll come and find you when the time is right. You have to trust me, Annese. This is the right decision.'

I could see his mind was made up and knew I had to trust him. We walked for a few more hours until we could see where the scrubby she-oaks gave way to mangroves and the sea glistened on the horizon. We stayed amongst the trees for the night, in the last of the cover. I slept alongside Macca, not daring to embrace him for I knew if we touched as lovers, I would not have been able to deny the need I had for him.

I woke at dawn to his gentle shaking. 'You'll need to put these on for this last stretch.' He held out Tottengarr's clothes.

The white uniform was far too big for me, but I rolled the skirt up at the waist and wedged Tottengarr's rolled-up pantaloons under the waistband covering it with a voluminous top. I certainly looked as if I was with child, and the floppy maid's bonnet disguised my cropped hair.

I was almost dressed when Kiani came beside me, grabbed my discarded clothes and cap, and put them on. The trousers were halfway up her calf but the shirt fitted and was loose enough to hide her breasts. Her hair, already cut short, fitted well beneath the cap. We began laughing as she danced a jig. Hearing us, the others came over. Even the usually serious Charlie joined in the merriment and, for one absurd moment, we five became a band of jesters. Five young people free of the constraints others would put on us.

When, finally, we fell down exhausted, Kiani approached Macca. 'I go with Annese dressed like a boy now. I want no bad name against me,' she said. 'Annese will know what to do.'

'If you get caught, they will send you back to Poonindie. You might be jailed, Kiani.' Macca's love for her was evident.

'I won't get caught. I boy now.' She smiled, her confidence undeniable, her determination unbeatable.

We joined hands and Macca knew we would not change our decision.

'You're free to choose, Kiani. But take it slowly. Don't make things worse. Annese, you must first find a way to check to see if the charges are still on record. No point drawing attention to them if they've been forgotten. You must say I made you leave Poonindie. Convince them that you didn't run away of your own accord.'

We agreed to his suggestions although I had no idea how I would do what he asked of me.

***

There was no pier at Tumby. I could see a schooner anchored offshore. A white man was on the shore loading a small dinghy when Macca, Kiani, and I emerged from the shield of the low sandhills. I expected him to be astounded at the sight of us but he showed only apathy; clearly, a man not easily flummoxed.

Macca went ahead and put out his hand. 'Murdo Macintosh. Have you room for my wife and her native boy? She is due to give birth within the month and needs medical assistance in Adelaide. The native boy is a trusted servant.'

Mimicking pregnant women I'd known, I cradled my fake stomach as if comforting the unborn child.

'As long as she doesn't drop it while we're at sea. We've no berths so she'll have to sleep on shore tonight at Port Lincoln.'

I stepped forward and feigned an Irish accent to sound like my mother. 'We've not the money for both room and the fare. I will stay onboard to sleep. The boy will be my companion.'

'Right you are then, Mrs MacIntosh,' he said, taking the coins Macca offered him.

Macca pulled me to him and gently kissed me on the cheek. 'Fare thee well, wife. I will be by your side by the time the baby is born.'

Taking the captain's hand, I stepped into the large dinghy, finding a seat on the wool bales that almost filled it. Kiani scrambled on behind me and sat opposite.

'Good thing you two are here. You'll help balance this load,' he said, rearranging one of the bales. As he pushed us off the mooring, I watched Macca walking back along the track. When he reached the point where he would enter the bush, he turned to wave. I raised my hand, fighting the tears.

Nearing the ketch, the *Lady Harvey*, I noticed a rope ladder hanging over its side.

'Ladies first.' I picked up my bag but Kiani grabbed it from me. Focussing on each rung, I was soon grabbed under my arms by two crew who hoisted me on board.

'Got more cargo than you bargained for, Captain,' one of them said.

'Aye, and you'll keep your hands to yourself. She's a married woman and carrying a bairn.'

I flushed as two sets of eyes looked me up and down.

Kiani scaled the ladder as if she had been doing it all her life. Passing me my bag as she boarded, she smiled briefly before dropping her head in the way of a servant. The captain indicated a pile of bales for me to sit on. 'Best you stay here while we load this lot. We'll set sail as soon as the wind picks up. Your boy can help us.'

'Charlie. His name is Charlie,' I said but I need not have bothered. 'Your boy' seemed to be all they needed.

***

We hugged the coast all the way to Port Lincoln. Kiani was soon adjusting the boom and raising the sails, tasks she proved well suited to. Her pregnancy was in the early stages, so did not impede her agility or balance, which were as good as they had ever been. I watched on with admiration as she helped bring us safely into Boston Bay.

The crew secured the vessel and headed for the hotel while the captain wrote up his log. Once finished he checked with me one last time that I would be safe before leaving us, Kiani as Charlie, on board until morning. The sky slowly sprang to life with stars. A rough bunk had been made for me from hessian bags filled with wool that had escaped one of the bales. Kiani was expected to lie on the bare deck and did so without complaint.

Exhausted from the day's walking, I quickly drifted to sleep and awoke early next morning to the excited crew coming back on board.

'Some natives have gone missing from Poonindie. Two women and a man. A couple of white folks went with them they think; a man who said he was police and a young girl pretending she was a lad. The publican says it might be a Malcolm Macleod and his offsider who stayed there just three nights ago.'

I feigned concern and shared a secret smile with Kiani. They'd made no connection to the heavily pregnant woman and the skinny native boy with whom they sailed.

***

We set sail for Adelaide at mid-morning after loading more wool. The wind was in our favour and before long we'd entered the passage between the mainland and Kangaroo Island. Trying to avoid seasickness, I stayed seated and kept my eyes on the sky. The crew nicknamed Kiani 'Lurcher', watching with amazement as she embraced the open sea travel with joyous excitement, as if the wind and waves were a stage for her to dance upon. I, too, marvelled at her will to not just survive but thrive, her connection with the natural world so plain to see.

By dusk, we were sailing up the gulf with Port Adelaide in sight. Macca had given me what few coins he had. My plan was to stay at the Temperance overnight but I knew Kiani would not be welcome there. As the sails were lowered, I managed a discrete conversation with her.

'Where will you go tonight?'

'Join my brothers and sisters. We will go to police tomorrow?' she asked.

Now that we were nearly back to a place all too familiar to me, where I would certainly be quickly recognised, where I'd once lived a normal life, I began to doubt my ability to carry through my promise to Kiani. The temptation to walk away from my obligation to her was intense.

Surely she'd be safe amongst her own people again. If she kept away from the police and stayed silent about the charges, maybe they would be forgotten over time. I allowed myself to imagine the relief I would feel if I simply said goodbye to Kiani and went back to Echunga. Back to wait for Macca with my family. Back to safety.

***

Kiani came up beside me, her shoulder against mine as if she'd read my thoughts. Every muscle in her body was taut and her eyes darted, checking no doubt for those that would have her put back in prison for crimes she'd not committed. She did not have my options. Her home taken over, her family decimated, pregnant to a half-caste, safety was no longer hers to choose. I leant into her.

'Stay dressed as a boy,' I whispered. 'Come to the Temperance Hotel at eight o'clock tomorrow morning.'

With a nod, she jumped onto the wharf and sprinted off.

'Look at the lurcher run. You'll not see him again, Mrs MacIntosh.' The crew laughed, and I wondered if they were right. A hollow feeling opened up inside me, a guilty emptiness. I would never be whole until she was truly free.

A crowd was gathering on the wharf, awaiting passengers about to disembark from the large clipper we'd followed up the gulf, an ocean-going ship from the mother country with a new horde of settlers. Some would come with money; most came, as my parents had, with nothing to their name. But all came with a promise that they could take up land, land that belonged to Kiani's people. I felt aggrieved for them too, for, like my parents, they had been lied to. The words of the Bible came back to me 'They know not what they do.'

But what will they do when they know, I wondered. What will they do?

CHAPTER 29

With the gangplank now lowered, the captain helped me ashore. 'Come, Mrs MacIntosh. Mind your step.'

I thanked him, relieved to feel the solid earth beneath my feet. Pushing my way through the throng, I kept my head low, longing for the security of a solitary room where I could once again become myself.

'Annese. Annese.' I kept walking, praying it was another Annese being called. The woman's voice called out again.

'Annese. Over here. It's Polly.' I looked up to see Polly's jubilant face as she waved her handkerchief at me. I hadn't time to remove my fake belly before she was at my side. Close behind her were Thomas and Frederick. As delighted as I was to see them, my heart sank. How would I explain myself?

Polly embraced me, glanced down at the bulge, and gasped. The less observant men took their hats off and nodded their welcome.

I pulled Polly to me. 'It's fake. Don't say a word.'

The intensity of my insistence stopped Polly's jubilance long enough for me to make up a story.

'I was invited to visit a friend, a Mrs Hale, at the Aboriginal training school. Mr Macleod accompanied me there but was unable to return.' It was not a complete lie.

'How adventurous you've become, Annese,' Thomas said staring at me, clearly not believing a word. 'Frederick, you know my little mouse of a sister. Do you agree she has changed?'

Before Frederick could answer, one of the crew walked past. 'Good luck with the baby, Mrs MacIntosh,' he said to me. The men's eyes went to my belly.

'It's not true,' I said once they had passed, unable to hide my shame. 'I'm not married nor am I pregnant.' I pushed at the bulge, showing its softness.

To my utter surprise, Thomas laughed. 'It seems you have some explaining to do, *Mrs MacIntosh*.'

I glared at him, angry at his light-hearted dismissal of my dilemma. He dropped his jauntiness. 'I'm sorry, Annese. I'm sure you have a good explanation.'

'You should be sorry, Thomas,' Polly said. 'Now go and get a bigger trap so we can all travel together.'

We were soon making our way towards Adelaide Town. My story came out in fits and starts, although I made no mention of my secret betrothal to Macca.

'So you see, I must get Kiani free of the charges. I have promised and she is a friend.'

I showed them the letter and the chess piece.

'You say Margaret Mayfield wrote this?' Thomas asked, clearly very interested. 'And Macca gave you and Kiani the two chess pieces?' I nodded and he engaged Frederick in an exchange I couldn't hear.

We pulled up at the Southern Cross Hotel. 'It has recently been refurbished,' Polly said, 'and is now Adelaide's most salubrious hotel.'

Thomas paid the driver and helped Polly and me down. As tired as I was, I couldn't help but wish I was in Joseph's clothes and could jump down on my own. Relying on a man for everything now seemed so unnecessary and, somehow, demeaning.

'We'll go up to my room to freshen up,' Polly said to me. 'Thomas, please let the manager know I have a guest. We will meet you soon in the tearoom.'

The room was on the third floor and was three times the size of the one I'd shared at the Temperance. Its walls were covered with embossed wallpaper and dark red damask curtains hid the windows. Polly drew them open to expose a small balcony overlooking King William Street, before pouring water into a bowl from a gold-embossed pitcher.

'Take off those dreadful clothes, Annese, have a wash and put this on,' she said, handing me a pale blue dress. 'It's what they call a Delaine dress. I bought it yesterday from Goodes Brothers. It's a little too roomy on me so I'm sure it will fit you. Here are some new undergarments too.'

She drew a screen around me and I took every stitch of clothing off, relieved to be free from not only them, but the façade they represented. The water felt marvellous as I sponged my whole body. The soap lathered easily, giving off the scent of lavender, and the towel she passed me was the finest I'd ever used. The contrast between Polly's life and mine could not have been starker.

'This hotel must cost you a fortune.'

Polly shrugged. 'I have no idea. Thomas organised it all.'

'He seems changed,' I said as I emerged from behind the screen in the underwear. 'Kinder.' I pulled the dress over my head and could not help but glance at my reflection in the mirror. Other than my roughly cut hair, I was pleased with what I saw. A strong woman.

'You see, I told you he would come good,' Polly said, pushing my clumsy hands aside to do up the many tiny buttons. 'Although he's still quite bossy.'

'Unlike you,' I said, not even trying to hide my smile.

'Oh me? I've always been bossy,' she laughed and gave me a hug. 'Thomas is a lawyer's clerk and has done a year of training to become a proper lawyer. Sometimes he acts as if he is fully qualified already. I must say, I think he'll be very good at his chosen profession.'

'A lawyer's clerk?' What on earth did he make of my pathetic attempt at seeking justice for Kiani, I wondered.

'Now what shall we do about this hair? Here,' Polly said, opening the wardrobe, 'this bonnet is quite acceptable to wear indoors and it sets off your eyes.'

I had to admit the aqua blue certainly looked well on me, although the gold trim seemed excessive. 'Thank you, Polly. I am not one to worry much about how I look.'

'You should. You do know Frederick is smitten with you?'

'Frederick?' The idea came as a shock and I knew I should have mentioned my commitment to Macca there and then. But I had not the courage nor even the words to describe our unconventional arrangement.

Polly didn't answer. Instead, she pinched my cheeks to bring up the colour. 'Tomorrow I shall go to my hairdresser. He sells wigs. It's quite a lucrative trade, I believe. They're mostly for ladies whose hair has fallen out from sickness.' She squeezed my hand. 'It'll be my gift to you.'

We made our way to the tearoom where Thomas was already seated. 'That's better,' he said after looking me over and pulling out a chair for me. Before I'd even settled, he began. 'I've been thinking. I need to take on a minor legal case, under supervision of course, to pass my next level of training. Do you think your native friend would let me take up her case? She would have to come with me to a meeting with the prosecutor tomorrow.'

'She has no money, Thomas. Are you allowed to represent an Aboriginal person?'

During my time in Adelaide Town, I'd seen plenty of her people lining up at the courthouse but I'd never seen one with a lawyer. The thought of Kiani meeting with Thomas made me shudder. He may have become kinder but even I was still a little frightened of him.

'Of course. Under our Proclamation, she is considered a British citizen. You can be with her while I question her, but you must remain silent. Where is she living? What is her address?'

I laughed at the naivety of his questions. He blushed then, realising the absurdity of his words.

'I've already arranged to meet her in the morning,' I said. 'We were going to go to the police together.'

'Good,' Thomas said, 'but you must not go to the police without representation. I will ask Jerome Crawford, my employer, to allow me to come with you tomorrow to take down her statement. But first, you should write out your statement and sign it. If the case goes to court, you'll be a witness.'

I stiffened. A witness in court? I'd not imagined anything so formal. But worse was the idea of having to write out a statement. I'd learned enough at school and at work to write lists, invoices, and the occasional short letter, but a legal statement was quite a different matter. I felt again the agony of my school-day struggles to make neat loops and hooks with my right hand. Even if I used my left hand, I'd never get the spelling correct.

'I am not sure I can do that,' I stammered. 'I can't write very well. Not like that.'

Polly and Thomas glanced at each other and tried to hide their pity. But I saw it plain and clear. And something else too. Without them saying it, I saw how grateful they were that they had not been left to suffer the poverty I had. Grateful too that Ma and Pa had agreed to them living with Mrs Scholz who'd given them the opportunity of a good education and an easy life. I wondered how much they knew of my role in their being taken and that the letter they'd recently read was a turning point in their childhood. But even as these thoughts formed, I realised that their fate had been sealed by forces much bigger than me. Our lowly status as workers, the struggling colony, and even Ma's Catholicism, had played a part in their removal. The letter, and Margaret's wrath toward me, was simply one episode in a much bigger story.

As they looked at me with both kindness and respect, the heaviness of years of guilt dissolved, and with it, the barrier I'd felt between us crumbled. They were truly my brother and sister.

'Sorry, I couldn't help but overhear.' I swung around. Frederick now stood beside me.

'Oh good. You're here,' said Thomas brightly. 'Frederick can write your statement for you, Annese.'

Frederick nodded. 'If you want me to, that is.'

'Perfect,' Thomas said before I could answer. I caught Polly's brief conspiratorial smile.

'Can we do it now, Frederick? That way I can be with Kiani tomorrow while she talks to Thomas.'

'Of course. But are you not tired?'

I was exhausted and wanted only to lie down and close my eyes. The gentleness of his words unhooked the final strands of my feigned courage, and relief flooded through me. Tears filled my eyes before I rallied enough to answer.

'Yes, I'm very tired, but I need to be with Thomas tomorrow when he meets Kiani. We must do it now, if that is suitable for you, Frederick.'

'This is all so exciting.' Polly giggled. 'Just like out of one of Miss Austen's books or even Mr Dickens'.'

'That's settled then,' Thomas said, standing abruptly. 'Polly, you come with me so Frederick can concentrate.'

Polly turned to me and shook her head, so slightly no-one else noticed. An awkward silence fell between me and Frederick.

'I'd assumed you and Polly were courting,' I said.

'No. Mrs Scholz would like us to be, but Polly is like a sister to me. She has no thoughts of settling and I must say I find her very…'

'Very Polly,' I finished for him, for I understood his dilemma in trying to describe her flighty way.

'Yes. Very Polly. Come, let's go into the side lounge. There's nobody there right now and I believe it has a writing table.'

I closed the door behind us hoping to dissuade others from coming in. The room was furnished with two red crushed-velvet settees and a mahogany table embedded with a variety of woods to create a diamond pattern. Embroidered satin cushions with tasselled trimmings were placed on each settee. Frederick lit the wick of a reading lamp and sat on the settee opposite me, the table between us. Answering a knock at the door he came back with paper, pen, and ink.

'I heard most of what you told Thomas and Polly in the trap, so if you like I'll write down what I remember and then we can go over that and you can add or change anything that I get wrong.'

I watched as he rapidly filled two pages, marvelling at his concentration and the precision of his work. Each word was evenly spaced and sloped perfectly as if leaning into the wind, strong and sure. His fine narrow nose and high cheekbones would have looked well on a woman and may have given him an effeminate look had it not been for his rough beard. His hair, no longer fair but not quite brown either, was fine, reminding me of an Irish setter I'd once played with. But what held my attention the most was his hands as they skipped across the page, his slender fingers elegant like those of an artist or pianist. They told the story of a simple life, a life without trauma and complication. I thought of Macca's hands, scarred by a life of struggle and conflict, etched with the darkness of untold and untellable stories.

I closed my eyes, the exhaustion of the day catching up with me.

'Annese.' Frederick's whisper drew me back. My bonnet had fallen to my shoulders. Feeling his eyes upon me, I scrambled to put it back on.

'Short hair looks well on you,' he said, with the kindest of voices. 'It gives you a clever, impish look.'

I pulled the bonnet back on anyway, unsure how to respond.

He read out what he'd written. I was astounded at how well he'd captured the details of my story and woven it with his formal language. His words gave Kiani's plight a weightiness, an importance. He'd neither slandered nor excused Margaret, simply stating the facts. I wondered if Macca would be happy with it.

Passing the written statement to me, I read it through for myself. There was one element I was unsure about. He'd mentioned Kiani's baby and the accusation of deliberate drowning.

'She may not have been charged with the baby's death. Macca, Malcolm Macleod, suggested that we not draw attention to it. We don't even know if the police are following up.'

He looked confused. 'I see. But I would have thought it was the most serious of the crimes being held against Kiani.'

I told him what I'd heard and Macca's thoughts. 'You see, to them, the authorities, it was just a native baby. I am not sure they even think of it as a citizen, or…' I choked on the words. 'Or even human.'

I remembered again his little body wrapped in reeds, his chubby arms gone limp, his deathly blue lips, once red with life. I began sobbing then and could not stop. I cried for all that Kiani's son would have been. I cried for Kiani and all that had been taken from her. I cried for all the evil words levelled at her people. I cried for Macca too and for the childish innocence I would never regain.

Frederick came beside me and put his arm around my shoulders until I recovered.

'You've seen things others have turned away from. You've heard when others have chosen not to. You've chosen actions that most would find too hard. But it has made you strong, Annese. And now you are not alone. You have your family to help you. And me.'

'And Macca,' I said wiping my eyes. 'We are to be wed.'

'Yes, and Macca.' He withdrew his arm and sat back, looking hard at the document.

'So do you want me to delete the passage about the baby?'

I thought about Kiani's determination to be free of the accusation.

'It is Kiani's decision, not mine.' And not Macca's either, I thought.

***

Kiani arrived at the Temperance Hotel in the company of five of her people: three men and two women. She wore a mish-mash of ill-fitting clothes and I could not help thinking how much prouder she looked when naked.

I asked Thomas to stay at a distance.

She pulled at my arm, desperation in her eyes. 'We go tell police now, Annese? Tell them I did not steal the chess piece or the horse. Tell them I did not kill my baby.'

'Yes, soon, but first we will get help from my brother. He will know how to tell them your story so that they will listen.'

'Brother Joseph?'

'No, I have another brother, Thomas.' I pointed to where he stood. 'He went to live with another family when he was little. Will you talk to him?'

'You trust him?'

Did I? In reality, I hardly knew him but somehow the answer was clear.

'Yes, I trust him. We'll do this together, Kiani.'

I signalled for Thomas to join us, pleased he'd not worn his dress suit. In his moleskin trousers and a regatta cotton shirt, he looked younger, less intimidating. I noticed how nervous he was as he approached and realised that he'd probably never spoken to an Aboriginal person before. Kiani lowered her eyes and she moved a little closer to her family when he got his notebook from his satchel.

'Kiani, is it okay if Thomas writes down what you say?'

She nodded and indicated a shaded area beneath a tree. One of the women sat in the dirt with her and Thomas and I found a fallen branch nearby. The rest of Kiani's family remained at a distance. Standing. Watching.

'You tell police I not a thief,' she said to Thomas, still looking at the ground. 'The chess piece given to me by Mr Macca.'

Thomas began firing questions.

'Slow down, Thomas,' I said. 'Maybe tell her a little about who you are.'

He looked at me with gratitude. 'I am Thomas. Annese is my sister. I am a lawyer's clerk. I work for Mr Crawford and I am training to speak for other people in the court.'

'You tell my words to the boss man at the court?'

'Yes. I tell them that you did not lie.'

'Why you not live with family?'

I saw Thomas hesitate. He looked at me but I let him find his own words.

'Our mother and father were too poor to keep me. No food. No bed.'

Kiani nodded. 'White man needs wooden bed. White man's food not good.'

He looked at me now, not knowing how to proceed. 'Tell her about Mrs Scholz.'

'I went with my twin sister, Polly, to live with another woman.'

'Aunty.'

I could see that he was about to explain she wasn't an aunty.

'Yes, aunty,' I said. 'Good person. She had plenty of food and beds. She helped Thomas become a good man. Strong man to help others.'

He looked at me and smiled. 'Annese is a good person too. She helped me when I was a baby. She is a good sister.'

'You can trust Thomas,' I said to Kiani, tears in my eyes. 'He is my brother.'

He began asking her questions again, about the chess piece and the china horse.

'No china horse. Macca's doll was the only white man's treasure I had. You show boss man Margaret Mayfield's letter.'

'I will show them, but it is not proof, I'm afraid,' Thomas said. 'Anyone could have written that.'

Kiani jumped up and two of her brothers came closer. 'No. Annese said Margaret Mayfield wrote it.'

I scrambled to my feet too. 'It's all right, Kiani. Thomas is just telling you what the police might say. I have made a statement—written to the police to tell them about the letter. And that Macca gave you the chess piece. Come and sit again.'

She relaxed and sat back down. 'You tell them about my baby too. I not kill my baby. He slip and the angry waters take him. That Margaret Mayfield, she a liar.'

Thomas turned to me now. 'I checked. The police are not investigating the baby's death. It was referred to the coroner but I could not find any record of a hearing.'

Kiani was trying to follow his words. 'What is he saying?' she implored of me.

'The police aren't...'

The horror on her face told me she understood what I was saying. 'My baby not important to them.'

I could not lie. I nodded.

She turned to Thomas and addressed him directly, her stance firm and strong. Her voice steady and direct. 'My baby part of me and my family. I not kill my baby. He slipped from my arms. The angry waters take him. That Margaret Mayfield, she a liar. You write that down. You tell police.'

Thomas nodded and wrote down her statement, word for word.

'I think we have enough. I will write this up in legal words. You must come to the court tomorrow and sign it.'

I saw Kiani hesitate. 'Thomas, I suggest you read out what you have written and get Kiani to put her mark on it today. It might be all we get.'

Kiani called two of her brothers over as Thomas read out the statement. I was astounded, and filled with pride, at how well he'd captured her words.

Kiani listened intently and looked at me. 'You think I should sign.'

'Yes.' I wondered if I'd been in her shoes if I would trust her as much as she did me.

She wrote her name in perfect letters as both Kiani and Kitty. It was her surname that surprised me. Macleod.

'Macca gave me his name. It is what police call me.'

When had this happened? And why? There was so much I still didn't know about Macca. So many sides to him I'd never seen.

Thomas carefully placed the statement in a folder. 'I'll take these to the court.' he said. 'They'll likely ask for a statement from Malcolm Macleod and one from Margaret Mayfield too.'

It hadn't occurred to me that there would be a delay. 'Will they agree to Kiani staying free till they get their statements?'

'I will certainly advocate for that. She will have to have an address. Maybe the destitute asylum?'

Kiani shook her head. 'No. That place full of dead spirits. I go with my family. You tell them, Thomas. I not thief. Not a killer. You show them the papers. I trust you. You Annese's brother.'

'Meet us here tomorrow,' I called as she walked away. 'We will go to the courthouse together.' She turned to wave and laughed, the laugh I'd always loved.

***

As promised, Polly bought me a wig and I borrowed her dress and bonnet again. My stomach churned as we waited for Kiani. When she appeared, accompanied again by her family, I was both proud of and fearful for her. She wore the same clothes as the day before, now soiled from having slept in the dirt. My rush of guilt for not arranging for her to at least make use of the luxurious washing facilities at our hotel, was quickly overridden by the knowledge that she would not have been welcomed there.

I feared that her wayward appearance would sway the court outcome and the reality that she could soon be taken back into custody gripped me like an iron lock. Why had I been so sure that justice would be done? Should I have listened to Macca and persuaded her to disappear back into the bush with her family?

Mr Crawford, Thomas's employer, met us at the courthouse and looked over the documents.

'You have been thorough in your preparation, Thomas. Is this the accused?' He looked at Kiani, unable to hide the uncertainty in his voice.

I was about to explain her appearance but Kiani smiled at him, her wide, optimistic smile. He smiled then too, taken aback by her confidence.

'Mr Thomas and Miss Annese know I am not a thief. Nor a killer.'

He nodded and looked at her now as if seeing her, really seeing her, for the first time. Was this his first conversation with an Aboriginal person too?

'You will be well represented by Mr Scholz at the pre-trial meeting, Miss Macleod. I will take up the case if it goes to trial.'

We went into the courthouse together: Thomas, on behalf of Mr Crawford, Kiana, and me. The prosecutor met us and looked over all the statements.

'Your statements are regarding two matters,' he said to Thomas. 'I have only one before me. That of a historical theft from a Miss Margaret Mayfield. The issue surrounding the death of a baby was not pursued.'

'The accused has asked that the death of the baby be declared unproven. She asks that the court declare it an accident.'

The prosecutor shook his head and looked at his pocket watch.

'I will only deal with what is before me. Regarding the charges of theft laid by Miss Mayfield, your statements, Miss Macleod, and Miss Laffer, provide me with enough evidence to cast doubt upon the accuser's version of the events. This letter, although unsigned, does throw significant doubt on the validity of Margaret Mayfield's accusation. Before I waste more of anybody's time, I will interview her. She will be shown your statements and the letter, and reminded that knowingly making false accusations is also a crime.'

For years I'd longed for Margaret to be publicly held to account for her lies, but now that it was to become a reality, I felt a stab of regret that it had to come to this. I feared Macca would not forgive me for presenting the letter and wondered, once again, what had passed between them on the day she'd rescued him. Why had he remained so determined to protect her?

'And the matter of the child's death?' Thomas asked.

The prosecutor packed up his files. 'Mr Scholz, I am aware that you are acting in Mr Crawford's absence, and that you are not yet qualified. You will do well to learn when to recognise a victory. In the absence of a case being brought against Miss Macleod regarding the death, the court has, by default, agreed that the death of the baby was an accident.'

My heart soared and I squeezed Kiani's hand. I could see she'd not fully comprehended what had just happened. 'They've agreed, Kiani. It was an accident. They know you did not kill your baby.'

She hugged me then and smiled at Thomas. 'You brother now.'

Overcome by relief, I nearly missed the prosecutor's next words.

'If Miss Mayfield wants to proceed against your client, Kitty Macleod will be required back in court for a trial. I sought advice from the Protector of Aborigines before this meeting. Unless you can provide a bail address while we progress the matter, he will arrange for her to go to the asylum awaiting her return to Poonindie.'

'No asylum,' Kiani said. 'Full of spirits.'

I knew Kiani would disappear rather than return to the asylum and Thomas's face told me he was unprepared for this situation.

'She… she has no fixed address in Adelaide,' he stammered.

'As I thought.'

'May I speak?' My voice came out a whisper but all eyes turned to me. 'I'll provide her with an address. She can live with my family who reside at Echunga on the land once owned by her people but taken from them.'

The prosecutor stood, clearly annoyed that such a minor case was taking so much of his time. 'Very well. Leave your details with the clerk, Miss Laffer, and make sure Miss Macleod returns if and when required.'

I was about to stand when Kiani's voice rose loud and clear. 'What has happened to my baby?'

The prosecutor turned on her as if to reprimand her but, seeing the sadness in her eyes, his demeanour changed.

'I don't know for sure, but usually in these cases, if no one comes to claim the body, it would be given a pauper's funeral and buried at the West Terrace Cemetery.'

'I could not come to claim my baby. My family came. They were told to go away.' She began her chanting, quiet enough for only me to hear.

***

Frederick helped us find the paupers graves; sad mounds with no acknowledgement of the lives of those who lay below them. Kiani turned to us.

'Thank you. You have done what was yours to do. Go now.'

We left her with her with family to undertake their ceremony. Arriving back at the Southern Cross, I was shocked to find Margaret sitting in a corner of the foyer. Thomas had told me that morning he'd made a few enquiries and learned that she was currently staying with her sister in North Adelaide. He'd informed the prosecutor, who'd quickly drafted and delivered a letter formally advising her that Mr Crawford would be defending Kiani Macleod and that he had in his possession new evidence in the form of a letter believed to be written by her.

I felt sick in anticipation of her anger. I could easily have left, but I knew I had to face her one day. I approached, expecting to see hate in her eyes. Instead, she began crying.

'Annese, I have just heard the horrible news.'

I knew without asking. Macca was dead.

CHAPTER 30

Kiani and I took our grief with us. We travelled back to Echunga, to her Country. Wordless, we sat side by side at the rear of the stagecoach, the only place Kiani was allowed. Arriving at Echunga, we went straight to the creek. Kiani began chanting and I wept, my body convulsing with the pain. When no more tears would flow, we waded into the creek, disturbing a grey heron. He looked at us before soaring away, his thin body flattened into an angry arrow.

Kiani started it, the splashing; tiny sprinkles at first until soon we were swooshing handfuls at each other, laughing and howling, hysterical in our grief. As we dragged ourselves back to the bank, soaking wet and exhausted, she dug into her woven bag and pulled out her chess piece.

'Police gave it back to me, but I don't need it anymore. Macca safe now, with his ancestors. You have it.'

***

Frederick stayed in Adelaide until the case was officially dismissed. Margaret had retracted her accusation, saying she could now not be sure which native person she had seen. Saying also that she may have been mistaken about the china horse. Regarding the baby, she said she had been in a confused state that day and was herself grieving the loss of a loved one.

She told them too that Malcolm Macleod would not lie and that I was a young woman with strong integrity. Learning of this, I recalled Macca reprimanding me about Margaret's character. Perhaps I had been mistaken all along. Perhaps there is good in us all.

Frederick brought the paperwork to Echunga for me and Kiani to sign, but Kiani had disappeared after that first day at the creek. He'd taken my hand in his as I passed the documents over and, on that day, declared his love for me. We courted for three months and when we announced our engagement to my family, no one seemed surprised.

'It's not how a marriage is usually arranged, young man,' Da said to Frederick, 'but Annese never was one to do things the way other folk did. You have our blessing.'

'I'm glad you found someone who understands your ways,' Ma whispered to me, hugging me so tight I thought I'd break.

'Me too.' I laughed. 'He says he likes my sideways slant on the world.'

Thomas and Polly came down a week later to say their goodbyes. Mrs Scholz was taking them to Europe to meet her family.

'Write to me, Annese,' Polly instructed. 'Tell me all about the wedding.'

'There'll not be much to tell,' I said, giving her the longest of hugs. 'Frederick has been accepted by the Friends. We will follow their ways and make our vows simply, at a regular Meeting.'

'Maybe you two can come to London one day,' Thomas said.

'No,' I said taking his hands. 'You won't see me there. This is my home. But you and Polly will always be near to my heart, no matter where you are.'

'Oh, I almost forgot,' Thomas said as they were about to leave. 'Do you want me to take your chess pieces with me to get them valued? I've been in touch with the British Museum. They're very interested in them. They think it is entirely possible that they are two of the missing Lewis Chessmen. They could be very valuable, Annese.'

But I couldn't part with the only tangible connection I had with Macca.

'No. Macca would have wanted me to keep them here, his new home. Maybe one day they will find their way back to his family's island.'

***

I take them with me, the chess pieces, when I go to Adelaide Town to visit Macca's grave. They help me bear the pain his death still left within me. The paper reported that he'd been with a small band of armed natives. They'd attacked two white men and he'd been caught in the crossfire. They'd brought his body back to Adelaide for burial. Da, Ma, Joseph, and I were the only ones at his funeral.

No mention was ever made of the fate of the Aboriginal people he'd been with.

I saw Kiani only once more. She was with her people at a gathering, a corroboree. Her baby was walking already and another man, not Charlie, was at her side. She wore feathers in her hair and paint on her face. Her body was as strong and wiry as always, her voice steady and sure as she sang their music.

I hear her laugh sometimes, down at the creek when the wind is playing in the leaves and the bees are humming.

EPILOGUE

Macca slipped the flask from the captain into his pocket as Annese and Kiani climbed into the dinghy.

'You look like you could use a dram,' the captain muttered, passing him a small flask.

Waving goodbye, Macca reflected on the years he'd known them, these young courageous women. He recalled their laughter as they played in the creek; innocent children then, with not a care to trouble them.

But that was another time, another world.

He drank long and deep as soon as they were out of sight. His body quieted as he rejoined Tottengarr and Charlie, who'd remained hidden in the bush.

He'd stayed with them, thinking he could protect them, but as they travelled further north, gathering berries and grubs, collecting water from hidden springs, he knew it was them who were saving him.

It was almost dark when they turned, sticking to the coast. Crossing an estuary, he followed their lead, staying silent as they set up camp among the mangroves. He watched as their hands flicked, their silent, secret language, wondering what they felt compelled to say without words. Understanding came when twenty men carrying spears surrounded them. Macca, mimicking his companions, stayed seated at the fire, his head hanging. They were on the land of others.

Charlie approached them. '*Kurra murka*,' he said pointing south-wards. Words were exchanged until the older of the men nodded and they slipped back into the bush as quietly as they'd arrived.

The three travellers slept until dawn. Continuing on their way, they left the coast in the early afternoon turning south-east. Signs of settlers dotted their way now: a cattle yard, a fenced-in water hole, a fire pit.

'Whitefellas not far,' Charlie said, pointing ahead where the other gulf could now be seen between the tangled bush. Macca's flask was empty and his craving surged, like a hungry dingo.

He persuaded Tottengarr to wrap her exposed rifle shaft in leafy branches, the butt hidden in her hunting bag. By midday, at the place where the limestone met the mangroves, Charlie's prediction came true: two settlers, sitting around a fire, a rifle and a half-full flagon of rum by their side. The travellers stayed hidden. Watching. Macca's body screamed for relief, but he had more pressing concerns.

'Give me the rifle,' he whispered.

Tottengarr glared at him. 'Mine.'

The men jumped to their feet at the sound of her voice, coming towards them, their rifle raised and loaded.

Macca stepped forward; his hands raised. 'Greetings. I'm Malcolm Macleod. These natives are under my charge.'

'What's your business in these parts?' the older man asked.

'I'm taking them to Oyster Bay to get a ketch back to Adelaide.' Macca tried to stay calm and assert his authority. 'Who am I talking to and what's your business?'

'I'm George Sutton and this is my son, William. Where's their chains?'

'I had to take them off to get to the ketch in time. I can tie them again if you want but they've been obedient enough. I've promised them rum once we arrive.'

Macca knew his story was thin but it didn't seem to matter; both men only had eyes for Tottengarr.

'Have you ever seen one that tall? Strong too.'

'She'd crush you in her thighs.' They laughed, leering.

'Not yours,' Charlie said, his voice barely above a whisper. Macca saw the shock on their faces turn to anger.

'Speak English, does he?'

Macca shrugged. William glared at him and spat.

'What about this one?' he said as he fronted Tottengarr, grabbing her hair and rubbing his crotch.

'Leave her.' Macca's command heightened the man's anger and his disdain turned to fury.

'Looks like we got a smart-arse black fella here and a lubra-lover with his whore.'

He pushed Tottengarr away from him, a push that would have sent most women to the ground. But she only stumbled briefly. Macca saw the rage take hold of her.

Righting herself, she pulled out her rifle. The concealing branches fell aside. She took aim.

Macca leapt forward, grabbing her gun, throwing it to George.

'Take it,' he said. 'We don't need it.'

'We'll take it alright, and her. Ten to one she's the one they've been talking about. Raided farms near Tumby. Shot a shepherd too. There's a price on her head.'

'I'm bringing her to trial.' Macca raised his voice. 'That's the law.'

'Trial?' George scoffed. 'There'll be no trial, lubra-lover. Administer summary justice without trial, O'Halloran said. So that's what we'll do, right here.'

'It doesn't apply. Not now,' Macca said, quelling his fear, trying to sound like the authority he was claiming to be. 'She has the right to a trial.'

The men laughed but exchanged a worried glance. 'What did you say your name was?'

'I told you. Malcolm Macleod.' His whole body was shaking.

George circled them. 'Heard about you. You're the one they call Macca. Left Tolmer in the lurch to go live with the natives.'

'That's one side of the story.'

The men, both armed now, looked at each other as if trying to make a decision. Macca knew he was no longer a white man in their eyes. Whatever he said next would determine their future. 'Take us all before the court then, if you don't believe me.'

William scoffed again but George moved forward, nudging Tottengarr and Charlie with his rifle closer to where Macca stood.

'You can all go in with the other prisoners at the wool shed.'

Macca looked to where he pointed and saw a stone building half a mile away. Weighing up the options, he nodded to Tottengarr and Charlie. 'We'll go.'

Tottengarr took the lead, Charlie and Macca directly behind followed by the men, their weapons raised.

A well-worn path led towards the wool shed. The bush around them was mostly low, tangled mallee. A few yards ahead stood one lone river gum. It creaked as they neared it. Macca saw Charlie glance briefly upwards before lowering his head again. His hands flickered. Tottengarr's flickered back.

Charlie stopped, his eyes to the ground, his voice quiet. 'Need to shit, boss. Now, boss.'

George shook his head, resigned. 'Be quick about it then. Will, go with him. And keep an eye on the cocky bastard.'

Charlie headed towards the scrub to the right, William's rifle in his back. Tottengarr continued walking past the gum, Macca and George close behind her. The tree creaked again. A loud crack. Tottengarr called out. Macca leapt sideways. A massive limb crashed down, knocking George to the ground.

William turned briefly and Charlie took his chance, thrusting him into a bush, discharging his rifle into the air as Tottengarr launched into a sprint in the other direction. Macca kicked the rifle out of George's grasp as Tottengarr reached the mangroves to the south, her feet skimming the muddy flats until she seemed to take flight, a heron, disappearing into the cover of the denser bush.

Into Country.

William struggled to his feet, smashing Charlie above the eye before starting after her.

'Leave her,' George yelled. 'We'll deal with these two first. She won't get far alone.'

William held the rifle to Charlie's temple, pushing him back to join Macca and George. One-on-one now, rifles reloaded and raised as they headed to the woolshed.

Macca entered first. He heard the thud as the door was bolted behind them. His eyes adjusted to the darkness. Three people, all Aboriginal, were corralled at the far end. One of them, a woman, spoke to Charlie in their language, pointing frantically at the wall.

Macca turned as a rock was removed from the outside. A rifle shaft appeared. He lunged towards it.

Author's Note

While writing *Stolen*, I have lived on, travelled across, and written about the lands belonging to the Kaurna people, the Peramangk people, and the Barngala people. I acknowledge that these lands, like all the lands of First Nation Australians, have never been ceded. The Aboriginal Australian people have inhabited this continent and its adjacent islands for more than 60,000 years, living according to their culture and laws. I acknowledge their leaders, past, present, and emerging, and thank them for allowing me to walk and work on their land.

Stolen was inspired by my own pioneer colonist family. In deciding to write a story set in colonial times I recognised that I could not, indeed would not, ignore the role they may have taken in the dispossession of the owners of the country they took over. With no evidence of them having actively partaken in the frontier wars, I have sought to describe a world, told through the eyes of a child, where the inaction of good people has had a lasting and devastating impact. I acknowledge that my white privilege, with easy access to education, food and housing security, has come about as a result of that outcome.

I am particularly grateful to Courtney Hunter-Hebberman for reading *Stolen* to ensure that my words would not cause offence to any Peramangk person. I also thank Mandy Brown for her poem *Stolen*,

2020. Her simple but passionate words inspired the theme and the central plot of this story and give added gravitas to the title of my novel.

I have been guided too by reading the works of many of our wonderful and talented First Nations writers, including Dr Anita Heiss, Tara June Winch, Dr Natalie Harkin, Tony Birch, and Karen Wyld.

Overseeing all my decisions has been the spirit of my friend, teacher, mentor, and challenger, Alma Ridgway. I miss her no less today than the day she passed and I feel her gentle hand on my shoulder at all times.

Feedback from a number of early readers helped shape my writing. These include: Sonya, Lynne, Josie, Helmine, Steve, Kerrie, Paul, Dean, Laura, and Wendy. My editor Victoria Steele polished and strengthened my words and my proofreader tidied up the last of those pesky errors. I am forever grateful to Josie Hage for the tour of the Poonindie Training School site as the spirits of the past watched over us.

Stolen is a work of fiction intertwined with historical records—records mostly made by wealthy white men. Drawing on primary sources, I have attempted to stay true to the timing of historical events, although some I have stretched a little to add colour and drama to my story.

I have named some real-life characters if their impact on the history of South Australia is both well-known and well-documented. In particular, quotations attributed to Archbishop Augustus Short are taken directly from newspaper articles. The quote from Quentin Agius in the prologue is used with his permission and was taken from the site of the historic woolshed near Port Arthur, Yorke Peninsula, South Australia.

Alongside those characters named from life, I drew heavily on the book *Chequered Lives* by Iola Hack Mathews and Chris Durrant (Wakefield Press, 2013) to understand the history of early colonial life at Echunga. The Hastings and Hogan families are fictionalised from their account of the Hack and Hagen families. The character of Margaret Mayfield is a fictionalised version of Margaret May and draws, for inspiration only, on entries in her diary and from her letters. The character Tottengarr is based on a letter Margaret May wrote in 1843 which I combined with records of an Aboriginal woman warrior, Tarenorerer. For authenticity, I have mostly used historically correct language, but with caution and in context.

I recognise the courage of the pioneering settler families, including my own Latter ancestors who settled in Echunga after arriving in South Australia, on the *Eden,* from Chichester, UK, in 1838. They left their homes and families with no hope of ever returning. By the time South Australia was colonised, the existence of Aboriginal people across the colony was well documented; yet still, most settlers came under the wrongful belief that the land they would inhabit was not populated and therefore not owned. *Terra nullius.* They came with the promise that land was readily available for them to farm and purchase.

I believe that most of these early South Australian settlers, along with those of us who now seek the truth about our colonial past, would have accepted the generous invitation set out in the Uluru Statement from the Heart:

"To walk with us in a movement of the Australia people for a better people."

Other novels by Jennifer Mackenzie Dunbar

MISSING PIECES published by MidnightSun Publishing June 2023

Inspired by the 1831 discovery of a hoard of priceless chess pieces on a remote Scottish Island, Missing Pieces tells the story of the women who created and protected the now famous artefacts.

When Marianne is coerced into leaving the security of her comfortable London life to curate an exhibition on the Isle of Lewis, she uncovers her own ancestral ties to the mysterious island. Her eerie connections to the past introduce us to Magrit, the artisan, beholden to a power-hungry bishop; Morven, the rescuer, who seeks intimacy with a mysterious stranger and Mhairi, the negotiator, fighting a greedy landlord to stave off starvation and eviction.

Missing Pieces is a story about women's determination, passion, and cunning, and the power of love to right the wrongs of the past.

Denise Newton Writes July 2023

This evocative novel by Australian author Jennifer Mackenzie Dunbar is a lively combination of historical fiction, multiple timelines, and a dash of magical realism, centred around the story of the Lewis Chessmen collection.

The characters (in Missing Pieces) are believable and relatable and the various settings of time and place brought vividly to life.

Missing Pieces is a terrific read, one I thoroughly enjoyed. It renewed my interest in the Lewis chessmen and spurred me to read more about them, and the island where they were re-discovered.

VIVALDI'S LOST CONCERTO

Fiona Sinclair knows she must do all that she can to earn her release from prison. A childhood of neglect, years of homelessness and drug abuse have all but eroded the good in her. When she is given a battered flute as part of her music therapy, she begins to hear a tune that has both haunted and enchanted her since childhood and she draws from it the strength she needs to carry on. By chance, she learns that her mysterious tune is a recently discovered Vivaldi concerto that has lain hidden in Scottish archives for three hundred years. But Fiona doesn't listen to classical music and this piece has not been played for centuries.

As Fiona tries to solve the mystery of Vivaldi's Lost Concerto the novel takes the reader back to 18th Century Venice and into the lives of the composer Antonio Vivaldi, his lover Paolina Giro, and Lord Robert Kerr, the young nobleman who bought the concerto while on a Grand Tour away from battle weary Jacobean Scotland.

www.ingramcontent.com/pod-product-compliance
Lightning Source LLC
Chambersburg PA
CBHW020909130726
47904CB00006BA/1794